D1579537

NICKEL'S STORY

A STEEL BONES MOTORCYCLE CLUB ROMANCE

CATE C. WELLS

Cover art and design by Clarise Tan of CT Cover Creations.
Edited by Kathy Teel.
Proofreading by Nevada Martinez.
Special thanks to Jean McConnell of The Word Forager, and always, Louisa.

❀ Created with Vellum

For Kristopher

1

STORY, AGE 15

"**A**w, hell yeah, Story, you should go to try-outs. If Anne Michelle sees your moves, she'll definitely tell the coach to put you on the team."

"I don't know." I shrug, hands in my pockets. "I don't think I'd make it."

Yeah, right. I *know* I wouldn't make it, and it'd have nothing to do with my dancing and everything to do with Anne Michelle thinking I'm trailer trash, but still...it's nice to hear someone thinks you rock. Especially if that someone is Ryan-freakin'-Alston.

He's the star running back of the football team and the hottest guy at Petty's Mill High, and like, *all* of Pennsylvania, and he thinks I should go out for cheerleading. This is pretty much the best party *ever*.

I don't even care that we're out in a field, that my high heel wedges are caked in mud, and there's nowhere to pee but an old tree-break full of sticker bushes. The full moon is out, making everything pretty and silver, and Ryan Alston is talking to me. *With* Bruce Miller and Keegan Olms. Bruce is the quarterback, and Keegan is a *senior*.

Ryan's the hottest, though.

"Now, why don't you think you'd make it?" Keegan scoffs. "We were watching you dance by the bonfire. You're amazing."

My cheeks heat. I can't believe they were watching me.

"Yeah, why not?" Ryan echoes.

I can't say the truth. I do live in a trailer, I'm in remedial English, and I've overheard the football coach gossiping to the cheer coach about how he's shoved dollars in my ma's G-string down at The White Van. No way they're letting me on their wholesome, small-town cheer squad. Not even JV.

"I dunno." I hunch my shoulders and look at my feet. "Anne Michelle doesn't really like me much." That much is true.

"Anne Michelle's probably jealous." Ryan eyes my chest. Under my jean jacket, I'm wearing one of Ma's tight, low-cut tank tops. She made me wear it. She says it makes my boobs "pop." She's always nagging me to make things pop. My eyes. My eyebrows. My butt.

"Yeah." I nod. If Anne Michelle were here, she'd definitely be pissed that her boyfriend is talking to me.

A lot of the girls hate me. Ma says it's because I'm super blond, I've had huge tits since sixth grade, and my body's tight from dance. I think it's because Ma's a biker chick and a stripper, and we live at Happy Trails down on the Patonquin flats. And then there's the whole rumor that I have herpes even though I haven't been with anyone yet.

I don't have many friends who are girls except at dance. Dance friends are the best. They don't go to Petty's Mill since I dance rec all the way out in Shady Gap. They don't know anything about how I'm in the lowest level classes and everyone thinks that I have an STD because some loser got pissed that I wouldn't give him a hand job under the table in art class.

Anyway, Ryan Alston has never even bothered to look down his nose at me before, and now he's talking about me going out for cheer. It's totally weird. Things like this don't happen to me. Ever.

"I could change her mind, you know." Ryan flashes his killer smile. "Get her to give you a shot."

"You could?" This is crazy. It's got to be the earrings. Ma lent me her pink crystal hoops tonight, and we both know they're magic. She won fifty bucks from a scratch-off the last time she wore them.

Ryan shoots a glance at Bruce and Keegan. "If all three of us ask Anne Michelle to give you a shot, she'd have to. We're...like...the heart of the team. Right?"

I nod. Everyone knows Keegan is being scouted, and Bruce's parents practically run the booster club.

"But what if her moves aren't good enough?" Bruce crosses his arms and frowns. He's not as friendly as Ryan and Keegan.

"They totally are!" A nervous giggle escapes my lips, and I press them together hard, trying to tone it down. I'm not very good at playing it cool.

I'm laughing, but my moves *are* awesome. Ma doesn't believe in TV—as if we could afford cable if she did—so I spend a lot of time practicing on the empty pad next to our place. It's the perfect stage. That's why I've been in show troupe since third grade. Practice, hard work, and no TV.

"We should give her a chance," Keegan suggests. "A tryout before the tryouts." He's way nicer than Bruce. He's not hot like Ryan, but he has a really sweet face.

"Maybe. Sometime." Bruce shrugs and grabs a beer from

a passing kid. The kid doesn't even bother to complain. Bruce is *scary* big.

Crap. I need to seize this chance. It's not going to happen again. It's not as if these guys will talk to me in school. Check out my rack, sure, but talk? Never.

"Why don't I show you now?" I arch my back so my boobs stick out. Ma's drilled it in me to work my assets which are—in order—my boobs, my ass, and my hair.

"Here?" Keegan raises an eyebrow, glancing around the clearing.

It is a little crowded. There's a huge bonfire, a keg, and kids hanging out, sitting on felled logs, horsing around. A couple guys have pulled up their trucks, and girls are dancing in the headlights.

If I weren't here talking to the cutest, most popular guys in school, I'd be over there. Dance is my life.

I'm about to suggest that I do a tryout in front of the trucks when the roar of engines cuts through the music and laughter, and everyone perks up. Shit. The bikers are here, which means the party is about to get crazy.

Crazy awkward for me.

I kind of hope it's the Rebel Raiders, even though those guys are gross. If it's Steel Bones, the club my mom hangs with, they might tell her what I'm doing. She wouldn't care, but that doesn't mean I want her to know my business.

Three Harleys cut their engines at the same time, and the guys duck walk them back into a line. I recognize Hobs and give him a little wave. He's the youngest brother of the Steel Bones' president, and we're in the same special reading class. I'm in there 'cause I'm not the best reader. He's there because some asshole took a whack at his head with a baseball bat a few years ago, and now he has a hard time remembering how to get places and tell time and stuff.

Hobs is a senior. He's with a guy named Creech who graduated a year or two ago. Creech is prospecting. I've seen him at club picnics. I think my mom has banged him. My mom's a sweetbutt so that's not, like, special or anything.

Then I catch sight of the third guy, and my palms go sweaty.

It's Nickel Kobald.

I steer clear of him. He's way older—like twenty-four—and he's an enforcer. Not even my ma messes with him. He's probably here to make sure no one fucks with Hobs.

I don't know how Nickel's not upstate. I actually saw him break a guy's jaw at a lake party once. I've seen him headbutt a dude twice his size and then do shots with the guy later, his teeth still coated in blood and his nose bent sideways. I've seen him lift a bike and throw it at a brother who pissed him off, and it wasn't a Sporty, either. It was, like, a Fat Boy.

I've known Nickel since I was a little kid and he was a prospect, and I've never seen him smile. I've seen him laugh plenty, but only when he's tryin' to kill someone with his bare hands. The man's not right in the head.

I turn back to Ryan so I don't accidentally make eye contact. Not like Nickel's ever paid me any attention.

"Sweet bike." Ryan eyes up Nickel's custom job over my shoulder.

Keegan shrugs and grins. "I'd rather be lookin' at something else sweet. Like Story's sweet moves." He winks. God, he's *so* cheesy. But cute, too.

"Well, here's not good, obviously." I glance around. This is really disappointing, but no way am I doing cheers in front of Creech and Nickel.

"We could take a walk," Ryan suggests. "Past the windbreak."

God, this is amazing. All the girls want to dance with

these guys, be with them, but here they are, hanging out with me. Willing to give me a chance.

I knew the earrings were lucky.

"Awesome!" I smile, and when Ryan makes an "after you" sweep of his hand, I walk off in front of the guys into the dark, away from the bonfire.

They lead me out to the windbreak—Keegan slings his arm around my neck—and I'm so nervous, I can't hardly remember any cheers, so I focus on high-stepping so the long grass doesn't wrap around my heels and trip me. That's the last thing I need, to fall on my ass in front of these guys.

The further from the bonfire we go, the more shivers prickle down my spine. If this was a horror movie, this would not be a smart move. Ma would definitely call me an idiot if she knew I was walking off into the dark with three guys. It's Ryan, Bruce, and Keegan, though. It's not a sex thing; they all have totally hot, *really* popular girlfriends, and it's not like virtually every other girl at Petty's Mill High isn't taking a number and lining up.

"Here's good," Bruce says when the noise from the clearing is faint enough that you can hear the crickets. "What do you think, guys? Here good?"

"Yeah, yeah. Looks good," Ryan agrees, smirking. He seems really excited. He's bouncing on his toes like he's about to take the field.

I take a deep breath and stand in position, feet hip-width apart, hands straight at my side. I'm going to *rock* this.

"Hold up," Keegan says. He's shaking a cigarette out of a pack. "I can't see with that jacket on. Why don't you take it off?"

Oh. That makes sense. I didn't even think about it.

I shrug my jean jacket off and look for a place to put it.

The grass is wet with dew, and besides, I need to wear it another week until we make a laundromat run.

"I'll hold it." Ryan reaches out a hand. He's such a gentleman.

The other two take out their phones and pull up a flashlight app so they can see me. They're only outlines now, and that makes it easier. I can pretend I'm alone on the pad next to my trailer.

I take another deep breath and clap once, loudly. I'm so nervous, butterflies are beating wings in my belly. I stare past the guys, into the dark, and I let my body take over.

"Be! Aggressive! Be—Be—Aggressive!" I do a dagger and then a high V. "B—e—a—gg—r—ess—ive!" I get so into it, like I always do when I'm on stage, that I'm not noticing anything but my muscles and the beat.

I finish with a herkie and a toe touch, and I am *so stoked* I finished it with no mistakes, not one, and my toe touch was really high, and I didn't wobble at all when I landed even though I'm wearing heels and the ground is spongy.

I blink, grinning widely, and the clearing comes back into focus.

"Look at her. The slut loves it," Bruce snorts. Keegan laughs, and it isn't friendly. It's mean, and it raises the hackles on the back of my neck.

Ryan groans, weird like he's hurt, and I finally notice.

Their phones aren't on flashlight anymore; they're recording.

And their dicks are out.

And Ryan Alston just came. On my coat. Which he's dumped on the dirty ground in front of him.

My jaw drops open like a fish, and Keegan says, "Let's get her on her knees. She can suck us off."

From the trees behind me, there's a low, raspy, "Fuck that."

And then it all happens so fast, I don't have time to panic or run. One second, they're all three facing me in a row, recording, and then it's like a tornado goes through them, and there's no light from their phones anymore, only the sick thud of fists on flesh and cries of pain filling the night air. There's a crack as Ryan Alston's head hits a tree trunk. He's out cold, crumpled near my feet.

I fall to my knees, desperately running my fingers through the grass and thistles and sticks. I feel a nail break. Goddamn. Where's his fucking phone? Where is it?

Finally, my finger grazes a smooth rectangle, and I snatch it up, shoving it into my pocket while I take out my own, much cheaper phone and hold it up, trying to sort out what's going on.

Bruce and Keegan are still on their feet. Barely. A man with a buzz cut and a leather jacket is taking turns on them, just pummeling the hell out of their midsections, mixing it up every few blows by sending a fist or an elbow into their faces.

It's Nickel.

Hobs and Creech are nowhere to be seen.

Nickel's strong, wiry and quick, but it's two against one. Biker against quarterback and linebacker. Not good.

I see a chance, and I jump in, landing a good kick to Keegan's nuts, but then the fighting gets up close again, and I can't see another opening. Nickel's all over them, though. It's all they can do to stay on their feet. One combo to Keegan's throat and gut, and he topples backwards, wind-milling his arms. When he hits the ground near me, I stomp my heel into his balls.

Asshole.

He wheezes, whistling like wind through a crack in the insulation. I drop down again, searching the ground around him and then dig into his pockets until I find another phone. Got it. Jacket pocket.

One more. All I need to do is find one more phone and this never happened.

It's just Bruce now, and he's weaving on his feet. I think Nickel might ease off, wind down, but he doesn't. Instead, he goes berserker, slamming his forehead into Bruce's face and driving his knee into his belly. The moonlight bathes Nickel's bloody face, and pure fear races through my veins.

This is not a guy in control of himself.

Nickel's mouth is drawn back in a grimace, feral and mad, his eyes glinting black. Blood splatter drips down his tattooed neck, and I swear I can see bone where his knuckles are torn. Bruce slams to his knees, and Nickel grabs him by the scalp to hold him upright.

"Come here, Story." Nickel swings his wild eyes to me, his voice raspy and deep.

Oh, God. Suddenly I have to pee *so bad*. I should run. I should get the hell out of here. Fuck that last phone. Bruce is obviously going to die now, so it's not like he's going to be able to post anything on social media.

When I stay where I am, Nickel's brow furrows in frustration, like he's trying to move me with his mind or something. Finally, he raises the hand not holding up Bruce's bloody head like *whoa*. Which is weird 'cause I'm not the one dripping with another dude's blood.

"Ain't gonna hurt you, Story," he says. "Come here."

And this is gonna sound strange, cause you'd think a man like Nickel wouldn't care to repeat himself, that he'd sound impatient or there'd be a threat in his tone. But I swear, he sounds just like when my mom tries to lure Poxie, the stray cat we feed, out from under the Henderson's truck.

Slow and patient.

So, Lord help me, I hobble closer to the scene of the crime.

I stop a few steps away, hugging myself around the middle. This close, I can see the hate in Bruce's one good eye. The other is swollen shut.

"C-can I just...can I just go, Nickel? I just want to go."

Nickel ignores me. Instead, he kicks Bruce in the ribs with the metal toe of his black boot. There's a crack, and Bruce shrieks, high-pitched. Then he throws up in the pine needles he's kneeling on.

Oh. There's his phone. Lucky for me, it's a good six inches away from the puke. I sneak my foot out and drag it toward me with my toe. Nickel's gaze flashes down, and he rolls his eyes. Then he jerks Bruce's head up so he can stare him in the face.

"Now you're gonna listen, you worthless piece of shit. You see Story here? Nod if you understand me."

Bruce whimpers. He can't nod without his hair pulling in Nickel's grasp, but he nods anyway.

"Story is property of Steel Bones. You understand what that means?"

Bruce blubbers something that sounds like yes.

"It means—" Nickel stomps the hand propping Bruce up off the ground. Bruce collapses to his side, sobbing.

"Don't touch." Nickel leans over.

"Don't look." Nickel spits next to Bruce's heaving body.

"Don't even fuckin' think about her ever again."

Then he sniffs, wiping a bloody hand across his face, and tilts his head until his neck cracks. The moon takes that moment to send a beam down to light his face. He looks insane. His eyes are black hollows; the slash of his cheek-bones and hard line of his clenched jaw make him seem more like a comic book villain rather than a human.

He's the most mesmerizing man I've ever seen. Strong. Fearless. Totally mental.

"Get out of here," Nickel growls at me. "And quit bein' so stupid."

"Nickel?" I don't quite know what I mean to say. Maybe *don't kill him*. Maybe *make it hurt*.

"Git." This time, there is a threat in his voice, and I do have a sense of self-preservation, so I bail.

I try to hurry back to the clearing, but it takes a while 'cause the clouds have drifted over the moon and the grass is really high. I hear a thud behind me, a few muffled snarls, and then nothing. When I'm a few yards from the bonfire, Nickel catches up. I know it's him because his tread is heavier than any of the boys. Besides, there's no way Ryan or the others are gonna be walking that quickly anytime soon.

Nickel slows down when he gets next to me, keeping a foot or two between us. His face is all shadows, but I can smell the copper of blood.

Should I say thank you? Sorry?

I should probably say thank you.

I open my mouth to speak, but he beats me to it.

"Why the *fuck* were you doin' cheers for three dudes out in the fuckin' woods?"

Yeah. I know it was stupid. I knew when I was doing it. Growing up where I have...I know how guys are. My skin prickles with embarrassment, and I'm happy it's too dark for him to see me blush.

"They said if I was good, they'd get me on the squad." I know how lame I sound.

He snorts and walks silently beside me a while longer.

Then he says, "Why the fuck do you want to be a cheer-leader? Thought you danced."

Huh? How would Nickel Kobald know that?

He must sense my confusion because he kind of grunts, and spits out all grudgingly, "When your ma was fuckin' Big George, five, six years ago, you had a charity thing up at the community college in Shady Gap. Big George made all us prospects go."

Five or six years ago? That was, like, my first or second show troupe recital. He saw that?

"Was I wearing a yellow body suit with sequins or a black-and-white polka dot tutu?"

There is a long silence.

"I have no fuckin' idea."

He must be sorry he said anything because he doesn't say a single word more until we're past the bonfire, close to all the trucks with their lights on.

"Story?"

"Yeah?"

"You want to be on the cheerleading squad?"

I don't really know. I thought I did. The idea of being on the team, in the middle of the other girls, girls no one ever looks down on—I guess the idea of that is what made me go off into the woods with three guys I didn't really know.

Cheerleading is fun and all, but I do pointe, and pointe's way harder.

"I guess not," I mumble.

"You want to be with those guys?"

The question makes my stomach sour. It wasn't like that. "No," I huff.

Nickel stops, reaches out all sudden and grabs my forearm so I stop, too. He leans down, so his face is almost level with mine.

He speaks real slow and clear. "Stop doin' things you don't want to do. And stay away from those motherfuckers. Hear me?"

I nod. His raspy, clipped voice echoes in my ear. I hear him, all right.

"And Story?"

I glance up.

"Give me the phones."

My cheeks heat while I wiggle and tug them from my butt pocket where they're all three wedged in tight as a drum. I lay them in his outstretched hand.

"What are you going to do with them?"

He shrugs a shoulder. "Toss 'em in the river."

Then he jerks his chin and stalks off toward his brothers.

The rest of the night, he doesn't talk to me once, but his eyes never leave me while he leans against Ryan's F150 with Creech and Hobs. When the guys finally hobble out of the woods, Nickel stares them down, daring them to say anything. They catch on right quick and tell everyone they were wrestling out in the windbreak. Letting off steam. No one believes them. Not when Nickel has his knee bent and the bottom of his mud-caked boot propped on Ryan's pristine driver's side door.

Even though I beg, my ride won't bail while the guy she's crushing on is still around, so I sit on a log real close to everyone else, my arms wrapped around my belly for an hour before another girl from Happy Trails offers to drive me home. Nickel and his brothers are still there when I go, so I don't know how it all ends. I hear later that Ryan had to say "please" to get in his truck.

You think the whole thing would've taught me a lesson. Keep your head down, stay in your lane, play it safe. Life's hard enough; you don't need to add the misery of wanting things you can't have.

But that's not how God made me. I'm the kind of weed that sprouts in concrete and makes a crazy bid for the sun. It's kind of stupid, straining for something you should know better than to want, but no one ever accused me of being too bright.

No matter what anyone said, after that night, I was a goner for Nickel Kobald. Talk about wanting things you can't have.

2

NICKEL, PRESENT DAY

I ain't never shot up or snorted shit, but I understand addiction. Hating something you can't resist. Knowing it's gonna do you in but still showing up for it, time and time again.

For the length of three songs every hour or so, Wednesday night through Saturday, I'm addicted to the doorway of the storage room at The White Van gentleman's club. Least ways, I can't seem to drag myself away from it.

I always know it's her comin' out from the first few notes blaring outta the sound system. Whatever she's gonna pick any given night, it ain't the hip hop the other girls favor. Tonight, I hear the twang of jumpsuit-era Elvis, and I know it's Story's turn. I settle back into the door frame, leaning as casual as I can, forcing myself to look like I ain't gonna pop off at the slightest provocation.

I *want* one of the motherfuckers in the audience to try and grab her. To call out somethin' wrong. The ugly is burning in my blood, my cock getting stiff just anticipatin' her long leg easing through the curtains, and I want to beat every asshole in this club blind.

The crowd don't never oblige me, though. Like tonight, the good ol' boys hear Elvis, and it's as if they all took a drag of the good stuff and the buzz hits them at the exact same time. They leave off their talk, lean back, grin all dopey. They got Story's number, too, and they know this girl gives 'em what they want. This is redneck country. Ain't nobody heard of Lil' Wayne, but everybody knows and loves the King.

Elvis begins cryin' about bein' caught in a trap, and when the drum starts poundin', the curtains part, and Story high-steps onto the stage, hands thrust high in the air like a magician's assistant, swishing her ripe ass from side-to-side, the widest smile in the world turning the place into something else.

A moment ago, it was all darkness and neon lights, black paint on the walls and floors, sticky imitation leather and grimy tables, all of it reeking of stale sweat, liquor, and cum. But when Story Jenkins is onstage, everything else fades to black. Dudes stewing in misery, carrying on with their buddies, or tying on a righteous drunk—they all leave off what they're doin' and watch like kids leaning forward in a movie theater, bringin' beers to their mouths without takin' their eyes off her.

Me, too. I'm watching. Anchored in place.

And I got the same dumb smile on my face as every other man in the whole damn place.

Story's got nothin' on but red tassled pasties, a red thong cut high—showing off the sweet divots under her sharp hip bones—red garters, and the highest red platform heels you've ever seen in real life.

We got pretty girls at The White Van, but don't nobody look like Story. She's got thick blonde hair down to her butt, high tits the size of bowling balls—more duckpin than ten-pin—an ass you can set your drink on, and a waist so little you wanna wrap your hands around to see if your fingers touch.

I wanna touch almost as much as I wanna watch, and I can't tear my eyes away. It's magic.

It's like—in this life—we hardly ever get to see people doing the thing they love. My brothers on a ride, Ernestine down at the club with her grandbabies...I can't think of no other times when I see pure human happiness. Looking around this room—dudes relaxing on a Friday night, drinkin', gettin' a lap dance—you see lust, smiles, hunger, worries set aside. Not bliss. Not on the floor.

But up on the stage?

Pure bliss.

Story dances, and she takes you with her. It's not like with the other girls when they make like they have eyes only for you. Story's lost in her music and her moves, and all of us sad sacks of shit only have eyes for her.

The ugly eats away at me at the very same time I'm high off watching her. I'd think it was jealousy or frustration if I didn't know myself better. It ain't as simple as that. What I got in me is the opposite of whatever God gave that girl when he made her. She's a flipped light switch in a dark room. I'm...

I'm the asshole lurking in a doorway, dick hard, scanning the crowd for a motherfucker, any motherfucker, to step out of line. I need to break my fists on a face and purge the devil ridin' me harder the longer she dances.

Call it blood lust. Maladjustment. Call it psychotic. You wouldn't be far off.

"Suspicious Minds" finally ends and "Take Me Home, Country Roads" begins, and it's fuckin' ridiculous, but by the second line, everyone's singin' along, even the businessmen who work up in Pyle.

Story's got the worst taste in music. She's like a dude, drunk off his ass, flippin' through a radio dial in some bumfuck county where they don't get any good stations.

I've seen her dance to "The Rainbow Connection." King Missile's "Detachable Penis." "All My Exes Live In Texas."

She's on a downhome kick tonight. I wouldn't be surprised if she ends this set with that one. Or maybe Johnny Cash. You ain't seen nothin' until you've seen an inverted pole spin to "Ring of Fire."

Her taste in music is a running joke around the club, and if she wasn't the biggest draw Cue's got, maybe he'd make her ditch the weirder choices. Listening to the dudes bellowing John Denver, arms thrown over each other's shoulders, the whole place breathing deeper like someone finally cracked a window, you can see why he don't.

Story Jenkins is magic.

It's almost like she hears me thinkin' cause her eyes find me in the doorway—like they always do—and she lets a smile break across her face, warm as sunrise. There's a twinkle in her eye. She's teasin' me now. She leaves off poppin' her ass and archin' her back, and she goes to her knees, resting her butt somehow on those crazy heels by twisting her ankles till her feet lay sideways.

She drags her fingers up her splayed thighs, and my eyes follow till I'm lost between her thighs where her red panties wedge between her puffy pussy lips. There's a collective moan from the crowd and a few yips and hollers.

Goddamn. She needs to stand back up. Push those knees together. Go to all fours and whip her hair around like she does.

Or spread those knees wider. Show me more.

'Cause there's no doubt. She's showing *me*.

She's reading my face, her lips twitching each time I shift my stance. She cups her tits and offers them to me, slowly easing her knees further and further apart until I catch a glimpse of pale pink on either side of the red silk.

I stiffen, fist my hands, but I'm stuck in place, my breath comin' shallow, desperate, and she's panting too, not from the dancing but from my eyes on her. She needs to fucking stop, but I'll die if she does, and then she slips one finger into her mouth, eases it between her parted, pink lips and—

A loud bang from the direction of the room we call the "Way Back" cuts through the room like a record scratch. It's followed by high-pitched screeching. Jo-Beth. The ugly perks up, and my body readies for action.

Thank the Lord. Shit's going down.

A man in a suit, belt unbuckled and jacket in hand, stomps past.

"You owe me twenty more!" Jo-Beth is in hot pursuit, her mascara streaked and her lipstick smeared like the Joker's.

"You got all I'm going to give you!" the man barks, pausing to buckle himself.

Jo-Beth reaches for his arm. He jerks his elbow back to avoid her hand, way harder than he has to, and Jo-Beth takes one in the stomach. She makes a little "oof" and staggers, but Jo-Beth don't go down easy.

By the time I cover five feet, she's taken her heel off, and she's whacked him a good one upside the head.

"Give me my money!" She swings again, way too close to his eyes.

Austin, the new kid, gets there the same time I do. He pulls Jo-Beth off before I can get my hands on the dude. It's only a split second, but the asshole manages to slap Jo-Beth

with his full force, knockin' her head back. She can't do shit
cause Austin has her arms pinned back.

The ugly floods my brain, mutes the music and the
shouts, and my body moves without my brain. I've got the
asshole in a headlock, and then I'm dragging him across the
floor. A table skids, a chair topples.

I use his face to slam open the swinging door, and then
we're in the parking lot. The ugly is throbbing, singing. I
land blow after blow, only vaguely aware that another man
in a suit and glasses has jumped in until he lands a
haymaker to the side of my head, setting my ears ringing.

The ugly rears up, and if it had teeth, they'd be drippin'
saliva like some alien monster. I smile, my split lip burning.
It feels so good—the pain, the clarity, the not-having-to-
hold-it-in—that I let the guy get a few jabs in for fun, don't
even raise my arms, cackling with release while I sway from
the blows.

This new guy is serious. He's studying up, his body
turned. He ain't soft like his friend. It's clear from his stance,
this ain't his first rodeo.

I wipe a thumb across my nose, and I dive in. There's a
few more minutes of glorious pain, scrabbling as we trade
the upper hand over and over. Then there's the bite of
asphalt as we take it to the ground, no longer a brawl but a
war, and the ugly almost, almost wears itself out—I think—
it ain't never had enough before so I can't be sure that's even
possible.

And then there's hands on me, dragging me off. Austin
has one arm, Forty has the other, and Cue's elbow is hooked
around my throat. I pull forward, make it a few steps, but
then Cue goes dead weight behind me, and I got to fall back
or lose air.

The guy I was fightin' climbs to his feet, weaving in

place. His glasses are cracked. His buddy's still curled on the ground.

There's a flash of purple, and Forty's only just able to catch Jo-Beth with his free arm before she goes to finish what she started.

"He owes me twenty!" she shrieks.

The rumpled ball on the ground whimpers, and the other guy pants, still catching his breath. He's holding his side like I got his ribs. I ain't gonna know what I've done to myself for another hour or so. Until the ugly wears off, I'm always numb. Even with Cue's help, it's hard enough to stumble to my feet.

"For what?" Cue asks from behind me.

"He wanted me to swallow," Jo-Beth answers. "I said twenty extra, and he said fine."

The dude on the ground whines something. It sounds like "bullshit."

"You negotiate up front?" Cue asks.

"He asked during." Jo-Beth is rounding her eyes, blinkin' her lashes. Ain't gonna work with Cue.

"You know the rules. All prices and services negotiated up front. Less hassle all around."

"Fine." Jo-Beth gives up the puppy dog and rolls her eyes. "You want me to eat the twenty along with his nasty jizz, then?"

Cue lets out a long-suffering sigh, and his cigar breath on my neck starts the chills to wracking me like they always do after I come down from a fight. I roll my shoulders and my brothers take the hint and drop me.

"All better?" Forty jokes.

I crack my neck and shake out my arms.

The dude with the glasses is eyein' me, and it's tense, but I know he ain't gonna call the cops. He's a man in a suit and tie, but I recognize his stance. He's got his own monkey on his back.

He limps over and squats by his buddy, fishing the dude's wallet out of his pants. He pulls out a wad of bills— way more than twenty—and hands them up to Jo-Beth. "Here."

She fists the cash, and she's halfway back to the club before the dude on the ground can groan a protest.

"We good here?" Cue asks, and glasses guy nods. "Your friend ain't welcome back."

"I get that." The dude in glasses helps his friend to his feet. The asshole starts muttering about the cops. He says he's gonna sue us, take us for everything we got.

"Eric. Shut the fuck up," the guy says. "They're Steel Bones."

Eric shuts the fuck up.

They roll off in an Audi while Austin and Cue go back in. Forty offers me a swig from the flask he keeps in his breast pocket. It's got an Army seal on the outside and Macallan on the inside.

I take it with a grunt and savor the burn. It's good to feel something besides the bone-deep cold that sets in when the ugly begins to recede.

We're quiet a long moment, watchin' the cars drive past.

"You could have killed him," Forty finally says on a long exhale.

I don't say nothin'. There's nothin' to say.

I've known Forty more than twenty years. This ain't the first time he's told me that. Nor the hundredth.

"I'm goin' in," Forty waves me off when I try to hand his flask back.

When he passes through the front doors, they swing wide enough that I can see Story working the floor. She's got two drinks in hand, a beer and what's probably an apple juice in a martini glass, heading for a table in the corner.

Her enormous blue eyes catch mine, and for a second, her dancer mask drops. Pink circles bloom on her cheeks, and her lips turn down a notch, plumping up her full bottom lip. She looks shy and worried and caught—all at the same time. She takes a half step toward me, and I shake my head once, raising the flask to my lips.

Her eyes beg. Ask me why. Her working girl posture—shoulders back, chin up, hip cocked to push her ass out—kind of shifts until she don't look like a stripper no more. She looks like that girl walkin' with me through a dark field, trippin' to stay in step, fearless 'cause I'm there beside her.

Pure terror socks me in the gut, and despite the lingering numbness, it rocks me on my heels.

I stalk off and the door finally comes to a rest, but not before I see her stiffen and disappointment flash in those big, beautiful eyes.

I feel that, too, and holy Christ, it hurts.

I should quit this job. I could pick up some more bounty work to keep me busy, and it's not like I need the money. I've had the thought a hundred times. I should walk away. I ain't normally one to run, but in this case?

The blows are gettin' harder and harder to take, and my skin ain't gettin' any thicker.

3

STORY, AGE 17

"Why don't you go talk to him?"

Fay-Lee wriggles up onto her elbows and lets her sunglasses slide down her nose. We're on the roof of a low outbuilding at the Steel Bones clubhouse. The pitch of the roof isn't too steep, and even though it's only April, the heat from the shingles makes it warm enough to wear a bikini top comfortably.

Nickel's over by the grill, drinking a beer, talking to Dizzy. Nickel's hot as shit in a white tank top and faded jeans that ride low on his hips. I've been ogling him behind my sunglasses all afternoon.

"He won't talk to me," I pout, pulling at the threads on my cut-offs.

"Have you even tried?"

"Literally every time I see him." And that's the truth.

I'm a junior in high school now, and I've spent almost two years striking out with Nickel Kobald. He doesn't even reply when I talk to him anymore; he just raises an eyebrow all sarcastic, tightens his jaw, and taps a foot until I wander off, mumbling and sweaty from humiliating myself. I wish the feeling would last so I'd learn my lesson, but that's not how I'm made. Ma says I'm a human bop bag. Get knocked over, pop right back up for more. I don't disagree. I ain't about to lie there.

"So what's your angle?" Fay-Lee asks, slipping down her swimsuit straps so she doesn't get tan lines. I don't worry about tanning. I'm wearing SPF 30 'cause I don't want color; I just like the feeling of the sunshine sinking into my skin and the cool, early spring breeze that whips past every so often.

"What d'you mean?" I ask.

"How are you reeling in Mister Tall, Dark, and Homicidal?"

"Well…" My cheeks heat, thinking about all my striking out. I've got zero game. "At Thunder in the Valley, I asked him if he wanted me to get him a bottled water."

"Smooth." Fay-Lee nods with fake admiration.

"At the bull roast, I asked him if he was into classic rock."

"Classic." Fay-Lee's laughing at me behind her shades. I deserve it.

"I've asked him to give me a ride somewhere, like, five times."

"Didn't work?"

"Nope."

"You need to get him drunk." Fay-Lee raises her beer to me, takes a long pull, and then tucks it back between her thighs.

"How would I even do that?" I huff. "I have to snarf beers off you."

"It's totally lame that Sunny cuts you off after three."

"I know." I'm lucky Ma's off trying to score with some dude named Wall. Usually, she sticks pretty close to me at the clubhouse. "When she was my age, she was following Phish."

"Old-schoolers suck." Fay-Lee shoots me a wicked grin. "Maybe not that one there, though." She makes a show of staring toward Nickel and licking her lips. "I bet he sucks so, so good."

I shriek and slap Fay-Lee's bare shoulder. We both break into giggles.

I love this girl. She's my first real, actual, female friend. She showed up a few months ago on the back of a nomad's bike, and even though the nomad left, she's still around. She's Dizzy's house mouse. I think she's supposed to be watching his two boys, but they're over on the pile of tires, trying to throw each other off, and she's hanging with me.

"Hey, get your dirty eyes off my boyfriend." I jerk my chin toward the boys. "Aren't you supposed to be watching those two?"

"You wish he was your boyfriend."

I do. I so, so do.

"As for the two last names." Fay-Lee's neck starts going, and her pointer finger goes up. "I told Dizzy. I said, I'm twenty-one years old, not nearly old enough to be their mama and not nearly big enough to whoop their asses. Which they both need, fuckin' desperately. So I'll cook, clean, and drive 'em where they need to go, but I ain't beating my head against a wall. He wants 'em to act right, he can step up."

"The two last names?"

"Parker. That's the older one. And Carson. That's the younger one. They've got fuckin' last names for first names."

"Okay, *Fay-Lee*."

Fay-Lee rolls her eyes. "Don't get me started on you. You ain't even got a *name* for a first name."

"Least of my problems. My boyfriend over there won't even give me his number."

"You're hopeless." Fay-Lee passes me her beer. I'm on number four of the day, but I ate a ton of hot dogs and spread the Buds way out, so I'm only a little buzzed.

I groan. She's right. "Everything is hopeless."

"Yeah?" Fay-Lee's listening, but her eyes are wandering now, too. First to Dizzy, then the boys.

I sigh. Nothing's been going my way lately. Not like it ever does. "I'm not gonna get the English credit. I'm gonna have to do summer school. Again."

"That sucks."

"My boss at General Goods is trying to make me work Thursday nights when I have dance. He says if I can't, he's gonna cut my hours."

"That really sucks."

"I should just call it a day, drop out, and go work with Ma at The White Van."

I've been thinking about it more and more often. It's not like I'll be able to get anywhere with a diploma. I still won't be able to read worth shit.

Fay-Lee rolls to her side and props her head in her hand, totally ignoring the boys shouting and wrestling across the yard.

"Or—" She flicks me between the eyes, and I yelp. "You could stop bitchin' about shit you cannot change and go get yourself a piece of hot and crazy."

My eyes wander back to Nickel, and a shiver shoots straight between my legs. He's so gorgeous, I can hardly breathe when I look at him. His cheekbones slash toward his soft lips, and even in the middle of a sunny Saturday afternoon, his black eyes glint and dart. He reminds me of a panther or something, searching for prey.

He's shifting on his feet, and he keeps crossing and uncrossing his arms. He never stands still for long. If I'm gonna make a move today, it'll have to be soon. He doesn't usually stay around long at family events.

"What do you suggest?" Short of flashing my tits, I'm all out of ideas.

Fay-Lee grins and waggles her eyebrows. "Get him alone and show him your boobs."

My mouth drops open. And then I slam it back shut. It's actually a *great* idea.

Nickel always shuts me down before I can even get started, but his eyes always stray down my front while he's doin' it. I'm not gonna lie. I'm a 30D. My boobs kind of have a gravitational pull on most dudes' eyeballs. Right now, a table full of prospects by the horseshoes are ogling Fay-Lee and me, tryin' to play it cool.

"How do I get him alone?"

Fay-Lee shrugs and rolls flat again. "I don't know. Follow him to the men's room."

I could do that. I slide my feet back into my flip-flops so I'm ready to go as soon as he makes a move toward the clubhouse.

A shout pulls my attention momentarily toward the tire pile.

"Oh, crap." I nudge Fay-Lee with my elbow. "Parker just threw Carson off the top of the tire pile."

Fay-Lee tilts her chin up to get more sun on her chest. "He still moving?"

I watch a second. The kid is slow to get to his feet, but a second later, he's halfway up the pile, cussin' a blue streak at his brother.

"He's good."

"Well, you better shake your ass if you don't want to miss

your chance." Fay-Lee jerks her chin toward the back door, and there's Nickel, walking through.

"Shit!"

I scramble off the roof, using a stack of pallets to get down, and I speed walk across the yard. Creech stares at me from a picnic table, licking his lips, and I go even faster. Creech creeps me out. He has a head tattoo, and he's always grabbing my ass.

When I get into the clubhouse, I pad down the dark hall to the bathrooms, grateful there's no one inside. It's a beautiful spring day, and everyone's out enjoying the sunshine.

My heartbeat doubles and then triples the closer I get to the john. Now that I'm on my way, I have to admit, this plan is not the greatest. Nickel lives upstairs, so he could have gone to his room. Also, there's the definite possibility that he won't be alone.

The idea causes me to fall back on my heels a few inches from the men's room door. This is stupid. I should go outside, climb back up on the roof, and tan my back. I hear a flush, muffled by the door.

Shit. If he comes out now, I'm going to be standing in the hallway, staring at the men's room door like a freakin' idiot. Shit.

I hear voices at the end of the hall. I make a split-second decision and push in. Go big or go home, right?

"What the fuck?" Nickel's washing his hands. The bathroom's otherwise empty.

My stomach wobbles like it always does when I'm near him, and my breath goes shallow. Good thing. It smells like piss and Pine-Sol in here. So not sexy. This is the worst idea ever.

"Story?"

Nickel shakes the water off his hands, his face darkening. Goosebumps rise all up and down my arms. He is *not* happy to see me.

"What are you doin' in here? You fuckin' meeting somebody in here?" His voice is sharp. Angry.

I shake my head. The buzz that fueled this dumb idea is well and truly gone. My brain is still slow from the beers, though, and I can't figure out how to get myself out of this.

While I stand there, speechless, Nickel's jaw gets tighter and tighter until a tic starts pulsing beneath his ear. He hasn't come closer to me; he's still standing by the sink, staring. My skin flushes hot; sweat breaking out behind my knees.

He's staring at my turquoise fringed bikini top. No, he's staring at my tits. All of a sudden, I'm super-aware of them. My nipples stiffen, straining at the nylon, and they kind of itch. I wriggle, arch my back, try to scratch that achy little itch, and the quietest exhale escapes Nickel's lips. His black eyes swirl. He's not in motion now; he's not scanning the distance for threats.

He's anchored to me, and he's into this. Oh, God. Now I'm even more into this. I slowly reach behind my neck and untie the top. He's tracking me, his hooded eyes burning as they slide up to watch my fingers work and then down to where the cups sag as I lower them inch by inch.

I drop the ties and square my shoulders. He swallows so loud I can hear it.

And for about three glorious seconds, he's eating me up with his eyes, and it's like my tits strain toward him. My belly flips like crazy and heat gushes between my legs. His entire body is taut as a spring pulled as far as it can go, and I know that he's going to break. He's going to come for me, and I'm trembling because I'm scared that he will and even more scared that he won't.

"You're so fucking beautiful," he mumbles, like he's talking in his sleep. And then his eyes are boring into mine; he's not even looking at my tits. "You're so perfect."

"I think you're perfect, too." It's true. To me, he is.

He laughs. An ugly sound. "You got no sense, do you, girl?"

"Don't need sense. I need you." That's true, too. I can't believe I have the guts to say it, but this moment is out of time. We're stuck in the eye of a tornado, swept in circles around each other, powerless.

"I'm a decade older than you."

"You're still hot." I grin, let him see me check out his six-pack abs. He broadens his shoulders, and his biceps flex. My grin widens.

"You're settin' yourself up for a disappointment, little girl."

"Maybe. You should let me find out for myself."

He stands there, lost for words, the beginning of a smile playing at the corners of his mouth, and then—without warning—a cold, metal knob knocks me right in the small of my back. I cry out, and Nickel leaps at me, slamming the bathroom door shut over my shoulder, scrabbling at my top, trying to put it back up.

"Stay the fuck out!" he roars, fumbling with the fabric, and all he's managing to do is press the twisted cups against my breasts, his calloused fingers stroking my flushed skin, setting off chills that race through me straight to my throbbing pussy.

He's breathing heavy, and his black eyes are drilling into mine, furious again and hungry, the half-smile well and truly gone. I can see the fight in them, and I'm hooked. I've never seen anyone fight themselves this hard. And it's over *me*.

"It's okay," I murmur. "You can touch them."

He beats his fist once against the door behind me. I'm not sure if he's warning off whoever just tried to come in, or if he's just pissed as hell.

"Fuck!" he barks. "Tie it back up!"

I lower my hands, which had been hovering at my sides, and I rest my palms on the door behind me. "It's okay. I want you to."

He rips his gaze away from mine and bores a hole into the wall with his eyes. "Tie it back up. Now."

"I'm seventeen."

"Not having this conversation, Story."

"You want to." I reach out to graze the hard length tenting his jeans. I've never touched a dick before, but I've seen plenty. I know he's got a hard on. For me. The feeling's so heady, twice the buzz I had going before. I stroke him through the denim. Once.

He hisses, a sound of pain, and grabs my wrist. Too tight. I suck in a breath. He holds on.

"You are going to tie that top back up, walk your ass back outside, go back to layin' on that fuckin' roof, and if I ever catch you doing something this stupid again, I'm going to—"

His face is a storm, dark and dangerous, and I wait, trapped right where I want to be, heat pooling between my thighs.

"What? What'll you do?" My mouth waters.

"Fuck!" He loses it. His body springs into motion, and before I can blink, I'm out in the hallway, the force he used to push me there sending me several steps forward before I'm in full control of my body again. In the bathroom, there's a crash, and then something shatters.

"What the fuck is that?" Boots, one of the older brothers, is wheeling himself toward me as I quickly do up my ties.

"Dude!" he shouts as he passes. "You wrestlin' out a shit in there or a fuckin' alligator?" Then he slaps my ass, cackles, and wheels himself into the ladies' room.

Later, after I hide in the kitchen for a while and help the old ladies clean, I snarf an almost full beer Grinder left on a picnic table and find Fay-Lee. She's still laid out on the roof. I pull myself up to sit on the edge, legs dangling. Nickel's nowhere to be seen.

"From that face, I'm guessin' you struck out."

I groan.

"How bad was it?"

"So bad."

"He barfed." Fay-Lee says it like *of course he barfed*.

"No. Asshole." I reach back to slap her baby-oiled thigh. She laughs.

"You puss out?"

"No. I showed him my tits."

"What, was he like 'meh'? He totally said meh, didn't he?"

A smile twitches at the corner of my mouth. I love Fay-Lee.

"No. He got really pissed off, kicked me out, and went ballistic."

Fay-Lee's quiet a minute, her head cocked to the side. "Cool."

"Not cool, girl. Not at all." I swing my feet, letting my flip flops dangle. "Embarrassing. Humiliating. The absolute worst."

Fay-Lee grunts as she does a sit-up until she's vertical. Then she scooches down so she's right next to me. She slings a skinny arm around me and rests her cheek on my shoulder.

"I don't know, Story. What is he? Like twenty-five?"

"Twenty-six."

She smirks. "I don't know any other twenty-six-year-old dudes who'd take a pass on seventeen-year-old pussy served up on a plate. Do you?"

She's right. I don't.

A smile trembles on my lips. "You sayin' he's, like, a good guy?"

Fay-Lee snorts. "Nope. I'm sayin' there's something wrong with him. But still. It's kind of cool."

And that's what I take away.

Not that there's something wrong with Nickel Kobald, but that my best friend Fay-Lee Smith, the coolest girl I've ever met, thinks the man I love is cool, too. From that day on, my course is set. I want what I want, and I'm not giving up. Of course, life is going to shoot me down in the end, but until then, I'm gonna elbow my way closer to the things that feel like sunshine on my face.

Like Nickel Kobald saying *you're so beautiful.*

You're so perfect.

4

NICKEL, PRESENT DAY

"Is she seriously dancing to 'Goodbye Yellow Brick Road'?"

Forty shakes his head and snaps for Starla to bring another round of beers. The White Van isn't very busy tonight. A new club opened up in Shady Gap, so business will be down for a while until the novelty wears off and dudes get tired of driving forty minutes to look at the same old tits and ass.

"That girl can dance, but goddamn. This fuckin' *song*."

My gut clenches, and I grind my jaw so tight my teeth shift a little in the gums.

Fuck. This is not going to work.

I don't need to look up to see who Forty's talkin' about. It's Story.

She should not be here tonight.

Cue's figured out to put her on nights I ain't bouncing, but shit happens. Dancers call in sick. Or there's times like tonight when we've got club business, and I'm here even though I ain't on the schedule. And—I ain't gonna lie—if it's been a while, I sometimes trade with one of the other guys cause self-control ain't really my strong suit, and Story's my weakness.

Cue's smart enough to be nervous—although not fuckin' smart enough to send Story home—and he's eyein' me from behind the bar. Bet he's worried about the glassware. His place got trashed by the Rebel Raiders not too long ago, and he's sensitive about his stuff.

And shit does tend to happen when Story and I are workin' the same night. Glasses do get broken. Chairs. Faces.

Truth is shit tends to happen whenever I'm around, but that's kind of my job. I'm the explosives, as Heavy, our club prez says. Either here, out crackin' skulls for Steel Bones, or backing my old pal Frisco, hunting bounties up in Pyle. I prefer the enforcer work. It feeds the beast, keeps me relatively steady. Or at least out of county lock-up on the regular.

This business we're doin' tonight, though...way out of my wheelhouse. If the order didn't come from Heavy himself, I'd have told Forty to fuck himself. Had I known Story'd be dancing tonight, this would have been a non-starter. She don't need to be near trouble.

That's why I try to stay away.

I sneak a glance at the stage. Keep my eyes above the neck. She's got that long, white blonde hair of hers done in two thick braids. Of course. Dorothy from Wizard of Oz braids. Yellow Brick Road and all. That's how she thinks. Like a kid playing dress up. I let my eyes drop all the way down. Yup. She's wearin' sparkly red high heels with a strap across the ankle.

My dick punches against my zipper, and my fingers start to twitch. She's got to get out of here. I cut my eyes to Cue, and he shrugs. I'm gonna break that motherfucker's shoulders if he shrugs at me again.

My body heats, and I'm itchin' to stand, walk over to the bar and make that asshole send her home.

"Drink." Forty presses a cold one in my palm. "You know how much is ridin' on this." Forty slaps the sides of my head. "Chill the fuck out."

I laugh. "We been rollin' together since sixth grade. You ever known me to chill out?"

Forty snorts. He sees my point.

I throw one back, knowing it'll only add fuel to the fire, while he rummages in his pocket.

"Heavy thought we might need reinforcements." He drops two white pills on the table in front of me.

"The fuck?"

I don't do drugs. I mean, I'll take a toke when Boots is passin' a blunt around the clubhouse, but that's the extent.

"It's a Xanax. No biggie. Deb takes one when she gets anxious about shit."

"What's Deb got to be anxious about?" Deb is Pig Iron's old lady. She does the books.

"The fuck I know. Menopause? Just take it. You cannot fuck this up, and we both know your fuckin' temper *will* fuck this up."

Sad thing is? He's right. He knows it; I know it. Charge, the dude who just plopped his ass down at our table, he knows it.

"So these pills are gonna calm my ass down?"

"Works for Deb," Forty says.

I down the pills with a swig of beer. "Next time I see Deb, I'm gonna ask her why she gotta take a pill to chill her out."

Charge chuckles. "You do like to live dangerously, don't you, my brother?"

I shrug. We're jokin' but there's truth in the statement. I

am how I was made. Fucked up. I wreck shit, which is why Story needs to fuckin' leave.

I can't drag her off the stage, make a scene. Forty's right. There's too much ridin' on this shit.

My hands are fisted, and I'm set like a spring, but Deb's pills must be magic, cause somehow, I stay in my seat, nursin' a long neck. I scan the room, wishin' to speed time, prayin' Story picked three short songs for once.

I should know better.

She's danced to "American Pie" and "Hey, Jude," with all the choruses.

I make myself shake out my hands, rest them on the table. There are no threats here—yet—just a bunch of truckers takin' a break after the weigh station, and the usual suits who work in Pyle and probably tell their wives they get stuck in rush hour. Every motherfucker in here is a pervert, and I'm the worst, 'cause I know how innocent the girl on stage is, and I still can't stop myself from starin'.

Her tits wobble and bounce while she does this cute half step around the pole. She's wearin' sky blue pasties 'cause this is Luckahannock County and besides the opioid epidemic and the unemployment, we still got the good old blue laws.

The pasties are huge, too. The sight of her nipples is seared in my memory. They were like saucers, so big, it'd be hard to fit 'em in my mouth. I'd manage, though.

My mouth waters, and I take a deep draw of my beer.

I need to look away.

Back when she was fifteen and looked at my loser ass like I hung the moon, I swore to myself I was gonna stay away. I ain't done a decent thing in my life, but I never took what she offered.

I've stayed true to my word. When she was seventeen

and showed me her tits at a picnic, I left it alone. When she turned eighteen and her ma started bringin' her to parties, I steered clear. And then when she showed up at The White Van last year and—in a moment of stupidity I made damn sure he regretted—Cue hired her? I banished myself to the storage room doorway, and otherwise, stayed the fuck away.

I can't help it if my eyes don't take orders from my brain too good. Especially tonight when this meet has me on edge, and Deb's happy pills are bluntin' my edges.

Story's strutting to the edge of the stage now, stopping every few feet so an asshole can stick a dollar in her garter. Under the table, my hand finds my knife, and I grip the hilt 'til it bites through the callouses on my palm. The only reason I don't get up and bash some skulls is that her eyes are roamin', too. Like they always do.

To find mine.

And damn but her eyes…they're like a cartoon character, the Japanese ones, too wide to be real, and as blue as a robin's egg. Her eyelashes are thick and long, and I know that females wear fake ones, but I've memorized this girl's body from age fifteen. Nothin' on her is fake.

She's blinking at me with those freaky, moon pie eyes, and her lips turn up, not like when a dude slips her a tip, but the way they do when I run into her at the clubhouse or back near the changing room. Her real smile. A little scared, a little shy, but mostly so fuckin' happy to see me.

It guts me like it always does. Sets my blood on fire. Incites the ugly and makes me want to beat that happy out of her before it ruins her.

I tear my eyes away and turn them to the door.

My cock is hard as shit, my temper's about to break, and my brother-by-blood is gonna be here any minute.

That thought alone is enough to douse my dick with cold water.

No way is Ike Kobald gonna see me starin' at Story Jenkins. It'd be like danglin' a bunny in front of a wolf. And then there's the small fact that he's a Rebel Raider hang-around from way back. That's why we invited him after all. To welcome him home from SCI Wayne where he served his sentence. And to pump him for intel on the war we seem to have brewing. See what he knows about the Rebel Raiders torchin' the Patonquin site and trashin' The White Van.

Ain't gonna lie. Havin' a Kobald brother on the outside again makes me twitch. My mind rests easier when they're all inside and accounted for. It's good I've got Forty to my left and Charge to my right. When I let the uneasiness drive me to something stupid, at least there'll be big motherfuckers to slow me down.

The double doors finally swing open, and I force myself not to check on Story. She's still up there. I can tell by the truckers singin' along to "Tubthumping."

"Baby brother!" Ike stomps in like he owns the place, bringing in the cold and the dank smell of cheap cigars on his jacket. He's gone bald on top like Dad, he's bulked up, and he's missin' a few teeth. So am I, but Heavy made me get bridges.

I stand, let Ike thump my back. He throws a few punches at my ribs like it's old times, and I do nothin', just tighten my obliques to absorb the impact. Heavy and I talked through how this needs to go. I stay chill and let Forty and Charge talk.

We sit, Starla brings over another round, and Ike leans back to take in the stage.

The ugly flares. Shit. Heavy mis-fuckin-calculated. Chill

is not going to be possible. I'm going to gouge Ike's eyes out of his motherfuckin' face if he doesn't—

Forty raises a hand, a C-note between two fingers, and waves Danielle over.

"A lap dance for our friend." Forty grins and slaps my knee, while Ike scoots his chair out so Danielle can hover over his lap. Don't see how we're gonna be able to talk like this, but it's a hell of a lot better than me sending him through a wall before word one.

"Steel Bones sure knows how to welcome a guy home." Ike smirks, his gaze darting between Danielle's tits and Forty. He knows something is up.

The fact that I wouldn't piss on him if he was on fire—and he knows it—probably clued him in.

"How long were you in?" Charge asks. "SCI Wayne, right?"

Ike nods a few times as if he's seen the war. "Thirty-six months. Got six off for good behavior. Would have been out last year if Jeannie hadn't come to the parole hearing and cried her fuckin' eyes out. Whaa-whaa. He broke my jaw. Whaa-whaa. PTSD. Had a cunt as head of the parole board that time. Bitch ate that shit up."

My knees start jiggling, and my throat burns. I know for a fact if the pills weren't mufflin' things, my hands would be around his neck. Fucker sounds just like Dad. *Whaa-whaa. Mommy's hidin' in her bed again. Cryin' like a bitch. Rather suck on a crack pipe than FEED HER FUCKIN' KIDS. WHAA-WHAA.*

The ugly churns my guts, kicking speed through my veins, and every part of me is itchy, jerky. I want to pull Danielle off his lap, slam his shit-eating face into the table. It would feel so good. My fingers twitch.

Charge stiffens next to me. He can sense it. He's been at

my side since we were kids, and he's backed me in enough brawls and pulled me off enough assholes that he knows the signs.

"Got a job lined up?" Forty changes the subject.

"With a felony assault conviction?" Ike shakes his head, and moves to grope Danielle's tits. She looks a question at Forty, and he puts another twenty on the table. *NO TOUCHING* is, of course, posted on every wall.

Ike cackles. "Perks of ownership, eh?"

"We might have a gig for you." Forty makes a show of tucking his thick roll back into his inner jacket pocket.

Ike pauses mid-grope, looks up.

"Do you now?" His smile is sly. Dad's smile when he talked to anyone outside of the family. Like he's getting one over.

"Wouldn't require anything but what you'd be doin' anyway." Forty raps on the table for a refill.

"This about Patonquin?"

"Might be."

"I ain't patched into the Rebel Raiders." Ike licks his lips and pinches one of Danielle's nipples. Hard.

She shrieks—pain, not surprise—but she's a pro. She slaps his chest, playful, and giggles, "Behave."

I wince, rise half to standing, ready to drag her away and behind me, and that's when I notice Ike's full attention is on me. Not her. He's smirking.

"What, Dudley Do-Right? What did ya think I was gonna do?" He leans over and licks the nipple he just tweaked, eyein' me.

Dudley Do-Right. Dad's way of fucking with me when I tried to get between him and Ma. *You gonna get her off the glass dick, Dudley Do-Right? You wanna take this belt instead, Dudley Do-Right?*

I shrug, thanking the Lord for Deb's little white pills.

"Don't know," I say. "But I think you should take Forty up on the offer. Minimal risk, maximum reward."

Ike grins again, slapping Danielle's tits so they jiggle. "What do you think, honey? Should I take my little brother up on his big deal?"

"Whatever you want, big guy," she purrs, tripping her fingers down his chest.

I make a mental note to slide an envelope into her locker. She's good people, club pussy from way back. We owe her big for this.

"All right." Ike sniffs. "I ain't gonna wear a wire or any of that shit."

"Don't expect you to," Charge says. "Do your business, and if you hear anything, call Forty. Shit pans out, cash upon delivery."

Ike curls a finger in Danielle's G-string, tugs it loose, and leers down. "Sounds good, sounds good. But one thing—"

He lets Danielle's panties snap back into place, and he turns that leer to her face. I want to beat it off him. I hadn't grown to my full height when he left home to shack up with Jeannie, so I don't have any memories of getting mine back with him like I did with Dad and Markie and Keith.

Every fiber of my body wants to make that memory now. I'm panting with it, negotiating with myself that if I hold one more second, then I can let it out. One more second. I can do one more second. The ugly is churning up a racket in my brain, though, and thinkin' is getting harder and harder.

"What's that?" Charge asks, easy as always.

"I wouldn't feel comfortable not dealin' with family. I go through Nickel."

I can almost see Forty swallow the *hell no.*

"After all, you can't trust family, who can you trust?" Ike sniggers.

I was holdin' on by a thread, but now that thread's shredding down to nothin', and my muscles tense, ready to blow, to wipe this fuckin' mistake of a human being off the face of the planet. Then I catch sight of Story in the mirror above the bar.

Strains of music filter through the chaotic mess of hate and memories and chemical urges moshing in my skull.

The end of song three. "Manic Monday."

Jesus Christ. It's fuckin' Friday.

And it's a Goddamn miracle but the chaos slows, and I can follow a train of thought. In less than a minute, Story's gonna do that stupid ballerina curtsy she does, and then she's gonna come down to work the crowd for drinks and lap dances. She's gonna head straight for this table like a bee to a flower 'cause she ain't never had no sense for danger, and she's under the misapprehension that I ain't the worst mistake a woman can make.

I stand.

Charge makes to hold me back, but I shake him off. I'm cool.

"Gimme a minute." I make a quick run behind the bar, grab a couple of Cue's Cohibas. I saunter back just as the last strains of the song fade out to a few drunk hollers and half-assed golf claps.

"All right, brother," I say. "You deal with me." I gesture to the door with the cigars, makin' sure he sees the gold of the label.

"Cohibas?" Ike's eyes go from Danielle's rack to what I've got in my hands. My stomach turns.

"Only the best," I say.

I fuckin' hate the things. Everything in that shithole I

grew up in reeked of cheap ass cigars. The drapes, the carpet, the dogs. When I moved to the clubhouse, I burned all my clothes. There's a point where you can't wash the smell out.

Ike follows me out front to the wrought iron bench underneath the neon *Live Nude Girls* sign. Forty and Charge don't give it a minute before they come out to babysit me. I hang for about an hour, forcin' smoke into my lungs, listenin' to my piece-of-shit felon brother talk about how he's gonna get back in the game, make Jeannie pay, buy a fuckin' Land Rover.

I got to give it to Deb's little white pills. Without 'em, there's no way I wouldn't have shut his ugly mouth with my fist. 'Course there's also the glimpses of white-gold hair I catch through the door every so often when a dude comes out to light one up. That keeps me shut up and in-line like a damn soldier.

That girl...she's always been a fairy-tale princess lost in a den of trolls. Too bad I'm the dragon in the story. And now I even smell like smoke and shit.

5

STORY

I had a *great* night.

I made two hundred and twenty-four bucks before Cue's cut, and sixty of that was from a lap dance where all the guy wanted to do was tell me how his Cavalier King Charles Spaniel needs an operation—which is *awful*—but at least the guy can afford it.

Anyway, then Nickel came in, even though he wasn't on the schedule. He was meeting some creepy dude who looked like him, but a decade older and bald. I know pretty much everything about Nickel Kobald, since I've been creepin' on him since ninth grade. It was probably one of his brothers. They're all bad news. I thought they were all incarcerated, but I guess not.

But the *best* thing tonight, though? Nickel let me see him looking at me.

He won't, usually. Since the bathroom incident, he goes out of his way to act like he's not watching, even though we both know he is. He's damn near worn a hole in the floor by the storage room. But sometimes—once in a while—he slips up. Either that or he gives up, and he doesn't hide what he's doing. What he's thinking...

He looks so angry when he owns it, like he can't help it and that makes him absolutely furious. I can't even tell you how hot Nickel Kobald is when he's seething and barely holding it together. He's got these perfect high cheekbones and chiseled jaw and these kind of half-sunken eyes. When he's pissed, all of the angles on his face go blade sharp, and he's so beautiful, I get shivers all down my spine.

I also feel totally guilty because I know he has an anger problem.

It's not like when people say, "Oh, such and such has an anger problem," but they really mean the guy's an asshole. Nickel has a real, serious, anger issue. Like the kind you need to see a shrink about. I didn't get that when I was younger, but I do now.

I know that's why he stays away from me. I don't know why he thinks I'd make him angry, but I've seen him lose his shit over a game of pool, an overcooked hamburger, and once when Pig Iron changed the channel when Nickel was watching Nat Geo Explorer so...his caution is probably legit. Still, it drives me crazy.

I want him, and he wants me, and all I get are these stolen moments when I'm on stage or when I stalk him at the clubhouse, and I feel his eyes burning into me, and even though they're black as pitch, I can see how he's starving. I'm starving, too, and I don't know how much longer I can hold out, waiting for scraps.

The dancing takes the edge off. It's amazing that I can get paid for doing what I love, and so what if The White Van's a little skeevy? So was the Happy Trails trailer park, and honestly, so was Petty's Mill High. I always knew I'd probably end up stripping like Ma, and looking back, I'm pretty sure my teachers knew it, too.

I know that sooner or later, something's gotta give—this is a stupid high school crush, and it's going nowhere—but for now? I'm still dopey when I change into my Juicy track-suit at the end of my shift, all because Nickel Kobald let me see him check out my rack.

When he looks at me, it's not like the other guys gawking at the merchandise. Nickel glares at my body and a war plays across his face. He wants to cover me up like he tried to in that bathroom back in the day, but he also wants to touch. He wants to get closer, but he won't, so his biceps bunch and his shoulders square like he's bracing for impact.

He fights himself over me, and it breaks my heart, and it turns me on, and it's so fucked up.

I am how I am, though, so it doesn't get me down for too long. I'm chill again by the time I'm near my car. Minus Cue's cut, I cleared one-fifty tonight, and with tomorrow night's tips, that's rent.

Besides, I have a bottle of Chablis at home that Ma's boyfriend, Larry, brought home from his family, and since Ma won't touch anything from them until they *accept her* and *accept the relationship*, it's all mine. I'm going to drink it while I lay in bed and think about Nickel, leaning back in that booth, that long neck pressed to his—

"Ah!"

Out of nowhere, a cold hand grabs my wrist like a vise. I swing my purse high, screaming, "Cue!"

Where is he? He always stands at the back door when we walk to our cars after close. There's a thunk as my purse makes contact and the thud of boots on concrete coming from the building.

"Fuck!" The voice is curt, growly. Nickel?

He's in the shadows by my Kia, his hand cupping his eye.

"Oh, shit. Did I hurt you?" My purse has a metal buckle, and it looks like it grazed his forehead, right by his left eyebrow.

"Why you attackin' the girls in the parking lot?" Cue bellows over from where he's stopped under a light post. He must have seen it was Nickel.

"Girls is attackin' *me* in the parking lot," Nickel calls back. Cue snorts and strolls back to the door, and then we're alone in the parking lot. Nickel and me.

My stomach swirls. Little bubbles pop and fizz all over my insides. He's staring at me, dead serious, and there's a trickle of blood at the edge of his eye socket.

"Oh, shit. You're bleeding. You want a tissue? I got some in here—" I babble, digging in my purse. Hair brush, tampons, wallet, a pen, Wet Ones, some acorns Ernestine's oldest grandbaby gave me—there! Tissues!

I hand the tiny pack to Nickel, and he takes it with two fingers, mystified.

"For your face." I gesture to the trickle of blood. "I'm so sorry. I thought you were a mugger."

Nickel hands the tissues back and swipes the blood with the sleeve of his grey Henley. "Why the fuck you stop then?"

Huh?

Nickel swallows, the cords rising in his neck. "You think you're gettin' mugged, don't stop. Don't you have mace in that thing? Somethin'?"

Nickel eyes my purse like it has teeth. I actually do have mace. I'd probably have to dump the whole thing on the hood of my car to find it, but it's in there.

"I wasn't getting mugged, Nickel."

"You got the survival instincts of a fuckin' toddler."

"You've got shit for manners." Fuck him. If I was a man, I'd be Clint freakin' Eastwood. I fight off a man in a dark parking lot, and I'm some kind of dumbass damsel in distress? Hah.

He stares at me, and I stare at him. Now is when he's going to stomp away. Roll his eyes, scoff, and turn his back, but even though he's being all bossy, I don't want him to. This close, I can smell him, and—gross.

"Why do you smell like Cue's office?" I wrinkle my nose.

Nickel blinks, thrown for a second, and then he dips his head to sniff his shoulder. "Oh. Cigars."

"You smoke now?"

Nickel clicks his tongue, irritated. He starts pacing in front of me, so I lean back against the car door and settle in.

Nickel is never at rest unless he's backing up one of his brothers. Otherwise, it's like he's got some Tasmanian devil under his skin, racing from limb to limb, trying to get out or else drag his ass somewhere. I love to watch him. He's like a tiger in the zoo, stalking his cage like he knows a way out, he's just biding his time.

"Fuck," Nickel grunts after a few moments and nails me with one of his meanest glares. "You got to quit this job."

"Not gonna do that, Nickel."

"You can't be makin' much. It's Friday night, and what did you clear? A C-note?"

"One fifty. That's over twenty bucks an hour. My day job at General Goods only pays eight." I might be shit at reading, but I can do math fine. Nothing in Petty's Mill pays as good as The White Van if you only have a high school diploma. Nothing I want to do, anyway.

Nickel's nostrils flare. "There's other shit you could do."

"I love dancing." I do. The music, the high of the applause and the hollering, the strange kind of drunken happiness in a room where a bunch of men are getting exactly what they want? It's amazing. The groping, the weird smells, and the asshole suits from Pyle who don't tip? Not so much. "What is it that you want me to do?"

He can't answer, and that pisses him off even more. His fists clench so tight, I can see the veins in his forearms pop where he's pushed his sleeves up to his elbows.

If he hits something, I hope it's not my car. It's made of aluminum foil; it'll definitely dent.

"Nickel, where's this comin' from?" I sigh, folding my arms.

This ain't the first time we've had this talk. When I started at The White Van, we had it at least once a week. He'd tell me to quit. I'd say no. He'd hit a wall or a locker, and storm off. It's pretty much the only conversation we've ever had if you don't count me coming on to him and him telling me to get lost.

"That man I was with tonight." Nickel stops his pacing.

"He your real brother?"

Nickel nods. "Stay away from him."

"Okay."

Nickel's told me to steer clear of certain guys before, usually pervs and drug dealers. It's nice to get a heads up since—and I will never admit this to him—I don't scare as easy as maybe I should.

"I'm serious, Story."

"I know. I said okay."

Nickel's shoulders flex. He doesn't believe me, so he's working himself up. I've seen this before a dozen times. It's usually the point Heavy or Charge hustles him out of the room or presses a beer in his hand.

"He's a bad man." Nickel snarls. "He hurts women."

"I won't talk to him." I take a step forward. I don't know

why. As if I'm gonna calm him down by getting close? I trigger this guy, and I know it.

"He asks you for a dance, you tell him your shift's over. He asks for your number, you tell him to fuck himself." Nickel's eyes dart in the sockets, as if he's seeing all these terrible things in his head. "You do not ask him to buy you a drink."

"I won't."

"And you do not walk to your car without Cue. Make that lazy fucker walk you." He pierces me with his manic gaze and grabs me by the shoulders, his fingers digging in hard enough to bruise. "You understand?"

I smother a hiss of pain. If I say let go, he will. I know. He'll turn all the rage on himself, and he'll bolt, and I don't want that 'cause I can feel the heat coming in waves off his body, and all I want to do is make him pull me closer. So I sneak attack.

"Hey," I say and smile, putting every bit of happy I have in it, and I have a lot, since Nickel is here with me, alone, in the dark.

He glances down, and I know the second I have him trapped. His eyelids drift closed like he's praying. I stand on my toes and wriggle my shoulders, loosening his grip. And then I bounce up and I—

I kiss his chin? Damn. He's too tall; I missed his lips.

"Huh?" Nickel drops his arms in surprise, and he goes very, very still. He's freakin' mind boggled. A jolt of pure feminine satisfaction runs straight between my thighs. I rest my hands on his rock-hard chest, stand back up on my tippy toes, and I plant another one on his jaw. The light beard he's growing out prickles my lips.

I slide a hand up and cup his neck, urging him down, but he won't budge.

"What are you doing?" he growls, his breath catching on his next inhale.

Since he's not bending, and I can't get to his lips, I work my way down, brushing kisses over the pulse that throbs under his ear and the cords straining in his neck. He hisses, as if he's in pain, but he keeps as still as a statue.

When I reach his chest, I inhale as deep as I can. Beneath the stinky cigar, there's the scent that unlocks my insides every time. Nickel's smell. Male musk, fresh-cut wood, and cheap laundry powder. My swirly stomach clenches and my pussy lips swell. I press closer, winding my arms around his neck, sighing as I rest my cheek on his chest.

"Touch me back," I murmur.

"You shouldn't do this." His voice is torn up, his arms ramrod straight at his side. His fingers twitch.

"Why not?" I stroke my fingers down the back of his neck, and I listen to his heart try to crack his rib cage.

"You know how I am," he growls, frustration finally trumping the element of surprise. I know I only have seconds left before he runs so I cant my hips forward, reveling in the feel of his hard length trying to punch through his jeans and press against my belly. This is for me. Only me. A whimper escapes my lips.

"What the fuck are you doing?"

"I want it," I murmur, punch drunk on his closeness, his scent, his raspy voice.

"Fuck, Story!" He jerks away, throws up his palms to ward me off. "Since you can't think so good, at least fuckin' listen. Stay away from my brother. Stay away from me. Fuck!"

He whirls back, slams his palm against Cue's truck. Good thing it's a Chevy or that would've left a dent.

Nickel's shoulders are heaving, and he has his back to me, but he doesn't leave. I know why. I'm not safe in my car yet.

"Nickel?"

He ignores me. It's so quiet I can hear cars whoosh down Route 7. I sigh and sort around in my purse until I find my key fob. The double beep breaks the silence, and I slide into my seat. I give it a moment, 'cause I'm an optimist, but he's shut down tight as a drum again. Won't even look at me.

"I'm not afraid of you, Nickel Kobald," I say, and he stiffens like I hit him in the kidneys.

"I know," he says, real quiet as he walks away, and he sounds so damn disappointed.

It takes me five long minutes of blaring the radio and singing along to "Uptown Girl" before I feel right again.

This is good. This is progress. A step forward.

Next time I'm gonna get a stool or something so I can reach his lips. He's so close to cracking; I can feel it. All I need to do is hold the course, and that man is gonna be mine.

6

NICKEL

The party's been goin' an hour at most, the clubhouse is only half full, and this night is already goin' to shit.

Story's hangin' by the jukebox like she always does, waitin' for someone to dance with her, and she's letting a prospect drape his arm around her like she's the bench seat of an Impala. The ugly, a wave of hot fury, washes through me, prickling my skin.

So it begins. The way every rage begins. The chemicals in my body surge, whipping my muscles into action and clouding my brain until beating something or someone to death seems like the only logical outcome to any given situation. It usually ends with blood splatter and Charge tryin' to talk down the police.

When I was younger, it was a high. Still is sometimes. But mostly it's tiresome and fucking depressing.

I don't want to kill the prospect. I actually kind of like him. He knows his way around an engine, and besides, I guarantee Charge or Forty told him to steer clear of Story— even though I ain't never said shit or made a claim—and dude still has the balls to rub up on her. I respect the cojones. I still want to rip his arm off, though.

"What's that fucker's name again?" I ask Wall as I break, sending the seven-ball hopping to the concrete floor.

Wall shrugs, chalks his stick. "One of the dead presidents."

We got four prospects around the same time. One's name is Roosevelt, so Heavy thought it'd be funny to name the rest accordingly. There's a Bush, a Wash, for Washington, and a Boom who started out as Eisenhower.

Road names are stupid.

Charge gave me mine off of one time I kept begging for a nickel so I could get a pop. Seriously. If I'd have been short ten cents, they'd be callin' me Dime.

The prospect hands Story his beer, and she takes a sip, eyein' me. Waiting. She hasn't tried this shit in a few years. Not since I sat in a bar stool and held her eyes, not blinkin', as she walked out with a hang-around named Dean.

Dean don't hang around no more.

I've managed to avoid her all week, had Forty cover the shift we shared, and until this moment, I'd only seen her every wakin' fuckin' moment of the day, in my mind, tilting her face back to kiss my cheek, snuggling to my chest, her silky hair tickling the crook of my neck. Another wave of fury crashes through me.

She acts like this is my choice. Like any man could have all that sweet and soft in his arms and decide to turn it down. It ain't a *choice*. If you're blind, you don't fuckin' drive a car. It's that simple.

Fuck.

I need air.

I need to see if Scrap is settin' up any fights out back; I need to beat on something. I need to hurt. But Story's over by the jukebox with a prospect's arm around her neck, and she's my anchor. My feet ain't goin' nowhere.

And damn, but she's so pretty tonight. She left her hair down, but she braided pieces on either side of her face and tied them back with a hot pink bow. She's wearing a dress to match—skin tight, cut low in front and almost up to her ass cheeks in the back—and white leather platform pumps.

The prospect thinks he won the stripper lottery, but he don't know what I know. Those are Fay-Lee's shoes, and they're at least a size too small. That's why she's favoring one foot and then the other.

She's wearin' briefs—the prospect definitely noticed that, impossible not to—not a thong or bare ass like another girl would with that dress. Every man here can see her panty lines, and she's oblivious. I guarantee Sunny, her ma, picked out the dress. Left to her own devices, Story shows up places lookin' like Punky Brewster bein' raised by Harley Quinn.

The prospect cracks a joke, Story snorts, and I can see the moment she forgets about makin' me jealous. She loses herself in the laugh, and every man in the room can't help but glance over and smile cause Story laughing is a raw hit of pure joy. Like when Ernestine's youngest grandbaby gurgles and shrieks when Charge blows bubbles on her tummy.

Ain't nothin' so beautiful, so perfect. This world is gonna kill that. Stomp it into the mud. Don't know how it hasn't yet.

She keeps this up, chasin' after me, workin' at The White Van, she's gonna be club pussy soon enough. And then she's gonna get burnt out and bitter, and a fucker like Ike Kobald's gonna move in, promisin' shit he has no intention of delivering.

She needs to get out of here. Out of Petty's Mill. Move to

some big city where she can teach rich bitches how to strip for a workout like I saw on TV. She stays here...it's a matter of time before I break. I ain't a good man. I will ruin a girl like her 'cause she'll think she can change me. That I'm salvageable. I ain't.

"Beer?" Danielle saunters over, handing a fresh one to Wall and me. She leans against the pool table, eyes it, then raises one of her weird, penciled-in eyebrows.

Yeah. Wall's about to run the table on me.

"You playing blindfolded tonight, Nick?"

"Hey. He's doin' better'n he usually do." Wall sinks the eight-ball.

Danielle winces. "I got loser." She pats Wall on the ass.

He sinks to a couch and takes out his phone. He's wide as a door and has fifty pounds on every dude in this place, but he's a chill guy. Only brother besides Heavy I've never brawled with over something stupid. Guess when you're as big as him you have zero to prove.

"You rack 'em," Danielle bosses and picks a stick. She's hot tonight, as always. We went to school together. She was two years ahead. Gave me my first blow job behind the concession stand at a pep rally. I lasted ten seconds, and she told everyone I had a monster cock.

Liked her ever since.

She breaks. Table scratch. She looks me a question, and I gesture for her to take another shot. She does.

"You know you didn't have to," she says.

I shrug. "I didn't have a clear shot."

She pops her gum. "I mean the envelope in my locker. That was you right? Two hundred bucks? You're fuckin' nuts."

"He touched you." I sink a ball off a bank shot.

"It was a lap dance."

"There's no touching."

"Bullshit. You watch me do more in the champagne room on the regular."

"You gonna give it back then?"

"Fuck no." She laughs. "I'll put a handy in the bank for you."

I snort, and catch a flash of blonde out of the corner of my eye.

Story's started for me. Her impossibly huge eyes are spitting fire. I know that look, even if I haven't seen it on her face before. She's pissed. Jealous.

My first instinct is to put my hands up, back off. Something deep in me needs her to calm down. Her upset cramps my guts and sends adrenaline roaring through my veins.

But hold up. I could use this.

Don't know why I never thought of it before. Maybe I've been hopin' I could keep her around forever, dangling. I could watch her like a pretty bird in a cage, and make sure no asshole got near her. When she was in school, it was easy. It couldn't be nothin' real. She wasn't even eighteen.

But she's a woman now. She's laid her cards on the table. She ain't out-growin' this. I keep letting her dangle, I'm the asshole. I need to make a decision.

"Can I cash in now?" I ask Danielle. I slide an arm around her waist, slow and deliberate. I'm so fucking awkward. I ain't never been one for PDA.

"Seriously? With Sailor Moon Barbie right over there?" Danielle raises a razor-thin eyebrow. "You gonna do my girl dirty?"

"You and me both know she got no business sniffin' after me."

"Yeah, well, you're gonna cause me work problems. I got no beef with Starshine. 'Cept her music sucks."

"Come on, Danny."

"Fifty."

"You said I got money in the bank."

"Okay, twenty."

"Done. Now stick your tongue in my mouth." I pull her in, and she's a pro, 'cause she has her hand on my dick and her lipstick smeared all over my mouth before I can think twice.

Or close my eyes.

So I get to watch Story's stupid, kid crush break in real time. Her eyes expand until they eat up her entire face. Her lips part. A soft "oh" floats across the room. Then her shoulders slump. Her knees sway, knock together, and her dress bags where her gut sinks in.

Oh, shit. I need to think.

Danielle guides my hand to her tit.

A cold sweat trickles down my back. This is the right thing to do. Isn't it?

The sick rising in my throat says it ain't, but my body's backwards. It don't know right from wrong. My daily life is proof of that. Danielle comes up for air, tries to wipe the lipstick from my mouth. Story stumbles over, closing the distance between us, the prospect doggin' her steps.

"What are you doing?" She stops in front of me, her fists clenched at her hips. Her voice cracks.

I need to fix this. I need to staunch whatever wound I just ripped open, but I don't know how. Tears gather along the bottom rims of her eyes, beading on her thick lashes. I have to make it stop. I can't breathe through her hurt.

But I got to. I need to let this play out. A little hurt now is gonna save a whole bunch of pain later.

This perfect girl can't be kissin' on head cases ten-years older than her in strip club parking lots. She needs to give this up, but she won't. She's gonna end up warping herself into thinner and thinner versions of herself—tryin' to fix the unfixable—until no one, including her, believes her life is worth shit.

I can see it clear as day. She's young; she has no idea, but I've lived this. Front row seat. I have to kill this thing now.

"Do what now?" I narrow my eyes, tugging Danielle closer to my side. I don't know where to put my hand so I rest it on her ass.

"What are you doing?" Story asks again, her voice almost a whisper.

"About to get my dick sucked. Why? Did you want to? Ain't waitin' for you to finish off the prospect first."

Each word scores my throat like acid. This is harder than listenin' to Ike the other night. Harder than watchin' her walk off with Dean the hang-around. Harder than puttin' her top back on and all the no's I ever told her put together.

"But..." Story glances over her shoulder, wildly, as if rescue is comin'. As if someone's gonna show up and let her down easy about how she's been barkin' up the wrong tree for years. The prospect should take her away now. Why the fuck is he standing there with his dick in his hand?

"But what?" I press forward. Embrace the pain. I deserve it. "You think I'm into makin' out in parking lots?" I force myself to laugh. It sounds like a death rattle. "I'm a grown man, little girl. Now, you wanna get down on your knees, or you wanna leave the grown-ups alone?"

"I—I—"

And for a moment, sheer terror seizes my chest. She's gonna say yes. She'll do it, she'll get on her knees, and I'll be damned a hundred times over. Too late, the prospect grabs her elbow.

I keep my eyes boring into hers, a sneer on my lips. My

stomach pitches, but I hold the line. Finally, she chokes on a swallow and shakes her head.

"You know what, Nickel? You could have just said. You could have said leave me alone."

Goddamn, but I have, a hundred times. Never meant it once, and she knows it. She draws in a deep, shaky breath and lowers her gaze to the floor. The ugly rattles my bones. Story shouldn't ever hang her head. And I did this to her. But hell, if I let her in, how much worse I would do?

She dashes a tear off her cheek. "You don't need to break things all the time, you know." She skewers me with those huge blue eyes. "You can just let things go."

That's where she's wrong. I do. And I can't. So I say nothing at all.

Then my beautiful, perfect girl wipes her palms down the sides of her dress, nods to Danielle, and hoists her purse higher on her shoulder.

"Well. You guys have fun." She lifts her chin, and she heads straight for the front door.

I force myself to kiss Danielle while she walks away. I've got another woman's tongue in my mouth while a gaping hole explodes in my chest.

When Story's finally gone, disappeared down the hall to the front door, I make it a solid five seconds before my fist slams into a wall. And you know something I never realized before now?

Doin' right and doin' wrong?

There ain't no difference. It all feels like shit.

7

STORY

I lose Roosevelt by the front door. I ask him to get me a beer, and I bail. I need to get out of here so bad. I'm crying, and half these people see me naked on the regular.

I make it to the Kia in record time, kick my heels off and drive, heading away from town. I have one hand on the steering wheel, and another pressed to my chest. I guess I'm trying to hold my heart in.

I've never been kicked in the stomach before so I'm not entirely sure, but this has to be close to how it feels. My belly aches, I can hardly breathe, and my heart feels like it's been fed to a shredder. And it's so much worse because it was *on purpose*. I've been kicked in the stomach on purpose. God, I'm so *stupid*.

I turn the radio up, but it doesn't help. I sing along, at the top of my voice, and that doesn't help either. I see Nickel's hand squeezing Danielle's ass. Red lipstick smeared across his face. Danielle's taller than me. She can reach his mouth.

I see his eyes, cold and blank, asking me if I wanna get on my knees. Well, he's put me there. This hurts so bad, and

I don't know what to do to make it stop. It's nine o'clock on a Saturday night, and I guess I could drive into Pyle and find a place to dance, but I'm weepy and alone and I don't want to dance. For the first time in my whole freakin' life, I don't want to dance. That's such *bull crap*.

I feel like a glass that somebody knocked over—on *purpose*—and I'm in tiny pieces, and I don't know what to do because I'm not a glass anymore; I'm shards on the floor. I'm obviously not thinkin' real straight, so I put on my clicker, pull a u-ey, and drive up to Gracy's Corner. I scrub my face with my jacket sleeve before I pull up to the gatehouse.

"Good eve—shit. What's wrong, baby doll?"

Lucian's working the gate. He's a sweetheart. A regular at The White Van. He tips real good.

"Boy trouble." I blink, puttin' on my stage face. More like delusional-girl-finally-gets-what-she's- been-askin'-for trouble, but he didn't ask me for all that.

"That's why you need a man," he jokes while the gate rises.

"They're double the trouble from what I hear," I joke back and wave as I pull off.

I guess I'm not totally broken if I can still banter with the customers.

Shit.

Now I'm sad that I'm not totally broken.

I drive toward my ma's new place, and I notice they've put up a new gazebo at the circle where all the streets in the development meet. It's real pretty, like the one from *The Sound of Music*. For a second, I get distracted, I forget about tonight, and then it's even worse because crash, bam, I remember again. Every painful second. Nickel tugging Danielle into his arms. The remark about leaving the grown-ups alone. How he didn't watch me leave 'cause his tongue was in my co-worker's mouth.

Even when I left with Dean, he watched.

I set my jaw, and then I break into a fresh wave of tears. I don't know how to do this. Normally, I buckle down and keep going. That's how I do life. But how do you buckle down through a broken heart?

When I roll up to Larry's place, I'm relieved to see Ma's new Lexus in the drive. She's terrible at parking so Larry puts her car in the garage at night and backs it out for her in the morning. Guess he hasn't valeted her yet tonight.

That's true love, I think. Parking your girlfriend's car so she doesn't ding her paint job on the garage door. And bam. I remember again, and more tears dribble down my cheeks. I haven't wiped them away by the time Ma throws open the front door, cocktail in hand, crying, "Oh, good God, Story! What's wrong?"

And then I'm in Ma's bony arms, enveloped by the smell of gin and apricot moisturizer.

"Is it the car? Is it work? Is Cue steppin' out of line? I'll cut his balls off." She drags me to the kitchen and shoves me onto a stool, calling, "Larry! Get a bottle of Cuervo! We're in the kitchen."

Then she rummages in a cabinet, finds a package of Oreos, and sets them between us. I love my ma.

I'm twenty-one, and she's only thirty-seven, so she's more like an older sister to me. She got together with Larry two years ago, and for a while, she tried to be all *mother-y* and make up for lost time, but we both got bored with it. I'm happy she's back to being wild and crazy Sunny Jenkins. I haven't needed a real mom in a long time, anyway.

Ma grabs three shot glasses from the cabinet, and then

she splays her hands on the kitchen island, a ring on all ten fingers, leaning back to take me in.

"It's that asshole Nickel Kobald." She purses her lips, holds one palm open as steps sound on the basement stairs. Larry enters a second later and slaps a bottle in her outstretched hand.

"Thank you, baby," Ma coos, and gives Larry a smooch while she untwists the cap.

"What's wrong, Ray?" Larry asks, brushing a kiss on the top of my head. He calls me *Ray* for *Little Ray of Sunshine* on account of Ma's name being Sunny.

It's a dumb nickname, but I don't care. Larry's awesome.

He's short, balding, and wears boat shoes with no socks. At the moment he has a white cardigan draped around his shoulders. He's a dentist, not Ma's dentist or mine, and she won't say how they met. Since she's been with him, she's quit dancing, stopped doin' the guys in the club, and she gave up smoking. Plus she sold the trailer, and she's living large in his McMansion.

That's not why I love Larry, though. I love him 'cause he thinks my ma walks on water, and he's not afraid to show it. Like now? He's gone back around the island to wrap his arms around Ma while we talk.

And *ouch*. A wave of hurt washes over me again, pooling in my tummy. I toss a shot back, trying to replace the pain with tequila burn.

"You gonna talk, or we gonna have to guess?" Ma prods. Larry reaches forward to refill my glass.

"Nickel," I grit out, and my face heats. Ma knows about my...well, she calls it a crush. She thinks it's cute. Reminds her of how she had it bad for a dude named Joey Lawrence back in the day. It's not like that. *I'm* not like that. No one seems to get it. They see me going after Nickel or dancing, and they think I make bad choices. Maybe, but it's 'cause I want *hard*. What I feel for Nickel? It's deeper than a crush. It's real.

You wanna get down on your knees?

Well, shit. Maybe it is like that. Worse than that, because whoever Joey Lawrence is, I don't think he'd talk to my ma like that.

"My baby." Ma taps my glass with hers and tilts one down the hatch. "Condolences."

"Nickel..." Larry's forehead furrows. "The angry one? With the crazy eyes?"

I sigh. That does about sum him up.

"He's the best of a rotten bunch," Ma offers, her nose wrinkling. "The Kobalds are pieces of shit. To the man."

"I'm not familiar with the family," Larry says.

"Don't surprise me. They're not big on dental work." Ma catches my eye, shrugs. "That one of yours is all right, but I grew up next to James Kobald down in Happy Trails. Nasty man. Nasty."

"You never said." I would have remembered. Especially in high school, I studied Nickel Kobald like a subject I needed to pass to graduate.

"Nothing nice to say." Ma sinks down onto a bar stool, and Larry takes the one next to her. "There were five of 'em in a two-bedroom single wide, and it sounded like they were constantly tryin' to fight their way out."

"Which trailer?"

"Gone for scrap by the time you would remember. The dad passed, and the boys drifted off. James, that's Nickel's dad, he married a girl who used to babysit me. Farrah. I always thought Farrah was the prettiest name." Ma smiles, and Larry swoops in to kiss her. He does that a lot. Kisses her smiles. The hurt flares in my gut.

How come she's tellin' me this now? I would've killed to know all this before. She saw the doodles I drew all over the inside of my binder. Nickel and Story with the *S* entwined with the *N*. I've still got the binder somewhere.

God, how hard I hold onto the impossible. He didn't want me then. He doesn't want me now. Or if he does, not enough. I need to let it go. And I will. In a bit. After gettin' good and drunk, and then crying myself to sleep.

"What was she like?" I ask. "Nickel's mom?"

Ma smiles. "Sweet. Too sweet. She lived with her grandma, and she wasn't allowed to date or even talk to boys on the phone."

"What's wrong with that?" Larry asks. He's in his late forties, and he's real conservative.

"What's wrong with that," Ma teases, patting his thigh, "Is that the only boys Farrah could chase were the Kobalds who lived across the way. And she caught herself a real asshole."

"What happened?"

I can't believe Ma's been holding out on me. She's had all these pieces to my puzzle all along and now she's handing out clues like Halloween candy when it doesn't matter anymore.

"She got beat on all the time, got hooked on pills, then smack, and then she kind of fell off the face of the earth. Toward the end, she worked at The White Van for a hot second, but Cue fired her. She stole from the till."

"That's freakin' *horrible*."

"She was so sweet." Ma fingers her amber beaded necklace like she does when she's praying. "She let me watch cartoons for hours and eat ice cream out of the carton."

Larry can't stand Ma lookin' sad for a second, so he

stands again and wraps his arms around her. His forearms are so hairy. And I'm so jealous.

I had stopped crying, my eye sockets are tender and my sinuses ache, but now another wave of tears is gonna make it all worse. I grab a paper napkin from the holder and blot like crazy. The last time I cried this ugly was when I watched *The Notebook* with Fay-Lee. At least that couple ended up together in the end.

"You gonna tell us what Nickel did?" Ma pours us both another.

"He hurt you?" Larry's forehead furrows and the muscles in his hairy forearms pop.

"No, he wouldn't do that," I say. Ma believes me—she knows the guys in the MC—but Larry raises his eyebrows.

"I myself have given that man two bridges for teeth he lost in fights."

I didn't know that.

"You're his dentist?"

Larry's eyes go shifty. "I do some work for Steel Bones on the side. Cash basis. At the home office."

"He's been here?" Tonight is blowing my mind. How do I not know all this? Ma is my best friend. I thought we didn't have secrets.

Hold up.

"Is that how you met Ma? Workin' for the MC?"

If so, that's got to be one hell of a story. Ma's worked her way through most of the brothers, like, at least twice.

Ma blushes bright red and fans herself with her hand. "Story for another time, Story." She grins like she always does when she works my name into something. "Now tell us what happened."

I drop it. For now, and I try to think of a way to put it. "The other night, I—"

What? Attacked Nickel in the parking lot with cuddles? Oh, God. This is so embarrassing.

"I tried to kiss him. And tonight he was hooking up with Danielle Martin."

"He was?" Ma frowns, surprised. "That's new."

The images flash in my head again, the world's suckiest photo montage. Here's his hand on her ass. Here's his tongue in her mouth. The tequila sloshes in my stomach.

"He was trying to get rid of me," I admit, and the words feel cold and hard and true. "He doesn't want anything to do with me."

"Well, I'd say what's wrong with him, but it's kind of obvious." Larry shrugs.

"What's wrong with him?" I know what I think, but I'm curious about how Larry sees it.

"Everything but his upper left second bicuspid and his lower right lateral incisor."

"Babe." Ma play slaps him. "Story has thought the sun rises and sets on that man since what? Ninth grade? He can't be all bad."

Larry nods, very serious. I bet he thinks we're both nuts, but he never acts better than Ma and me. Another reason why I love him.

He pats my hand. "I guess what I mean is that he's obviously wrong for our little Ray. She should always be smiling and sunny. Like her Mama." Ma melts into him, but he keeps his eyes level on mine. "I'm serious."

I know. And then bam, crash. The weight of it all slams down on me again. I'm going to see Danielle on Wednesday. Nickel too, maybe. I'm gonna have to get mostly naked and dance. They might be all over each other, and I'm going to have to dance to it. Oh, Lord. My stomach heaves.

"Bathroom that way!" Ma shouts, but I suck down a few deep breaths and the nausea goes away.

"This is the worst. I can't go back to The White Van."

Ma cuts a loaded look at Larry.

"Why is that, baby?" She nods toward the counter by the fridge, and Larry goes to get whatever she's after.

"Because..."

I can't say it. I'll sound too weak.

Because I don't want to look at Danielle's bare ass knowing Nickel's been all up in it.

Because it's one thing when Nickel's there, tryin' to hide the fact he's watchin' me and failing. It's another thing when he's decided he's got to make me hurt so I'll go away.

Because I can't dance with a broken heart.

Yeah. I sound stupid. It's not like he was my boyfriend. He never led me on. Well, not with his words. His eyes though...

But what? I'm gonna be heartbroken 'cause of a man who stares at me? And that's enough to be my bliss? I hardly ever win in life, but when I see a shot at better, at happy, since when do I sit around and wait?

I'm silent, lost for words, when Larry slides a colorful brochure across the counter and takes his seat again next to Ma. They both grin at me like hyenas. I glance down.

Four very fit young people in polo shirts and backpacks are laughing by a fountain.

"Luckahannock County Community College?"

Ma and Larry bob their heads in unison, smiling almost as wide as the cover models on the brochure.

"They have a two-year program in dental hygiene," Larry says. "When you finish, you could work in my practice. Starting salary is forty thousand. If you wanted to move to a city like Pyle, you could make more."

"Think about it." Ma's eyes go wide. "You'd only have to work one job. Health insurance. You wouldn't have to work nights."

I'm shaking my head already. "Ma. You know I hardly graduated."

"That was then. This is now."

"What's different?"

I'm at a loss. I know Ma wants more for me now that she's doin' so good, but community college? Does she not remember how I had to retake English 10, like, three times?

Ma's eyes narrow, and her voice drops. This is as serious as she gets.

"One. We've got the inside track." She hitches a thumb at Larry.

"Two. You were always just fine at the practical stuff. And three. You've got to stop dreaming so small."

Ouch. That feels harsh, given the night I had.

Ma sees me cringe and sighs. "I blame myself for raisin' you in that small-ass trailer in this small-ass town. You should have been dreaming about dancing in the ballet. Getting famous on the internet. Fallin' in love with some prince."

I hear what she doesn't say. She thinks I should want better than strippin' for truckers and holdin' out for a biker with anger management issues. I do have dreams, though. A real one. I want to dance, and maybe it's not high class, but I am dancing.

It's like this test Mr. Anscomb talked about back in high school. They put a marshmallow in front of a kid, and they tell him if you don't eat it, when I come back, I'll give you two. The good kids wait, and the bad kids eat it. That's bull-shit, though. The *smart* kids grab that marshmallow. 'Cause in this world? You ain't promised anything else, and you better take what sweet you can.

Today, though, dancin' at The White Van and crushin' on Nickel Kobald don't taste so sweet. But dental hygiene?

"How's dental hygiene dreamin' big, Ma?" I glance at Larry. "No offense."

"Maybe it's not big, per se." Ma sniffs. Is she tearing up? Oh, no. If she cries, I'm gonna start again. "But it's my dream for you. An easier life than I've had."

"I love dancing."

"You'd still have your Swinging Seniors class."

I teach adults one night a week at Shady Gap Rec. The rec people know where I work so they don't ask me to teach the kid's classes, but I have fun with the seniors.

"I'm not really interested in teeth." I mean, I'm grateful I have all mine, but beyond that, it's not really something I've thought much about.

"Truth be told, neither am I." Larry lifts a shoulder. "I dropped out of med school during my fourth year, and getting a dental degree was the easiest way to make use of my credits."

"You went to med school?" This night is blowing my mind.

"Dentistry is honest work, and you help people. It's a good job." Larry dodges my question.

"I don't see how I'd pay for school, go to classes, and work two jobs." I'm considering it—it's a new idea, but it's not crazy. Maybe it's time for a new dream. A new direction. I don't know how it'd be possible, though. I have bills.

"We'd pay for school." Ma and Larry say it at the same time.

I open my mouth to argue. I've never asked anyone to

pay my way, and I'm not starting now. Ma doesn't let me get a word out though.

"Yes, we will, and you'll take it. We'll also front you some cash so you can drop one of your jobs."

I shake my head.

"Yes, you will. You'll work for Larry when you finish, and that's gonna pay him back in the long run. You'd be replacing Amy when she retires, and she makes a hell of a lot more than forty thousand."

They've really talked about this.

"Come on, Ray. Say you'll think about it." Larry grins, and I can't help but smile back.

I guess I will. It's not like I want to think about what's on my mind at present. I can think about going back to school. It sounds ridiculous. Still, dental hygienist is a good job. And Larry seems pretty confident that I can pull it off.

While I mull it over, Larry excuses himself to bed. Ma and I take the party to the overstuffed couch in the den. We crank up WFIV, *Top 40 from the Past 40*, and we kick off our shoes. We're drinkin' from the bottle now.

"I'm so sorry, baby." Ma grabs my feet and cradles them to her belly. She used to do that when I was little. "I know you really liked him."

"He likes me, too."

I've never told anyone this part before. Fay-Lee and Crista and Jo-Beth, all the girls at the clubhouse and at work, they think I've got some unrequited crush. I let them think it, 'cause what am I gonna say? He looks at me hungry? He nags me to quit my job?

"He thinks he's not good enough for me."

Ma gives me a boozy half-smile. "I know, baby."

"Yeah?" My mouth twists. She's humoring me.

"Of course. He told me as much."

"What?"

Ma raises her palms. "Now don't blow a gasket."

"Tell me!" I dig my heels into her stomach and she shrieks.

"Okay, okay. It was when you turned eighteen, and you started coming to parties at the clubhouse. He cornered me. Told me to leave you home. Said no man around there was good enough for you, and I needed to start being a real mother, and if any man touched you, he'd kill 'em, and it'd be on me."

Ho-ly. Shit.

"Why didn't you tell me?" I throw a pillow at her head, and she drunkenly bops it aside.

"'Cause I knew this is how it would all end, and I didn't want to encourage you."

A cold settles in my chest. When Ma says it like that, the whole thing sounds doomed.

"What did you say? To him?"

Ma snorts. "Said if I left you home, I wouldn't know what worthless piece of shit men were creepin' up on you, and besides, I now had it on good authority that you'd be safe and sound at the Steel Bones clubhouse, seein' as how if any man touched you, he'd kill 'em."

"What did he say?"

"Put his fist through the kitchen door and went to pick a fight with Creech."

That sounds about right.

"Why's he like that, Ma?"

It's getting hard to keep my eyes open. I set the tequila bottle down on the floor so it doesn't spill if I pass out.

"I dunno. Why are you so much like me? Some of it's got to be in the blood. Some of it's how I raised you. That ain't the question that comes to mind when I think about Nickel Kobald, though."

"What is?"

"I wonder why *ain't* he like the other Kobalds."

There's a long silence while I think about this. My thoughts are coming real slow from being tired and heart-sick and most the way to drunk.

"*Is* he different though?" Maybe he's not in jail now, but he's done some time through the years.

"I don't know, Story-girl. Don't think any other Kobald would have gone out, bought a new kitchen door, and hung it that same night."

Oh my goodness. I *remember* that. It was my first club-house party. I was giddy. Fay-Lee was pissed at Dizzy for something, and we were dancing together, buzzed as hell, and I'd noticed Nickel with a tool box, hangin' a door. Thought it was weird as shit.

"You think he'll ever—" I don't know the word I want. I grasp around, but my tipsy brain won't cough it up.

"Change?" Ma supplies. A corner of her lip rises in a sad smile. "No, baby. I don't."

"W-why not?" A last, sad sob escapes from deep in my chest.

"He'd have to believe a person can change. And I don't think he does."

Those words follow me down into a restless sleep. They haunt me the next day, and the day after that. They should be hopeless words, but they're not. I'm just not a hopeless kind of girl.

Nickel Kobald needs to believe a person can change. And as they say, seeing is believing.

On Monday, I get Larry to drive me up to Luckahannock County Community College to register for classes. We buy a whole bunch of books, and later, Larry gets on the internet and gets me audio versions of all of them. On Tuesday, I give my two weeks' notice at General Goods.

That was not the job Ma was hopin' I'd quit, but she's always let me make my own choices.

Nickel Kobald likes watchin' me. Well, I'm gonna make him watch me change. I'm gonna be a fuckin' dental hygienist if it kills me.

Maybe he's made me give up on us, but I sure as shit ain't givin' up on him...or myself.

I'm just not that kind of girl.

8

NICKEL

S tory's ignorin' me. Which is good.

It's two weeks later, the first time we've been on the same shift since that night with Danielle, and she's actin' like she can see through me. She hasn't been around the clubhouse, and even her girls have been icin' me out. Fay-Lee and Crista gave me the cold shoulder at the poker run last weekend. Radio silence. It's all good. But it's makin' me jumpy.

She's on break now, and instead of givin' me those big eyes or tryin' to slide up next to me like usual, she's back in Cue's office with a book and headphones. A *book*.

I ain't never seen her with a book before. It looks like she's studying which don't make no sense. There's no way she's tryin' to get a degree or somethin'. She was in Hobs' classes in high school and that brother is missing a piece of his frontal lobe.

Story *is* smart, though. Not book smart, and not street smart necessarily, but—ain't there a kind of smart where you don't let shit get you down? If there isn't, there should be.

She sure as shit ain't lettin' me get her down. She hasn't said shit to Danielle, and when she was dancin', she didn't look at me once. Which is good. It's what I want.

My right eye twitches.

After Story left that night at the clubhouse, I went twelve rounds with Johnny Walker and picked a fight with Scrap out back. Scrap was all too happy to take the action since he's on the outs with Crista since his release from upstate. Heavy tells me the odds were ten to one against me since I wasn't blocking at all. Next day, he cut me in on his take. Apparently, I headbutted Scrap at the end by accident and knocked him out cold onto a picnic table.

Heavy's been sending me out with Forty, following up leads on the Rebel Raiders who trashed the Patonquin site, but nothin' has panned out. The time on my bike is good. I can blank while I fly down the highway, but then there's every other waking moment when I get to remember Story crumble, piece by piece, over and over like a highlight reel of my greatest fuck up.

And I did fuck up. I wasn't *wrong*, per se. But what I did...it wasn't right. I woke up the next morning, hung over with a pit in my stomach that felt like I took a steel toe boot to the gut. I expected it to go away, but it hasn't.

I hurt her. She never did nothin' to me except try to get close, and I ain't even functional enough to just talk to her about why it can't happen. So instead I rub her face in Danielle? Yeah, blood shows. It's exactly the type of asshole thing Ike or Keith would get off on doing.

I should say sorry. Duck back to Cue's office. Real quick. Keep it short and sweet. I didn't need to talk to her with disrespect. She had that part right.

I definitely gotta move, do somethin'. My body's primed with adrenaline, and all I'm doin' tonight is walking the floor, watchin' a handful of retired steelworkers nurse twenty-five cent drafts. I wander closer, keeping quiet so she don't notice.

Her head's bent over the book, headphones so big they dwarf her head. Two long waves of white gold hair frame her face, the rest pulled up in a bun, and she's biting her lower lip. My dick rises to attention. Her lips are so full, and they're the palest pink, almost exactly the color of the inside of a seashell. She truly is made perfect.

Every so often, she drums on the desk with her pencil eraser. Then she grunts, aggravated, and huffs so the hair hangin' in her face flutters. She moves her finger back to the top of the page. I don't think the studying is goin' so well.

I should speak up. Tell her I'm sorry. Find out what book she's reading.

She'll tell me to fuck off.

She'll probably be mad if I interrupt her.

Nah. No, she won't. Story's never mad. She's the reverse of me. It's like God sat down and thought, "What's the exact opposite of this piece of shit?" And voilà. Story Jenkins.

I should leave her alone. It's the smart thing to do. My body's stupid, though.

My feet drag the rest of me the few feet to Cue's office, drop me in his doorway. This close, I can see all the way behind the desk. She's wearin' a short, silky white robe over her costume. She's slipped off her heels, and she's sitting all tucked up like a little kid.

She startles when she finally notices me, and a quick flash of hurt expands her pupils, the black eating up the blue. My fists tighten. This was a terrible idea.

She slowly tugs the headphones off, bein' careful with her hair. She taps the pause button on her phone. I wait for her to say somethin'.

She don't.

"I—" I swallow, but my throat's totally dry. What was I going to say? Shit. I didn't think that far.

She blinks up at me. She makes her face hard to hide the hurt, but I can see her knuckles whiten where she grips the headphones.

"I—" I look wildly around the office, but there's only pinups plastered on the walls. No cue cards.

Story slowly unfolds her legs and slides her tiny bare feet back into her white heels. She's not helpin' me here, and she sure don't have to, but damn. I wish she'd pick now to be her soft, sweet, pushy self.

"Look. I'm sorry about the other night," I manage. My voice sounds weird. Too low.

She stares down, into her lap, and chews on her cheek.

"I mean, I'm not sorry about what I did. But what I said..." The clock ticks in the silence. She gives me nothing. "Fuck, Story."

She glances up, and her eyes are swirling with betrayal and confusion and disappointment, and I realize that comin' back here was the worst mistake of my life because her eyes are gonna kill me.

"Okay, Nickel."

She slides a piece of paper into her book and gently shuts it.

Dental Hygiene: Theory and Practice.

What the fuck?

"What are you readin'?"

She shrugs, slips the book into an enormous bag resting on the floor, and stands.

"I got to get past you, Nickel. My break's almost over."

I'm blocking the door, and I should step back, let her put her purse back in her locker. I'm an asshole if I don't.

"Forgot your headphones." I wave at Cue's desk. She scoops them up, winds the cords, and tucks them into her purse.

"Thanks." She folds her arms right under her chest.

She's standing by Cue's chair. I'm still blocking the door. There's maybe two feet between us, and she's tryin' to look everywhere but at me, but all I can do is take her in.

Two weeks is forever. Sometime during the past couple of years, I've grown accustomed to her. We don't talk. I ain't much of a talker, even with my brothers. But her bein' nearby, her dancin' for me while I stand in the shadows? It makes me steady. I feel all right 'cause she's all right, and I *never* feel all right.

I'm standin' here, waiting for that feeling—like a cold beer on a hot day—to hit, but it ain't comin'. I check her closer. She's obviously unhappy, but is that all? Her skin's usually pale, but is it paler tonight?

I think she's lost a few pounds. It's hard to tell, but if her upper arms get thin, she ain't been eating good. She looks so delicate in the silk gown. I bet she ain't been eating right.

"Nickel?" She gives a meaningful look past me to the hall, raising her eyebrows again.

"Are you okay, Story?"

She exhales, the slightest sigh. "You don't get to ask me."

I understand this, but I still need to know. I try another tack.

"I didn't fuck her. Danielle."

"Ain't my business one way or another."

I swallow a snarl. I'm getting frustrated. Not with her. With myself. My skin starts itching with it. I really need to move. Pace. But if I do, she'll be out of here. I need to let her leave, but my body's a firm *hell no* on that.

"I just wanted you to stop comin' after me," I go on, but I

ain't makin' it better. That perfect, plump lower lip is wobbling now, and I feel like I got a kitten in my hand, and I'm tryin' to pet it, but I can't help but squeeze too hard.

"I know. Message received." She firms her chin to stop the wobbling, and that only ends up making her look sad as hell.

I roll my shoulders, try to stave off the ugly. I can feel it gathering in my arms and legs; I know it so well I can predict it like weather. Cloudy with a one hundred percent chance of me losin' my shit.

"I'm no good for you," I say.

"I know you think that."

"Fuck's sake, woman," I raise my voice. I don't mean to, I don't want to, but still, I'm almost shouting when I ask, "Can you say anything besides *I know*?"

She sucks in her cheeks and crosses her arms tighter. "Seriously, Nickel? Now you want to have an actual conversation? Two minutes *after* my break's ended, after I've spent literally *years* trying to get you to talk to me. Now?"

"Now." I am aware that I'm being a complete asshole, but she's talkin' to me, ain't she?

"Well, okay."

She straightens her spine. Her eyes spit fire, the hurt disappearing as bright pink spots bloom on her cheeks, and a weight lifts from my chest. She's pissed, and by some magic, I settle.

"For one, *I* get to decide who's good for me and who isn't. You don't get to decide *nothin'* for me. And second, I deserve a man who will kiss me when I smile. Buy me a big house on top of a hill. Who'll park my car in the garage if I need it, which I don't, 'cause I can park just fine."

She pauses. I don't know what the fuck she's talkin'

about, and she looks like she kind of lost herself there for a minute, too.

"Oh. And three. I *know* I'm better than this. And you are, too."

A cold wave crashes through me. It's so strange, it takes me a minute to place. It's fear. Her words terrify me. I don't want her to decide I'm not good enough.

And since I asked for the words, I need to make them stop, and I don't know how, so I do the only thing I can think of. I close the space between us in one stride, walk her back into the wall, and shut her mouth with mine.

I don't kiss women. I mean, I have in the past if that's what it takes to seal the deal, but it's not really my thing. So maybe I'm not the smoothest, but the instant her soft lips meet mine, I'm converted.

She's so warm, so sweet. She tastes like the apple juice Cue pours for the girls when the customers buy them a drink. She's open to me, and I'm so hungry, all I can do is take.

I cup her cheek, but she wrests her head away, clamping her lips tight together. She gives me the side eye.

"What was that?" she asks, breathless.

I need to back up, back away, but this girl's my anchor. I'm locked in place, her chest heaving against my ribs. I rest my forehead lightly on hers.

"Kissin' you," I answer low like a confession. I hold her hands, twine her fingers in mine. *Please don't make me stop.* She furrows her brow, clearly thinks I'm talkin' nonsense, and then she raises her mouth.

"That's not kissin'. Lean down." Her voice is low, bossy.

I do.

She sips at my top lip, gently tugging. I plunge my tongue into her mouth, and she ducks her head away again.

I'm trailing her, desperate for another taste, and she pulls a hand free to press a finger to my lips.

"Stop."

I force myself still. It's so fucking hard.

"Like this," she whispers, and then she brushes her lips across mine, and after my brain goes fuzzy, she deepens the kiss, suckling, tasting. My dick throbs, beating a rhythm against my cold zipper, and I want to thrust into her sweet mouth, take everything she's offering like a greedy bastard, but I don't. I stay stock-still and let her show me what she likes.

She likes soft kisses. Nibbles. Fuck, but I guess I like that, too.

She's moaning between kisses now, squirming against me, and I crowd her, so scared she's going to shake this spell off and go back to ignoring me.

Oh, Lord, what am I doing? The taste of her is a drug, the kind when you know with the first hit that this is a hole you could happily fall down forever.

"We can't do this," I mumble into her mouth.

She slips her sweet tongue past my lips, and it tangles with mine. Precum dampens my boxers.

"We got to stop." I'm clinging to that like a drowning man, even as I know I couldn't back away if I was on fire.

"This can't happen."

And then her hands, which were tentatively exploring my chest, slam against my pecs. Hard. Once, twice, and a third time.

"Stop," she says, jerking her lips away again, and the loss is so sharp, I whimper like a kicked dog. "Uh, uh. No way. Nope."

She shoulders past me, grabs her purse, and books it to the door before I know what's going on. She stops in the doorway, pupils blown, chest rising and falling as if she's run a mile. She holds up a finger, and I swear, she looks so much like Fay-Lee in this moment that I'm expecting that mountain twang when she speaks.

"You kiss me, you're gonna say sweet things. Not 'we can't do this,' 'it's soooo wrong,' blah, blah, blah. I deserve better. I deserve someone who feels so damn lucky he gets to kiss me that he praises the God- damn-Lord while he's doin' it and thanks Him after!"

She's almost yelling, and she never yells, and it's so weird, it's kind of...soothing. The ugly is totally quiet, and I actually feel like...laughing?

"You're right, baby." I chuckle.

She blinks her big eyes at me, her chest heaving. She's speechless.

"Come back over here," I say. "Take me to church."

I grin, and her face turns beet red. She shrieks, whirls around, slams the door, and I don't see her again that night.

I'm in such a good mood, though, that at closing, when Cue waves me over to the bar, I go. He pours us both a shot of Jameson 18 and leaves the bottle out.

"Saddle up, young'un," he says, dusting off the seat of the stool next to him. I oblige. "I see you chased off my best dancer two hours before the end of her shift."

I shrug and take a sip. "Story chases me."

"Hard life, eh?" Cue cackles, and then he grows quiet, staring into his glass. "You know, she's gonna smarten up one day."

"Yeah."

"Yup," Cue goes on as if I didn't say anything. "She's gonna finally say yes to one of these stockbrokers from Pyle. He's gonna buy her dinner, bang her a few times, knock her up, and then dump her for his real girlfriend."

"Shut the fuck up." The ugly raises its head, my mellow blown.

"Creech is always sniffin' around her. Maybe she'll finally let him hit that. He'll give her the world. And by the world, I mean the clap, but nothin's perfect."

"What are you doin', Cue?" The ugly's roiling my belly, and it burns twice as bad since I had a few hours break from it.

"Pointing out that a gainfully employed brother who worships the ground she walks on ain't really the worst Story Jenkins is likely to do."

His words. They reach deep and stir up shit I ain't felt in years. Hope. It almost worse than the hopelessness. Hope's got the taint of fear in it. You can lose hope.

"I ever tell you about Bananas?" I ask.

"If that's what you call your dick, I don't wanna hear."

I shake my head, help myself to another shot of the good stuff. "Bananas was a goldfish. I won him at the St. Andrew's carnival."

"Your folks took you to the carnival?" Cue went to school with my dad, so he knows that shit's unlikely.

"It was walking distance. My brothers and I would spend all week there, causin' trouble, sneakin' back in once they kicked us out."

"Good times."

I nod. In relation to everything else, it was.

"Anyway, I won Bananas. I stuck him in big ass pickle jar, and I fed him bread crumbs. That little dude was tough as shit. Ike and Dad put out cigarettes in his jar, he swum past. Markie thought it'd be funny to put him in the toilet and take a piss on him. Little dude kept swimming."

"Don't tell me how you got him out."

I grin. "I won't. Anyway, this goes on for months. At one

point, Keith hides him under the trailer to fuck with me. I don't find him for three days, and he's still swimming. It was, like, November, and there was ice in the jar, but Bananas did not give a shit."

"This story don't end well, does it?" Cue lights up one of his Cohibas.

"I got pissed off. Don't even remember about what. Probably some petty shit. Things got ugly, and after, when I've got out the broom and dust pan, there's Bananas. Dead on the floor. Half squished from where I stepped on him. I didn't even realize I'd knocked his jar over."

Cue nods, his thick brow wrinkled. "I take your point."

My shoulders slump. I knew he would.

"Yeah," Cue hacks and slaps my back. "You probably shouldn't keep your bitches in a pickle jar."

"Not what I'm gettin' at." I'm losin' my patience. I'm sittin' here, spilling my guts, more than I ever do, and Cue's makin' it into a joke.

"Yeah, yeah. I get it." He smirks. "Moral of the story is fry your bitches up and eat 'em before your brother gets a chance to piss on 'em."

"The fuck, Cue?" I set my whiskey down hard. He winces. He's really sensitive about the glassware since the break in.

"So is it that you shouldn't even bother bringing your bitches home from the carnival?"

I'm pissed, the ugly's got me out of my seat, and normally I'd have bucked at this point, shoved Cue in the chest at least, but something is holding me back. Maybe 'cause kissing Story somehow eased my hair trigger a touch. Maybe 'cause Cue ain't laughin'. He's dead serious. Braced for impact, but dead serious.

"Or, and you can call me crazy, but maybe—" He says

this slow, as if I'm hard of hearing. "Bitches ain't carnival goldfish."

It's the dumbest shit I've ever heard. I sink back onto my stool.

Cue freshens up my glass. "You break that, I don't give a fuck. I'll fire you."

"I own a stake." All the Steel Bones brothers do.

"Then I'll shove the glass up your ass."

We sit in silence for a few minutes, listening to the filler music echo in the empty club. Trudy, Cue's niece, has closed out the till, and she pads back to his office to put the take in the safe. Austin, the other bouncer for the night, hangs out at the back door, waiting for her to finish so he can bust out, too.

The place is sad with the lights up. You can tell the booths with the high, tufted leather backs are made of plastic and the stage is only plywood painted black. Ain't nothin' sadder than a strip club after hours.

"Shit, Cue. You know me. I don't know how to be with a woman."

"You're around women all the time." Cue gestures around the club with an open hand.

"You know what I mean."

Cue sighs and swipes a hand over his bald head. "You think you'd end up beatin' on her."

The words are a blow to my guts, so much that I sway back and hiss in a breath. But he ain't wrong.

"She drive you crazy, then?" he asks. "Push your buttons until you lose it."

Never. I mean, she does drive me crazy, and she does push my buttons. All the fuckin' time whether she means to or not. But...

"That don't matter," I say. "Beatin' on females is fucked up no matter what."

Cue nods, his big fish-lips turnin' down. "See, I do know that. Not surprised to hear you know it, too. So why do you think you're gonna end up like your asshole father and those piece of shit brothers of yours?"

And ain't that the heart of the matter. Cue might look dumb, but he's wise for all the brain cells he's burnt breathin' in hair spray and body glitter.

"'Cause I am like them. The ugly gets loose...there ain't no brake, Cue. There ain't no second when I can make a choice and take a deep fuckin' breath." I laugh, and it sounds bitter as hell. "She's standin' around when it happens...she might as well be a goldfish in a pickle jar."

"Yeah." Cue nods his fake solemn, smart-ass nod again. "No legs to get out the way, cain't speak so no way to talk sense to you, no pretty titties to remind you that she ain't the one you're pissed at. Just like a fuckin' goldfish."

"You know I'm right."

"I know you're a pussy." Cue stands, slaps me on the back, and shuffles behind the bar. "And considering my profession, I do know a pussy when I see one."

9

STORY

I blame Nickel's kiss.

Not the first few. Those were truly heinous. So much tongue. But after. When he caught on. Dear sweet Lord. Even now, in this quickly spiraling situation, my clit tingles. I agreed to come with Fay-Lee on this misadventure to clear my mind, but instead, I'm distracted, and it looks like I'm about to be in deep, deep shit.

I clutch my purse tight in my lap and scan the empty linoleum dance floor at Twiggy's one more time. Twiggy's is the dive bar we drove an hour into the boondocks to reach, an hour and a half if you count Fay-Lee getting lost and turning down that rural route.

"I don't want to be a pussy or anything," I whisper. "But is the vibe in here kind of...?"

"Every roadhouse movie when the fresh meat walks in and all the scary biker dudes stand up and crack their knuckles?" Fay-Lee offers.

"Uh..." I take another quick peek around. "Yeah?"

"Pretty much." Fay-Lee scrunches further back in the corner booth.

The clientele is seriously grizzly, and to top it off, three Rebel Raiders just stomped in through the swinging, western-style doors.

We only came with Roosevelt, the prospect. We wouldn't have even brought him except he guilted me about ditching him at the clubhouse after the thing with Nickel. Anyhow, he's up at the bar getting us beers, so if the Raiders see Fay-Lee's Steels Bones cut that says she's Property of Dizzy, we're fucked. And if they see Roosevelt's cut, he's fucked.

We're basically fucked.

"Why are we here again?" I ask.

Here is all the way out by the county line near Gifford. I've never been before, but Fay-Lee knows the joint from her travels with the nomad.

"Well, I'm doing that thing where Dizzy pisses me off, so I run away and make him chase me, and then he spanks my ass red, and we have crazy monkey sex."

"And what am I doing here?"

"Probably driving my corpse home in your trunk." Fay-Lee's joking, but she's tearing up her napkin and rolling the pieces into balls.

She's worried. So am I.

"I thought you said this place was all rednecks and cowboys. No bikers."

"It was."

"When?"

"I dunno. Like six years ago?"

I groan, and I will Roosevelt to abandon the beers and come back to the booth. I can't phone him cause the ring would draw attention, and I don't want to text him and distract him from getting his ass back here.

"You got anything in that bag of yours? Knife? Gun?" Fay-Lee looks hopeful.

"Expired mace and a nail file."

"Get to diggin', Story-girl. I'll take the nail file when you find it." Fay-Lee's head is down, her fingers flying over her cell phone. She must be texting Dizzy.

I open my purse in my lap and start going through it by feel, all the while praying the Raiders don't notice Roosevelt. He's a good guy, my age, and he'll dance to whatever, even the two step. He's never put the moves on me 'cause he says he's into older chicks. I think it's more like he's into one particular older chick—I've heard him drunk-cry over some lady named Camila—but he don't talk about it, and I don't ask.

The bar is filling up, slow but sure. Every time the door swings open, I hold my breath. The more people, the less likely the Raiders are to make us. On the other hand, what if three Raiders sidled up at the far end of the bar are meeting friends?

After what feels like forever, Roosevelt grabs three long-necks and heads back to our booth. I keep my eyes glued on the Raiders.

"Come on, come on," I mutter under my breath. It takes him thirty seconds to cross the bar, but it feels like an eternity. The Raiders don't turn in their stools. They're watching the game and talking amongst themselves.

I stand as soon as Roosevelt gets to the table so he can scoot past me. He winks. "You want me in the middle? Guess I can do that."

"Sit the fuck down," Fay-Lee hisses.

"What?"

Oh, dear Lord. I grab his pant leg and tug. "Sit!"

He finally catches on and slides in, scanning the room. I can tell the instant he sees the Rebel Raiders. His face blanches, making his chin strap seem even darker.

"Fuck." He reaches under the table real slow. He's easing a knife out of an ankle holster. "You call Dizzy?"

"Yeah." Fay-Lee checks her phone. "He's coming with the guys from the clubhouse."

Nickel won't be coming, then. It's Saturday, and he's working. I'm relieved. I think. I don't want him killing anyone, and if this goes south, he will. But still, I'm scared as shit, and I want him. For some reason, my brain still sees him as my pit bull, my personal loaded gun.

Damn, why did I go along with this? Heavy told all of us we need to play it smart, travel together, stay close to home. I totally would have—I'm not a rebel in the slightest—but Fay-Lee didn't seem worried, and she's an old lady. I figured she'd know if shit was seriously serious.

Besides, I desperately needed a break from Nickel Kobald and dental hygiene. All week, I've been struggling. Class goes too fast, and there's no one I can ask for help. I can't raise my hand as much as I need to 'cause if I did, I'd look like an idiot. I can't hardly follow the teacher at all. She'll start saying something, and then she talks about a patient she had back in the day, and I'm lost.

And Nickel...I have no idea what's going on in that man's head. I know for a fact he switched shifts with Forty on Tuesday and last night so we'd work together. He didn't try to talk to me, but I kept catching him staring at me. And not when I was on stage, either, but like, when I was brushing out my hair in the locker room. Or when I was reading that fucking textbook that both makes no sense and also keeps saying the same thing over and over. He didn't even try to act like he wasn't looking.

By the weekend, I needed a drink in the worst way, so when Fay-Lee suggested we head up here, I was game. So that's why I'm gonna die. 'Cause school sucks and boys are confusing. What am I, sixteen?

"How far out are they?" I ask.

Fay-Lee checks her phone, scrolls down. "Forty-five minutes."

"What's Dizzy sayin'? He gonna kill you?"

A shine appears in Fay-Lee's dark brown eyes. Oh, shit. Is she gonna cry?

"He says he loves me. That I made his world when I—" She sniffles. "When I said I'd be his old lady."

Somehow, I know that isn't exactly what he texted, but it ain't my business.

"Oh, shit," I whisper. This is bad. Dizzy should be ripping her a new asshole, and he's giving her last words type shit? We're in real trouble.

Roosevelt's grip tightens on his knife. "If they come over, when I stand, you girls go under the table. Fay-Lee, your keys in your hand?"

"Yup."

I see now it was stupid to seat Roosevelt between us. He's pinned in.

We sit there in silence, Fay-Lee and Roosevelt sipping their beers. I can't get anything past the lump in my throat. I don't know why the beef between Steel Bones and the Rebel Raiders began, but I know it goes way back, and every so often, like the past few months, it erupts. It's been fairly quiet since Heavy became president and focused the club on construction and the other businesses, so I don't really remember things getting real ugly, but my ma tells stories.

Hobs taking a baseball bat to the skull. Crista…what happened to Crista. Scrap came home not long ago for the dime bid he did on the back of that shit.

And now, the Rebel Raiders are riding again. They

trashed a Steel Bones Construction work site, and then they
sent two assholes to toss The White Van. Nearly broke Cue's
heart when he had to put out two thousand on repairs. He'd
wanted to give Trudy a raise.

The door swings open, disrupting my chain of thought,
and my gaze flies up, hope in my heart. It hasn't been long
enough to be Dizzy and the brothers, but I can't handle
waiting for the other shoe to drop.

The man who enters isn't Steel Bones, but he is familiar.
He's got Nickel's sharp cheekbones, and his hard expression,
but he's older. The top of his head is shiny, and when he
gives a chin jerk to the Rebel Raiders in greeting, I can see
he's got a full neck tattoo.

It's Nickel's brother. Ike. The one he warned me away
from. He sits down at the bar, talking a mile a minute, but
unlike the Raiders who respond without peeling their eyes
from the game, Ike's gaze is darting all around the place.

My body freezes, and I grip the mace so tight it slips in
my sweaty palm.

Fay-Lee whispers, "What?"

I don't dare say. Ike's eyes have found my rack. They
linger there, and I can't help the flush that turns my chest
bright red. He smirks. And then, eventually, he looks up,
and his gaze sweeps to Roosevelt and then to Fay-Lee. His
eyebrows raise, and he smirks so wide, I can't believe the
Raiders don't notice.

I know what Nickel said, but I shake my head, ever so
slightly, begging him with my eyes not to say anything. He
winks at me—fuckin' *winks*—and he slips out his phone,
texts or searches something, and then he spins around and
slaps the counter to get the bartender's attention. The relief
leaves me shaking.

"Do we know him?" Fay-Lee whispers.

"Ike Kobald. Nickel's brother."

"He a Rebel Raider?" Roosevelt asks, his jaw clenching. The stress is getting to him. He smelled like Acqua di Gio when we came in, but now he smells like armpits.

"I don't think so. I think he's just a hang-around. Nickel says stay away from him."

"No problem." Roosevelt smiles through the nerves.

We go back to staring at each other and the table, trying not to startle every time the door opens or someone walks toward us. We're sitting right next to the jukebox and the quarter machine, so there's a bit of traffic.

It's torture. Even though I haven't touched my beer, I have to pee so bad. I'm too afraid to move, though. I try to distract myself, think about dental hygiene class, but that puts me even more on edge.

"Time check?" I whisper to Fay-Lee.

"Ten. Maybe fifteen minutes left."

I'm thinking we can do this, that it'll be another crazy story to tell around the bonfire at the clubhouse, when shouts ring out in the bar and boots stomp the hardwood floors. I nearly piss myself.

"Ten to six, motherfuckers!" A deep voice booms, and a few scattered claps punctuate the excited chatter that grows as chairs scrape and people stand and stretch.

Fay-Lee exhales. "The game's over."

Our relief is quickly eclipsed by panic. The Rebel Raiders are standing, and they're making their way toward us. Oh, shit.

"They're just gonna get quarters for the pool table," Fay-Lee hisses. "Act natural." She gives me an enormous fake smile and blinks like she's got a lash in her eye.

"Remember," Roosevelt says. "Go under the table."

But when it happens, it happens so quick, there's no

time. One minute, the three bikers—a fat guy in a red do-rag, a skinny guy with a weird white eye, and a guy with two tear tattoos on his left cheek—are filing toward us, followed by Ike Kobald. Then the skinny guy elbows the fat one, points at Fay-Lee, and says, "That's Dizzy Jones' bitch."

"What did Knocker say?"

"Two large."

"Ca-ching," the man with the face tattoo says, and then there's a clatter, hands on me, and then I'm in the air, the mace slipping from my hands. I drop like a sack of potatoes. A boot toe catches me in the stomach while the Raiders drag Roosevelt from the booth, stomping his wrist into the floor until he screams and drops his knife.

The skinny guy wrestles Fay-Lee to her feet by her hair, and the Raiders muscle Roosevelt and Fay-Lee across the floor and down the hall toward a back exit. I'm on my ass, gasping for breath, my hands scrabbling on the sticky floor, and Ike Kobald looms over me, chuckling.

"You should stay down." He stares down at me, flipping a toothpick in his mouth.

My gaze darts wildly around the bar, searching for a friendly face, anyone who can help, but no one will meet my eye. Ike Kobald just stands there, his arms crossed over his chest, smirking, flipping that toothpick.

My purse is under the table. The mace has rolled all the way under the bench. Roosevelt's knife is on the floor, a foot away.

Ike must notice the second I see it because he goes to kick it, but I'm quicker and closer. I grab it, and I bounce to my feet. I don't know what to do, but they've got my best friend, so I make a mad dash after them.

Ike Kobald's hand wraps around my forearm, grinding

the bones together. I whimper. He puts pressure on my arm, forcing me to bend into a squat, and he looms, leering.

"You should sit back down, girlie."

"They have my friends."

He laughs, and ice trickles down my spine. He has Nickel's voice, his face, his eyes, but it's like whatever makes them alive in Nickel is dead and rotten in this man. I expect him to hit me, but he lets me go.

"You're dumb as shit, aren't you? Well, don't let me get in your way, then. Go for it."

He laughs again, and it's not a cartoon villain laugh, it's worse than that. He's truly amused. He thinks I'm running off to get raped or murdered, and he thinks it's funny. I bolt for the back, grab my purse, and it's actually not as scary as it was, 'cause I'm more scared now of what's at my back than what's ahead of me.

10

NICKEL

W *3 Rdrs at Twgys 1 SB & Dzzys btch & blnde btch w tits No blod yt but its comin theres a bounty*

My phone chirps. It's Ike. In an instant, I'm dashing to Cue's office, grabbin' his keys.

Blonde bitch with tits. That's Story. My Story-girl. A red roar of terror and rage swamps my mind.

"What the fuck, brother?" Cue follows me.

"Emergency," I tell him. "I need your car." My bike is fast, but on sharp turns, I can pull more speed out of the Mustang. Twiggy's is out in the boondocks. I need four wheels.

Adrenaline spikes through my limbs, and as I kneel in front of Cue's safe, I have to shake my fingers loose before I spin the combination lock. He keeps a piece or two in here, and I need more than the 10+1 rounds in my Glock. As I'm opening the safe with one hand, I'm dialing Heavy with the other. He answers on one ring.

"You've heard." His freaky-low voice is calm, and as it always does, it beats back the madness stoked in my brain, giving me room to think. Cue crowds in behind me. He takes the Smith and Wesson from the safe and loads it with his steadier hands. I've never been so grateful for my brother.

"Ike texted."

"Our information is three Raiders up at Twiggy's. They haven't made our people yet, but it's probably a matter of time."

"Are you moving?" As I ask, I'm taking the gun from Cue, tucking it in the small of my back, and jogging for the parking lot.

"Already in motion. I've got Dizzy, Forty, Charge, the prospects. Fourteen men. ETA forty-two minutes."

That's too fuckin' long. Anything could happen in forty-two minutes.

"Don't we have anyone closer?" I'm peeling onto the road, fingers clenched on the steering wheel.

"It's in Bumfuck."

"They have Story?" Say no. Say no. Jo-Beth is blonde besides the purple streaks. So's Angel when the mood strikes her.

"Yeah. Seems Fay-Lee got a wild hair and took her girl with her."

"Stupid. Stupid." Pictures are flashin' in my head, like at the end of an old school filmstrip. My stomach knots, and I try to accelerate but my boot is already to the floor. "Which prospect?"

"Roosevelt."

The one with her that night at the clubhouse. Petty jealousy beats at my ribs, but my brain clings to this information like a life raft. He's into her. He ain't gonna run; he ain't gonna let her get hurt.

"Anything else from Ike?" Heavy asks.

I glance down at my phone on the passenger seat. Nothing.

"No, brother."

"Call if you get more information."

"Right." I pull up to a red light, and I strain forward, inching, my muscles burning from the effort of holding back. Cars are comin' too fast to run it. My heart's beatin' so hard, it echoes in the cab.

"And Nickel?"

"Yeah, yeah." Green! I slam on the gas.

"Your girl's gonna need you steady."

We ain't never talked about it, but I'm not surprised Heavy sees the way of things. I always thought he was made as big as he is so as to fit his monster brain.

"If she's hurt—" I can't hardly say it, but it needs said. "If there's one hair out of place on her head, I'm callin' chaos."

"That's a given."

The reluctance that pissed Cue off so much after the attacks on the site and the club is gone. Whatever angle Heavy was workin', tryin' to negotiate with Knocker Johnson, he's done with it now. The Rebel Raiders are a clear threat to our women now. Blood will flow.

"If she's hurt bad—" The words stick in my throat. "You need to knock me out or somethin'. Keep me away. She don't need to see me like this."

There's silence on the line. I can hear Forty barkin' orders in the background. My entire body feels like it's going to combust into an inferno of panic and rage.

"That ain't gonna be what she needs." Heavy sighs. "You're gonna have to level up real quick, brother. No losin' it."

A wave of impotent fury crests over me, suffocating, buffeting my control and draggin' me under. I need bones to crunch under my fists. I need to take the flesh and blood that caused this and pulverize it into dust and mud.

Heavy sighs again. "See you in thirty."

"Thirty," I repeat.

I vibrate in my seat, drum the dash, rock my hips as if I can urge the car faster.

Story's so fuckin' small. She has the curves and all, but the rest of her is so fragile. What the fuck is she doin' at a roadhouse out in nowhere? All the girls got the talk from Heavy.

It's fuckin' Fay-Lee's fault. I swear that girl put her up to flashin' her titties at me at that picnic back in the day. My memory offers up an image amid all the churning gore. Story in the bathroom, her bikini top hanging to her waist, and her big eyes hypnotizing me, a mischief-makin' smile curving those sweet, pink lips.

I didn't mean to say anything but "Get the fuck out." I knew she had a thing for me. I wasn't stupid. But I also thought she was a kid, that she'd take a hint, move on to the next brother. But she was so beautiful. So perfect. This giggling, wide-eyed, sneaky little thing with no fear, no darkness to her at all.

I beat my fists on the steering wheel, and when I feel a slight give, I have to pull back with all the force I have in me. I can't break the fuckin' car.

I don't know how, but I wrestle myself in check. I ain't got no room in my mind for light anymore, though. The ugly spits up pictures like it always does, stoking the fires, beating me down until I follow it off the ledge.

Me whaling on Keith, slamming him into a wall, over and over. Ma's hand touchin' my arm so gentle, and then her cry when my elbow drives into her jaw. Her hands flying up to her face, but keeping her eyes glued to mine.

"It's okay, Nickie. You didn't mean it. I know you didn't mean it." The blood on her teeth.

I see Story's sweet face, beaten, bloody. Acid burns my throat. I know what might be waiting for me.

I know how many pieces a human can break into.

I know what men can do to women, and I can only hurtle forward, my lips moving in prayer, no sound coming out.

11

STORY

When I bust through the screen door, the sun is blinding. It's almost five o'clock, but it's real dim in the bar, and it takes a minute for my eyes to adjust. Screams ring out, and I can't wait, so I run half-blind through the high grass behind the parking lot, pumping my arms to catch up.

Fay-Lee is flat on her back, kicking and twisting as the skinny guy with the weird eye tries to drag her toward a truck parked way in the back. He stops to slap her, and she jolts up, headbutting him. He kicks her in the ribs, and she howls in pain, but at least he's not dragging her now.

Roosevelt is worse off. The two other guys are taking turns on him, and he's so far gone, he's staggering from one to the other, hugging onto them like a boxer in the middle of a fight.

I see the fat guy register me, but he doesn't even bother to turn. He doesn't think I'm a threat.

Am I? I fight to calm my breath and tighten my grasp on the knife with a sweaty hand, my grip slippery.

Fay-Lee screams again, and I stop, gazing wildly back

and forth. Am I strong enough to stab through the leathers the guys are wearing? And if I only get one shot, where should I take it—the neck? the side? Do I go for Fay-Lee or Roosevelt?

I need to be smart here, and I've never felt so dumb.

Fay-Lee's eyes lock on mine. She screams, "Run, Story!"

The men beating on Roosevelt look up, and I see it. A floor pathway. The field is a stage, and I see the movement phrase. The choreography.

I don't think, I just run, straight at the fat man, and the moment before I collide into him, I leap into a barrel roll turn, flinging my arm wide, past the fat man's grasping hand, and I flip the knife and slide the handle into Roosevelt's open palm.

Roosevelt reads my mind, and he shouts, springs forward, and sinks the knife into the shoulder of the man with the tear tattoos. Blood spurts from the wound, splattering Roosevelt's face. The man grunts in pain, and drops to his knees, trying to staunch the blood. He's not dead, but he's hurt. Bad.

The fat man hurls me off of him, and this time, I land hard. My ass bounces when I hit the ground and my teeth snap together.

"Okay, okay." Roosevelt crouches, shifting from foot to foot. "Come on then, motherfucker."

The skinny guy drops Fay-Lee and sprints over, pulling a knife—a lot longer than Roosevelt's—from a sheath strapped across his chest. I roll to my knees, scan the dirt for a stick or a rock or a broken bottle.

There's a thud as bodies collide, a scream, and then the sound of a dozen engines and tires churning up asphalt. A cloud of dust rises from the parking lot. The skinny guy bolts, making for the tree line in a flat-out sprint.

Three gunshots ring out in quick succession.

"Hands in the air!" Fat Guy raises his hands above his head. Skinny disappears in the undergrowth. Fat Guy checks himself for bullet holes, and I do the same, until I see Heavy, wild hair wind-whipped like some kind of Neanderthal giant, gun still raised from where he fired it in the air.

Steel Bones swarms the grassy yard, guns trained on the Raiders, each man's face blank, his eyes cold and hard.

"In the woods! In the woods!" Roosevelt is shouting, but it comes out weak and wheezy. I'm pointing, shouting, too, and several brothers peel off and run into the trees.

Dizzy stands facing us, his finger on the trigger, aiming straight for the Fat Guy. I see his index finger squeeze and then ease off. His gaze swoops over my shoulder, and I turn to see Fay-Lee limp up from behind me, her arms opening wide.

"Baby," she moans. "My ribs hurt."

Dizzy engages the safety, and then he scoops up Fay-Lee, so impossibly gentle for a man his size, and he carries her off to a truck, shouting at her the whole way.

"What the fuck were you thinkin', girl? You ain't gonna sit comfortably ever again. Goddamn it!"

Fay-Lee snuggles into him. "You're gonna have to wait 'til my ribs feel better, baby, before you beat my ass. I kinda just got my ass beat, you know."

I fall back on my butt, and I sit there, dazed, while Creech and Wall carry off the dude with the knife in his shoulder, moaning and limp, and Forty and Bullet wrestle the fat guy into Heavy's Range Rover. There's no sign of the brothers who took off after Skinny.

A whole bunch of guys are milling around. Wash and Boom are givin' Roosevelt shit about how bad he's fucked up, and Heavy's givin' orders, sending Gus and Eighty into the bar to make sure no one saw nothin'.

I'm sure they didn't.

No one but Roosevelt's payin' me much mind. He stumbles over, gives me his hand, and I take it. As soon as I stand, a wave of dizzy crashes through me, and I sink back down onto my butt.

"Gimme a minute?" I suck down a deep breath, willing my stomach to chill out.

"Sure thing, dance partner."

"That was a pretty slick move, wasn't it?"

"Yes it was." Roosevelt smiles. His teeth are coated with blood. I think he's lost one.

"I know someone who can help you with that." I wave my hand toward his face.

He laughs and glances toward the SUV where they've put the guy with the tear tattoo. "I think the dentist is gonna be busy tonight. Maybe tomorrow he can fit me in."

Shit. Does everyone know about Larry but me?

I let my eyes drift shut. It feels like I'm spinning circles even though I'm sitting still. The adrenaline's wearing off, and I'm getting weak and trembly. I want Nickel. I want him to stand, watching over me like he does when I give a lap dance, making me feel safe, like I've got a super power in human form backing me up.

I'd rather have that than dumb luck. I don't kid myself— if the fat man had anticipated my move, it'd have been over. Shivers rack my body. I need to get up, get myself a jacket. My arms and legs are weights, though, and I can't get myself moving.

Eventually, someone hauls me up, presses a bottled water into my hand, and half drags me toward a truck in the parking lot. It's Gus. I guess he's givin' me a ride home.

I lean against the truck, waiting for Gus to unlock the door, when Cue's yellow Mustang turns sharp into the lot, sending asphalt skittering. What's he doin' here? Except for catching Skinny, the situation seems handled.

The mystery clears when the door flies open and Nickel jumps out, his eyes swirling black pits, every visible muscle tight, roping, veins bulging. His lips are peeled back, rage and violence painted across his face.

This is the man I saw in the moonlight all those years ago. The one who plowed through three football players, sheer bloodlust and madness in his eyes.

I didn't think I had any left, but fear floods my limbs, priming me to run. It's the only natural reaction to this man. All around me, brothers straighten their spines and eye Forty. He's the only guy who doesn't seem fazed. Forty approaches Nickel, slow and deliberate, hands up.

Nickel sees me. He rocks back on his heels.

I hold my breath.

He looks back to Forty. "Where are they?"

"Taken care of," Forty answers. "Or about to be."

"Where the fuck *are* they!" he howls. His eyes dart frenetically from car to car.

"Gone already." Forty lowers his hands, and he stands in that weird way he always does, feet an exact width apart, arms straight, his finger and his thumb almost touching.

"Where?" Nickel demands, his rage a living thing beneath his skin, the motion of it accentuated by Forty's stillness.

"Story's over there." Forty jerks his chin in my direction.

Oh, shit. I'm really feeling weak-kneed and a touch barfy, and I'm clinging to the truck's door handle to keep myself upright. I'm not at all prepared for Nickel in a rage.

He turns the whole force of his demented, black glare on me.

"How bad is she hurt?" he snaps at Forty.

He jerks his chin at me. "Ask her."

Thanks, Forty. He's throwing me to the wolf. My stomach flops around like there's a fish in there, and I try to swallow it down.

Nickel rakes his gaze down me, and I can only imagine what he sees. My hair is springing from the bun I had it in, there's grass stains all over my jeans, and there's a bruise where Ike grabbed my arm. I can tell when he sees it because every muscle in his body strains.

It's so weird. He's frozen in place. All the brothers are frozen in place. We're all waiting, holding our breath. He's going to blow. He always blows. It almost looks like he's waiting for it, too.

But it doesn't come.

Instead, he rolls his neck. Then he shakes out his arms and tosses his head as if to clear it. He takes a measured step toward me, and then another, and my grip tightens on the door handle. He stops a foot away, reaches out, and then his hand stills mid-air. He drops it. His eyes aren't swirling anymore. He looks almost...lost.

"You hurt?" His voice is low. Just for me.

And the fight just drains from me, seeps out, and I sway, but before I can even stumble, he has me. He holds me up, propping me against the truck.

"Where are you hurt, baby?"

"I'm okay."

He searches me again, head to foot, his rough hands skimming over my arms, my sides. It's like getting patted down at a football game when you set the metal detector off.

"You're okay?"

"I want to go home."

He can't seem to compute this. His gaze sweeps the area again, searching for the enemy, but they're gone. He has to return his gaze to me, and when he does, he moans and gathers me closer, tucks my face against his chest.

"Please, baby," he begs in his soft, raspy voice. "Tell me they didn't hurt you."

My head's woozy, my stomach's queasy, and there's a dozen aches and pains in my ass and back from hitting the ground.

"I'm fine," I say, my words muffled by his cut. "Please take me home?"

In this moment, I finally understand something. I'm stronger than Nickel Kobald. Nothing owns me like his rage owns him. I always felt smaller, like I was some pesky kid dogging his footsteps. That's not the truth, though. I'm the one who can rescue him. I'm the one who can make it okay.

I draw back, watch as his palm hovers above my shoulder, all the want in the world pouring from him, and he's too afraid to touch.

It's backwards, this dance we do. I chase him. He follows me, watching. I'm wearin' heels, but I'm going to have to be the one who leads. Neither of us know the steps, but I can hear the music. I'm gonna have to make this work for the both of us.

"Are you gonna take me home, Nickel?" I sigh. "Or do I gotta ask someone else?"

He searches the area one last time, desperate—it seems to me—for a problem he can solve with his fists, but he must see what I do, nothin' but a bunch of Steel Bones brothers and beat up trucks.

"Okay," he finally grunts and grabs my hand. "Can you walk?"

"Standing just fine now."

He guides me across to the Mustang, walks me around to the passenger side, opens the door, and carefully hands me in. Then he pushes my hands aside so he can buckle me in himself.

He stalks back around, slides in the driver's seat, and I relax, expecting this all to be over, but he doesn't turn the key in the ignition. Instead, he sits there, staring at the console. Seconds tick by. I'm not sure what's happening.

"Nickel?"

His head jerks up, and even though his pupils are still blown to hell, he seems calmer now. "Where's your purse?"

My purse? He's been sitting here wondering about my purse? Well, shit. I was about to leave it here in Bumfuck, Egypt. Maybe I shouldn't judge.

I remember dropping it when I launched myself at the Rebel Raider. "Somewhere in the grass out back."

He nods. Then he turns on the car and rolls the window down.

"Prospect!" He calls Wash over, tells him to get my purse, and then he backs out of the parking lot, and finally, we're heading for home, fast but not too fast. I lean against the headrest, and try to breathe through the aftershocks shuddering through me every so often.

Nickel breaks the silence. "Don't tell me what happened."

I blink my eyes open. He's staring at my forearm, at the bruise from Ike.

"Not until we get home." He squeezes the steering wheel, knuckles white. "I need to be calm. To drive you safely. Okay?

"Ten-four, good buddy." I pat his thigh. Right now, I don't want to talk at all. I want an aspirin, a bath, and a drink. And I want to bask in this moment, Nickel's clean, woodsy smell filling the car, my entire body wrung out.

I'm safe now.

What would have happened if he'd gotten there first? I shiver. There would have been bodies dropped in that field.

All the way back to Petty's Mill, I sneak peeks at his face. I've never seen him like this before. It looks the same as when he fights himself over me. There's a wildness in him. You can see it in the throbbing pulse in his neck and the slapping of his palm on the dashboard when we hit a red light and a dozen other tics, a frantic energy spoiling to burst out.

But then there's this other thing. It flexes, forcing the wildness to stay contained, controlling it. I think he's trying to manage the anger. I've never seen anything more beautiful. The wildness dancing beneath his skin, and the strength directing the motion. He's mastering himself, and it's so fucking beautiful.

12

NICKEL

"Where are you?" Heavy barks.

I pull the phone away from my ear. Brother is big everywhere, especially his mouth.

"Story's place." I'm standing in the middle of her living room. Pink shit has me surrounded. Candles and pillows and a damn blanket shaped like a mermaid's tail on her couch. The place smells like her, fresh and sweet. I have a semi just from bein' this close to her, but even so, the place makes me uneasy.

"She okay?" There's concern, but also respect for what's mine. The brothers all know now. I've staked my claim as sure as if I've put my name on her back.

That should make me uneasy as fuck, but it don't. I want everyone to know she's mine. It'll make it easier to prevent what happened today from ever goin' down again.

"She's banged up some. She took an aspirin for a headache, but then she asked me to order a pizza, so I guess she's feelin' better? She's in the shower now. How are Fay-Lee and the prospect?"

"Fay-Lee has bruised ribs. Roosevelt's gonna need some work. Broken wrist. Cracked ribs. Lost a tooth."

"He earned his patch."

It ain't my call alone, but the kid has my vote. That boy-band-lookin' motherfucker took a man's beating, and he finished hard.

"That he did," Heavy agrees.

There's silence on the line for a while. He's probably thinkin' what I am. When Story gave me the short version of what went down, I nearly lost my shit again. She's got the survival instincts of a suicidal lemming. What would have happened if she hadn't come through with the knife? If the brothers had been even a minute later? My stomach balls into a tight knot.

"What's next?"

"We lost the skinny guy in the woods. Forty's taking lead on hunting him down. With that freaky eye, people will know him. It won't take long, and then, 'There will be retribution, and it will rain snares and fire and brimstone and burning wind will be the portion of their cup.'" Heavy's quotin' the Good Book again. His ma was a Bible thumper, and what with his perfect memory, we get treated to this shit on the regular.

"You better fuckin' call me when you find the asshole." If there was any space for anything in my mind 'cept Story, we'd be havin' words about that right now. I shouldn't have had to call him.

"I was unaware you were so...invested. How did you know, anyhow?"

"Ike."

"The fuck?" Heavy don't like this anymore than I do. Ever since our sit-down at The White Van, we haven't heard shit from our *inside man*. Until today.

"He texted me."

"You think he was involved?"

"He was hangin' around the Rebel Raiders."

"Which is what we asked him to do."

"I don't trust him, Heavy."

"Story tell you what they said before they grabbed Fay-Lee?"

"Yeah. Two-thousand-dollar bounty."

"We're goin' on lock down. Bring her in."

Ah, fuck. I eye Story's dresser through the rainbow bead curtain that separates her bedroom from the rest of the place. There's literally a hundred bottles and tubes covering it. I look down. I'm standing on a pink shag rug. She's got a *carpet* on top of a *carpet*.

"You want an escort to bring her in?" Heavy asks.

"Nah." I think about my room at the clubhouse. She's gonna be very disappointed.

Of course, she's going to be disappointed. My digs are only the beginning of the let-down. I ain't made for an old lady. Ain't outfitted for one, neither.

"You run into anything on the way over, call Forty. He's coordinating."

"Ayup." The shower shuts off, and my adrenaline spikes. She's in the next room. Naked. Soft. My dick tries to punch its way out of my jeans. "I'll find you when I get to the clubhouse."

"Take care, brother."

I hang up, and I turn to the bathroom door. It opens onto the room where I'm waiting.

Story's whole place is laid out weird. It's over one of the old retail spaces on Main Street, the ones with paper covering the display windows. The businesses have all gone bust, but people still rent the apartments overhead. Must be like living in the attic of a ghost town. Still, she's got a separate bedroom and a kitchenette, which is more'n I do at the clubhouse.

When's she comin' out of that bathroom? A hair dryer starts goin' and my dick goes back to half-mast.

I spend the next several minutes thinkin' about when the last time was I got a house mouse to change the sheets on my bed. Story needs rest, and once we get to the clubhouse, she ain't leavin' my sight. I don't want her sleepin' on used sheets.

I text Jo-Beth real quick to see if she'll straighten my room. She owes me from beatin' the shit out of a client of hers who busted a nut and didn't pay. She'll do it if she gets the message. Or she'll pretend she didn't see the text. I'm standin' there, fussin' with my phone, when Story finally comes out.

Fuck.

She's only wearin' a towel. She's got it tucked, but her curves are so bangin', the edges don't quite meet. There's this narrow gap straight down her belly and past her pussy lips where I can catch a flash of pale skin and light blonde curls.

Oh, fuck. She doesn't shave her pussy totally bare. There's a little patch of curls over her slit. I love that. Blood rushes to my cock, and it's pulsing now, beating to get loose. I want to see. I want to stroke those curls, collect beads of her pussy juice on my fingers, taste her.

I realize I'm standin' like Forty, a soldier waitin' on inspection. She's standin' still, too, watching me watch her.

"You want to see?" She cocks her head.

I nod without thinking. "Show me." My voice is so low, it don't sound like my own.

"You gonna start all that 'I'm no good for you' bullshit again?"

She rests her hands on her hips, and the towel spreads another quarter inch apart. I can make out lips now. Plump. Slick.

I groan.

"I ain't. But I'm gonna be."

"Huh?" She drums her fingers on her hips. I'm gonna be grabbin' them before this night is done, holdin' on while I plow her so deep she loses the ability to speak anything but my name. I'm done holdin' back. That ride from hell used up all my restraint and left me raw with needing her.

"I'm gonna be so fuckin' good to you," I promise, licking my lips. "Now show me, baby. Please."

She shoots me the cutest warning glance, like I better not be shittin' her, and then she reaches up and undoes the towel. She's a pro, so she don't just let it drop to the floor. Instead she lets it drop bit by bit, showin' me creamy skin I've seen before, but never like this. Never knowing it was all mine.

Her nipples are puckered in the cool air, dusky pink and big as saucers. I probably couldn't fit all of one in my mouth at once, but I want to try. She keeps on, revealing her taut, white belly and the curves of those hips, so ripe. And then she stops.

"You're sure, right? You're not gonna say 'this is so wrong' when I open up my pussy for you for the first time, are you?"

I've been so distracted drinking every perfect, creamy inch of her in that I hadn't noticed the corners of her mouth kick up. She's teasin' me.

For a second, I think of teasin' her back, but I've had enough of pretending. That drive, the ugly raging in my chest, tossin' up the worst of my shitty life, shorting the circuits in my brain, and there wasn't a damn thing I could do but drive. Couldn't even pray 'cause I didn't know the words or who to talk to anyhow.

Now that my miracle is in front of me, alive and well, trusting me with what I know is the whole fuckin' world...I ain't gonna lie to her no more.

"Well?" My girl's getting impatient with me.

"I ain't gonna say that. You're perfect. This is perfect. Every time you're around, it hurts to take my eyes off you. And it ain't 'cause of your body, which is perfect, but 'cause there ain't anything in the world that makes me feel the way I do when I look at you."

"And what's that?" Her hands have stilled, but she's trembling.

"Like there's good in it." And I said it all wrong somehow cause her big blue eyes fill with tears. My heart cracks. There it is. I can't be trusted with nice things. I break shit. It's how I was made.

"Fuck," I say and make for her bedroom. "We don't have time for all this. The club's on lockdown. We got to head out. You got a duffle bag?"

"Nickel." She calls me back. She ain't moved from the spot. "What the fuck?"

I can't stand to look at those tears, so I stare over her shoulder. "Just wipe your face, would you, Story? It's been a long day."

She swipes at the tears, seeming surprised they're streaming down her cheeks. I hand her the handkerchief from my back pocket.

"Is it the tears? They bother you?"

I don't dignify that with an answer. After a few moments, after she realizes I ain't gonna say shit, Story smiles.

"You're sweet as hell. You know that?"

"So you gotta cry about it?"

She huffs and elbows past me to her bedroom. "You ain't got a clue about women, do you?"

"Never claimed different." I follow my girl and stand there while she throws her crap in a bag. My dick's still hard, but it's clear the moment's passed, and I ain't pressed. She's here, she's safe. She's stopped bawling. It's all right.

13

STORY

Nickel Kobald is really absolute shit with women. You'd think my tears were the plague or somethin'. I let him off the hook and pack a bag. I'm disappointed—my clit is aching—but I'm figuring out that getting closer to Nickel isn't about getting naked.

I wish I could remember every word he said in the right order, but I'm sexually frustrated, still a little woozy from falling on my ass earlier, and I'm starving. I haven't eaten since breakfast.

Nickel calls to have the pizza sent to the clubhouse, and I don't fuss when he gets all bossy and tells me I'm gonna be stayin' there with him until this business with the Rebel Raiders is settled, and that's that. I've spent years trying to get into his bed. I don't know why he's acting like I've been drafted for some shit job.

I'm tempted to "accidentally" leave my textbooks at my apartment so I can take a break from 'em, but I pack them, too. Ma and Larry are so stoked about this community college thing. I don't have the heart to tell them I've found something I hate more than English Lit, and that's the theory and practice of dental hygiene.

I wish there was a way to dance for a living and leave my clothes on. I don't need to be on a stage; I just want to be moving to music, with people, sharing the bliss. Is that too crazy? Probably, yes, in Petty's Mill. If I want insurance and an income that lets me make rent without working myself to the bone, I need a skill other than dancing. I know that's what I'm supposed to want—and being a dental hygienist would make for a good life, a better life than any Jenkins ever had at least—but I can't help but feel sad.

Nickel's jittery on the drive to the clubhouse, broody and quiet. He keeps checking the sideview mirrors, but I don't think it's the Rebel Raiders that have him all twisted up. I find out I'm right about halfway there.

"Look," he breaks the silence. "My bunk. It ain't nothin' special."

"All right." I've seen the rooms at the clubhouse. The nicer ones have an en suite, but you can't get around the fact that the building's a rehabbed diesel garage built in the 50s.

"I got a bed and a sh— a bathroom. That's about it."

"Okay."

"Ain't like I'm poor."

I know this. All the brothers get a cut from the businesses, and Steel Bones Construction is a big name now. They don't show it off, but everyone in Petty's Mill knows they make bank. All you have to do is drive past the clubhouse and look at the parking lot to figure it out.

"I got no need for a house or anything. I can't cook worth shit."

Neither can I, but I don't volunteer the information. "I'm not gonna judge you, Nickel."

"Yeah. Well. Maybe you should."

"We back on that again?" I huff. "I don't think you want to go there."

"Yeah? And why's that?"

I roll my eyes. "I'm just gonna tear up again, and then you'll puss out, and it'll be a whole thing."

He tries to make his face mean, but he can't stifle a snort. "You got a mouth on you, don't you, woman."

I really don't, but there's something about this man, vicious as a junkyard dog, that makes me want to mess with him. I want to see what I can get away with because I have the sense I can get away with *everything.*

He's not a charmer like Charge, and he don't dog on women like some of the other brothers. It's like he's a total relationship virgin, and I kind of see why guys get hot for the innocent girl. Most people don't ever get to be first in line, but I'm gonna be. I'm planning on being first to plant my flag on Nickel Kobald's heart, and that...that's a hell of a rush.

I'm so into it, I forget my growling stomach, and I turn down Wall's offer of a drink when we get to the clubhouse. I make Nickel take me straight up to his bunk, where I've never been, and I've got these ideas of ripping his shirt off or him ripping off mine and us going to town on each other and then—

He opens his door, and I have to blink.

Damn. He wasn't lying. His room is *empty.*

It's at the end of the hall, and it's big. About as big as the combined kitchen/living/dining room in my apartment. And there's literally a bed, and that is all. Oh, and a chin up bar hung in the doorway to what I guess is his bathroom. I've slept a drunk off in one of the guest rooms a few times, and they share a communal bathroom by the stairs. Nickel's digs are nicer, but...bare. No pictures. No chairs. No dresser.

"Where do you keep your clothes?"

He walks over to the bed, fishes underneath, and yanks out a plastic tub with a bunch of folded t-shirts and jeans.

"Where do you put the dirty clothes?"

He walks to the bathroom door, swings it open, and I see a laundry bag hanging from a hook on the back of it. He stays over there on the far side of the room, arms crossed, a mulish expression on his face.

I shrug and drag my duffle bag in. He'd set it in the hall when he unlocked the door. Have to admit, I'm not sure why he bothers locking up a bed, a chin-up bar, and a laundry bag.

"You ain't gonna say anything?" he finally mutters.

I look up. I've dropped to my knees, and I'm rooting around for my makeup bag. I don't like to leave it 'cause once I had a bottle of baby oil leak, and I pretty much had to throw a hundred dollars' worth of makeup away.

"Well?" he says.

I'm not sure what to say, but then my eye catches the bed.

"Those sheets clean?" I don't want to lay down where some other girl's bare ass has been.

He sidles up to the bed, grabs a pillow, and sniffs it. His shoulders relax. "Yup."

Thank the Lord for small favors. I stand and start poking through my makeup, checking for leaks, when it strikes me. I glance over. Nickel has perched on the edge of the bed, watching me, wary, as if I might bolt at any minute. I look around the room again, really closely. At the walls.

There.

And there.

You can't tell at first, but once you see, there's dozens of them. Patches, painted over, the white just a tad less dingy than the rest of the wall. I know why he doesn't have any furniture.

Will he tell me? Butterflies shake to life in my belly. I want him to tell me. To trust me.

"How come you don't have a dresser or a desk or somethin'?"

He skewers me with those black eyes, and he chews the inside of his cheek. He knows that I know.

"I'll get pissed off, and I'll break it."

"How long since you had any furniture?"

He exhales, and his shoulders loosen. I bet he thought I was going to bail. He still doesn't get that I know what I'm dealin' with. I saw him launch that Fat Boy. Drag that man out to the parking lot. Lose his shit over a documentary on sea turtles.

He shoves his hands in his pockets. "Broke the shit that was in here when I patched in and got the room from Grinder. Haven't bothered to replace it."

So at least ten years ago. He had his patch when he rescued me at the field party.

"That was a while ago."

"Same man I was then."

"A danger to men, walls, and furniture alike?" I try to make it a joke, even though I know it isn't.

He sniffs, and a flush creeps up his neck. "I know it's stupid. Immature."

There's shame in the bow of his head, and he seems so damn lonely, standing on the other side of his empty room. My heart twinges. I don't want to leave him all alone.

"I still play dance class."

"Huh?"

Oh, shit. Maybe I should have thought this out. No one knows about my daydreaming. Not even Ma. I can't believe

I'm telling him, but I know if I reach out with my arms, he'll bolt, so I have to do it a different way.

"When I was a kid, I used to pretend I was a dance teacher. I'd have all these imaginary students, and I'd choreograph these elaborate dances. Then I'd teach the steps to an empty room. Correct pretend mistakes." My face is on fire. "I still do."

He could roll his eyes. Snort like I'm crazy. It is more than a little nuts. I'm twenty-one years old. Way past the age when playing pretend is acceptable.

"Don't you teach a dance class?"

"Yeah. Swinging Seniors. At the rec center." How does he know that?

"But this is different?" There's no judgement in his voice. Just curiosity.

"Yeah. Instead of being in the rec center basement, I've got my own studio. Natural light. Floor to ceiling mirrors. A barre. A pretty locker room with wooden cupboards painted white and a chaise lounge with pretty pillows."

"You really got a thing for pillows, don't you?"

I cock my head.

"You got more pillows at your place than I ever seen before. What do you do with them?"

He's not making fun of me. Well, he is teasing me about the pillows, but not the whole *play pretend* confession. He seems less set apart, too. He's in motion again, like he usually is, and he's working his way closer to me.

"They're for decoration."

"Babe, I do not get that."

I gesture around his empty room. "I can tell."

He's real close now, leaning a shoulder against the wall, watching me so intently like he does, as if he wants to read me but the writing's all smudged.

"Is that what you want? To have your own dance studio?"

I duck my head, tucking my hair behind my ears. I need a breath. The moment feels so raw, so strange. This isn't how we are together, Nickel and I. We're magnets with the same ends pushed together. We don't touch. We don't get close. We dance on the edge of a force that keeps us apart.

He reaches out, tucks away a strand of hair I missed. His fingertip whispers over the shell of my ear, and I shiver.

"Is that what you want?" he asks again.

"It's just pretend."

I'm Story Jenkins. My real dreams are too big to come true. Suddenly, this conversation feels too real. Too dangerous. This time I'm the one to step back.

I survey the room again, fist my hands on my hips. "Well, I'm going to need somewhere to sit."

If Nickel's thrown by the sudden change of topic, he doesn't show it. "What's wrong with the bed?"

"I need a table, too. I'm going to need somewhere to put my face on."

"You can't use the counter by the sink?"

I glance through the open bathroom door. He's got the kind of sink where there's no cabinet underneath, just pipes. He's filled up all the counter space with a cup with a toothbrush and a tube of toothpaste.

"Nope. Sure can't."

He shakes his head like I'm the one who's nuts, and then says, "Stay here."

He's out the door without ceremony, and I'm left in the weird, empty room, a funny feeling in my belly. I didn't really realize there are parts of me I hide. Not 'til I laid them out for Nickel just now. If this is trust, trust is scary as shit. I felt less exposed when I was flashing my pussy.

Nickel disappears for a half hour or so. When he comes back, he has two prospects in tow. He's brought a folding table, two chairs, a few empty milk crates, a lamp, a Yankee candle, and a hot pizza with napkins and two Cokes.

"Pizza!" I relieve him of that in a hurry—my stomach's been grumbling, and it echoes in this bare room—and in short order, the table's set up, the crates are stacked along a wall as a makeshift chest of drawers, and the lamp is plugged in next to the bed.

Nickel lights the candle with his Zippo and sets it in the middle of the table. The scent of lemon lavender fills the room.

"Where'd you steal that from?"

"Deb's office." Deb does her bookkeeping in an office in the annex. She does all the club's finances, even though Pig Iron is treasurer. It's pretty much an open secret.

"Deb's gonna hatch an egg."

"You ain't gonna snitch on me, are you?" Nickel retreats to sit on his bed and watch me eat.

"Deb asks, I'm not covering for you. She scares me."

Deb's almost as badass as Harper Tripp, Heavy's sister and the club's lawyer. Neither of those ladies are particularly fond of club pussy, and since I'm young and I strip, they lump me in with the girls like Angel and Danielle who spread it around.

"Aren't you gonna have any?" I gesture toward the pizza, folding a slice and going to town.

He shakes his head slow, and a wolfish grin reveals white teeth. "Nah. I'm hungry for somethin' else."

The butterflies that had been snoozing in my belly take wing, and suddenly, after only one slice, I'm full.

"You think I'm a sure thing, Nickel Kobald?"

There's so much tension radiating from him. I bet he hopes I am.

"I fed you dinner, haven't I? Candlelight dinner no less." He's teasing. He's got the dumbest smirk on his face.

"I ain't cheap."

"No, ma'am."

He leans back on the bed, eyein' me up, and I push the pizza box away. I want him to come to me. Pick me up and throw me on the bed. Tear my clothes off. Lose control. I am past ready.

He bounces a knee, all nervous energy.

I pull my shoulders back, thrust my tits forward. I didn't put a bra on when I got dressed at my place, and I know he can see my nipples.

He swallows.

I lean forward in the folding chair, press my knees and thighs together. A throb has started in my pussy, just from being here alone with Nickel. The bed is so close. It's time. No more dancing around each other.

He scrubs a hand over the back of his head.

I wait.

He sits there. Staring at me.

What the what?

"So...are we doing this?" I gesture between him and me. "'Cause I thought we were doin' this?"

He sighs. Looks down. "Fuck, Story. I don't know what I'm doin' here."

Oh, no. We are *not* doing this again. I'm going to rip him a new one, get up and kick him in the shins, and then the balls, and then the *face*, but then he says, "I ain't exactly... you know...*good* at it."

"Good at what?" I already know he's shit at communication.

"You know..." His knee bounces faster, and a tic pulses where his jaw meets his neck. "Fucking."

"Fucking what?" I wrap my arms around myself, trying to hold in the shriek of frustration.

"Just *fucking*."

Fu— oh. Huh.

"I don't— it's just—" Nickel's face is actually flushed. He's *blushing*.

I did not see this coming. I know he fucked pretty much everyone back in the day—Danielle and Jo-Beth and Angel and Cheyenne and Claudette before Harper ran her off. Since I've been going to parties, I haven't heard of him hooking up with club pussy, but he's been to rallies. I know what goes down.

But thinkin' about how he kissed me at first—like a raccoon gettin' in a trash can—I can kind of see it. He's not exactly smooth.

"So..." I tread lightly. Nickel doesn't have that sensitive male ego like some guys, but before today, I've heard him talk about personal shit exactly zero times. This might be really new territory for him. "How's it usually go?"

He shrugs. Glances at me out of the corner of his eye. "The chick gets me off. I get her off. I buy her a beer."

That's the saddest damn thing I've ever heard.

"Don't look at me like that. That's my whole point. I don't want to do you like that. You're—" He loses steam and his shoulders slump. I want him to finish that sentence so bad, but I'm afraid if I drop this thread, I'm never gonna end up in those worn but clean plaid sheets he's sitting on.

"So...how do you usually get off?" I ask.

My pussy pulses. Part of me hates talking about him with other women, but that hungry, nasty part of me wants to hear every little detail. I want to know this man inside and out, all of it, everything he's ever done.

"Really?" He cuts me a look of disbelief.

"If we're gonna do it, we should be able to talk about it." I sound prim and preachy, like my health ed teacher.

"I don't know. Get my dick sucked. Fuck her in the pussy. In the ass."

Whoa. I've never done that before. In the ass.

I'm actually not that experienced. I only ever slept with two guys, a dude named Dean—huge mistake—and this guy Evan. He was the only guy in show troupe. He was like my lab partner, but for sex. The summer after high school, we just went crazy. I felt guilty, but Nickel was in the wind, and my curiosity won out. Nickel growls, apparently uncomfortable with how long it's taking me to reply. I shake the memories away. Where were we? Oh yeah. *In the ass.*

"What positions?" I ask.

He shrugs his hands. "You really want to talk about this?"

"I really want to talk about this." My pussy's so wet I can feel it leaking past the elastic of my panties.

"Doggie. Her on top. Whatever works. Usually space is an issue."

"Why's that?"

"Bathrooms are tight. Back seats are tight."

"You don't bring women back here?" A little flame flickers to life in my chest.

"I don't let anyone in my space." The little flame flares and warms me to my toes. I'm in his space. I'm *all* up in it.

"So how do you get a woman off?" I make myself focus back on the conversation.

He's clearly uncomfortable, but he's humoring me, and I love that he's doing it for me. After thinking too hard a little too long, he says, "Get out of the way so she can play with her clit. Lick it if she don't cum before I do."

Wow. I don't know what to say. My naughty, wild-child, hippy brain, the one that gets a kick out of dancing on the stage at The White Van, is turned on, but I also feel sad.

The sex Nickel's talking about sounds like when I trade shifts with Jo-Beth. This for that. No emotions allowed. (Bitch does not care if you're sick or if your car broke down. She'll trade if she wants to, and if she doesn't, *too bad, so sad* for you.)

I think sex should be a dance. Fun and sweaty, body-exhausting and soul-warming. If this was a cartoon, a light bulb would be flashing over my head. I grin wide, and Nickel looks very worried.

"What?"

"I have an idea."

His brow furrows, and he seems to be puzzling something out. "All right, baby. I'll eat you out if you want."

I laugh, suddenly sure of myself again. I stand and twist at the waist, stretching my arms above my head.

"What are you doin'?" Nickel's lookin' at me like I'm nuts.

"Stretching." I grab my phone and open the music app. "You don't have to worry about anything. You stay right there. I got this."

I scroll through the Os and the Ps until I hit the Qs. This'll be perfect.

"Story?" He's getting to his feet, and that's not gonna work for me.

"Sit back down. You're so worried about making it good for me? Then just sit. I know how to make it good for me. You want it to be good for me, right?" My voice is husky, seductive. It's not how I talk with customers, but it's not my usual voice, either.

Nickel nods, swallows, his Adam's apple bobbing amid the cords of his neck. All of his muscles are straining; his sleeves so tight over his biceps you can see the definition. He's so built.

He's amazing, this man. As hard as rock, thrumming with pent up energy, his stark and beautiful face entranced. By *me*. I feel powerful. Sexy. Happy.

I hit play, male voices harmonize a capella, and I tug my tank top slowly over my head, fluff up my hair, and with a little flair, I drop my shirt to the floor. For a moment, Nickel is frozen, and then he bursts out laughing.

"Is this 'Bohemian Rhapsody?'" His eyes are watering.

Was this not a good choice? No. It's awesome. It's a great song. Six minutes long, guaranteed sing along, guaranteed good tips.

"You have a problem with it?" I play like I'm put out, but the truth? Hearing Nickel laugh? Worth a million dollars.

"Not at all," he grins. "Go on."

He leans back, his gaze shifting down to my chest, and he licks his lips. I sashay toward him, letting my hips swish and my tits bounce. I usually have six-inch heels on when I do this, but I slipped my shoes off earlier. Good thing my ass is big enough it bounces even when I'm barefoot.

I come to a stop between his knees, resting one hand on his shoulder. I run the other between my tits, over my belly, and then I pop the button on my jeans. He groans.

I slowly pull the zipper down, and then I shimmy my hips, but these pants were not made for stripping. "A little help?"

I rest both hands on his shoulders, and he gently tucks his thumbs into my waistband and tugs my panties down with the jeans. I step out of them and kick them aside. He groans, and heat floods my pussy.

He doesn't know where to look. His gaze flies from my face to my tits to the V between my legs. I shift a few times, loving the feeling of my slick lips rubbing together while Nickel watches me, his eyes darkening.

I run my hands down his hard chest, and then I drag his shirt over his head. He raises his arms to help me, and I sink to my knees.

"Scooch back." I push on his rock-hard pecs. He lays back on his elbows, still watching, and I unzip his pants and drag them down, boxers, too.

"You like me like this?" I ask. "On my knees?"

"I like you," he says. "Any-which-way."

His dick is bobbing between us, hard and thick. The tip is angry red, and a vein runs down the shaft. My mouth waters. He's huge. Like, call-a-friend, take-a-picture-or-it-didn't-happen *huge*.

I want to try that. I want to take all of that in me, and he's going to let me. I feel a surge of pure power, and I rise and climb up his body, dragging my tits along his chest, my nipples aching from the friction. I whimper.

He raises up to take my mouth, and I think he's going to try to eat me like he did before, but he doesn't. He sips instead, and then coaxes my lips apart, slipping between them and tangling his tongue with mine. He raises a hand to cup my neck, and he's gentle and it's wonderful and...not him.

It's like he's pretending to be a guy on a soap opera or something. There's no way Nickel Kobald fucks like this. I want more. I want *real*.

I go looking for it, spreading my knees wider until that

throbbing cock slides along my folds, back and forth, not penetrating, nudging my clit with the ridged head.

I moan, and he stiffens. He's even more restrained now, but it feels so good, I don't want to stop, and so I rock, smearing my cream all up and down his shaft. He's looking, so I look too, and we're both mesmerized by the sight of his cock glistening with my juices.

"You're so fucking perfect," he breathes, stroking his hands up my thighs so softly the callouses on his fingers almost tickle. I don't want to be tickled. I want him to grab me so hard I have bruises tomorrow. Touch me like he needs to hold on tight so I never get away. I almost growl in frustration. I want him in me, so bad. I don't care if he's being weird and careful.

We need a condom.

"Be right back." I smile, hop off, and make for my purse.

Oh, shit. Some prospect has my purse. I glance around the room. No help there.

"In my wallet. Back pocket." Nickel's chest is rising and falling like he's run a mile, and he's dug his fingers into the bed sheets. He's strung so tight, his grimace looks like pain.

I fumble in his wallet, pull out a foil wrapper, thanking the period gods that my monthly friend just took off. If this all went down two days ago, well...it would've been awkward.

When I get back to the bed, Nickel has scooted up, propping himself on his pillows, and I saddle back up, unrolling the sheath down his dick. We both watch my hands work, and I reach under to cradle his balls. He hisses, and his chest jerks forward, but then he stills.

I glance at his face, and there's a war going on. The wildness that I love, the crazy energy that reminds me so much of how I feel when I dance, is there, sparking in his black eyes, but the control has it locked down. His body is stone-like with the effort of keeping himself in check.

This isn't what I want. I don't want him controlling himself for me. I want him to lose it over me. I always have.

I lean over, take his mouth, nip at the tongue that searches for mine. I grab his hand, guide it to my tit, hold it there while I glide his cock along my pussy, rocking ever so slightly, teasing, pushing, pushing. I want him to break.

I want him to give me all of himself, not whatever he thinks is worth something, but every piece.

"What are you waiting for?" I goad him. His hips pump, seeking my entrance, and then he stops so quick I imagine brakes squealing.

"Come on, baby," he groans. "Give it to me."

"This?" I slide, let the head of his cock notch at my opening, and then I back off, pulling forward to raise a tit to his mouth. "Or is this what you want?"

He leans up, pulls my nipple in his hot mouth, suckling and flicking with his tongue. I almost give up, sink down on his hard shaft, soothe the ache beating a rhythm between my legs. But I'm the strong one. I just need to hold out a little longer.

I crawl closer, far enough so his cock can't touch my pussy without him really moving, and I straighten my back so my tit comes out of his mouth with a pop. I slip a finger into my slit, swipe it through the juices that are leaking down my thighs.

"If you want this—" I run my finger over his lips then slip it into his mouth. "You have to take it."

And then *I* freeze, hands on my hips. Waiting. I don't have to wait long at all.

He almost roars, an animal sound that sends jolts of adrenaline down my spine, and then he twists, rising from the bed, pulling me under him, dragging my arms over my head and pinning them with his rough hands. He doesn't speak, one look at his face tells me he's past words as he lifts one of my knees and slams home, stretching me so bad I whimper from the brief pain, as he makes me feel every inch. Then he pulls out, and before I can even draw in a breath, he slams into me again, bottoming out.

Over and over again, he thrusts, grunting, nipping at my neck, clasping my ass and dragging me up so he can go higher, deeper, battering my G-spot like he's a piston, not a man. I want to chase the pleasure gathering low in my belly, but I can't move. He's holding me in position, mastering my body with each frenzied stroke. He makes a false move, misses, and the head of his dick grazes my clit. That's all it takes. My pussy clenches, and the first wave of heat unfurls in my belly. He doesn't stop. He fucks through my pussy walls spasming around him, sending another orgasm racing through me, priming me for another.

I'm keening on an endless loop, so loud there's no doubt people can hear. It feels so good, I can't keep it in, and he's going so hard my voice vibrates from the thrusts. All I can do is hold on. He's got his head tucked into the crook of my neck, so every feral sound he makes echoes in my ear.

Minutes, maybe hours later, he raises up and tilts the knee he's still holding wider. He stares down where he's pummeling my pussy.

I want to see, too. I struggle against his grip, and when he finally lets go, feeling rushes back to my fingers. I push up on my elbows.

He slows, not much, but enough that I can catch a breath. I watch my swollen, red pussy lips cling to him as he strokes in and out, his six-pack rippling as he fucks me like it's his job.

He's braced on one arm above me, and I glance up, wondering if he has the same dopey look on his face that I must have on mine. I expect him to still be watching my pussy take his cock, but he's not looking down. His gaze is riveted to my face.

The wildness is there, but he's not mindless with it. He seems different. Intense, but in a whole new way.

"Can you do it again?" he gasps between pants. "Please?"

"Do what?" I'd do anything for him right now.

"Cum on my cock. You're so fucking beautiful when you cum." A wave of warmth that has nothing to do with what our bodies are doing fills my chest.

I want to see him cum, too. I am kind of amazed at his stamina. He's almost thirty, so I guess it's true about older guys being able to last longer. I don't know how much more I can take. Each orgasm has wrung me like a washcloth.

I don't know if my body can do it again, but I can't tell him no.

"Give me this." I grab his hand, suck on it, and then I tuck it between us. I guide his fingers to the raw nub pulsing with each slow thrust. "Be gentle. It's really sensitive."

"Like this?" He brushes the rough pads of his fingers over my clit, and I squirm.

"Yeah. Do circles, too."

He does, light and slow, and an urgency builds in my belly, giving me energy to raise my hips, to take him deeper. He smooths my hair away from my face and dusts kisses across my forehead and my cheeks, leaning back to gaze into my eyes.

"Beautiful girl. Give it to me. One more. Come on. This is all I ever wanted. Give it to me now."

His words are all it takes; I tumble over, heat pulsating, belly fluttering, my thigh muscles totally giving out. He rides my orgasm, battering my cervix once, twice, a third time, and miraculously, he drags another spasm from my core. I collapse, put-a-fork-in-me done. He shouts, and his body jerks as he cums inside me. I imagine I can feel the heat.

He pulls out, falls flat on his back, and about two seconds later, I hear a soft snore. I don't want to laugh, but I can't help it. *Of course,* Nickel Kobald passes out after sex.

To be honest, I'd like to pass right out, too, but I have the presence of mind to reach between my legs. The condom got stuck, and Nickel's cum is leaking down the crack of my ass. It's easy to fish out, but when I go to tie it up, I notice it's ripped, too.

Well, we did try. I'm not too freaked out. I just had my period, and it looked like most of it didn't get inside me.

I'm going to tell myself that Nickel's most likely clean. His dick looks fine. I am totally not going to think about anal and bathrooms and backseats right now. I'm not going to let anything ruin this moment. The man of my dreams is snoring beside me after giving me the best sex of my life.

I go to the bathroom to drop the condom in the trash and wash up. My body's tired, but I can't stop my feet from dancing on the way back to the bed. There's a massive wet spot, obviously, so I wedge myself in on Nickel's other side and let myself drift off, a stupid grin on my face. Everything's finally going in the right direction.

Nickel let me in.

There's no going back now.

14

NICKEL

Story's asleep when I wake up, so I creep out of bed and pull on my jeans. She's all the way on the edge, her hair fallin' to the floor like Rapunzel or something, and I can see why. There's a huge wet spot in the middle of the bed. I wonder if she squirted. I didn't feel it, but at the beginning there, I was out of my head.

My skin feels tight, and uneasiness prickles down my spine. She don't look hurt. She's got a silly smile on her face, and I grab at that, hold onto it like a life raft.

When I lost it, when I started pounding into her, she didn't say stop or nothin'. And she would have if I hurt her. Wouldn't she? I scrub a hand across my face. No. She probably wouldn't. That girl has been doggin' me for years, thinkin' I'm some kind of knight in shining armor. I kissed Danielle in front of her, and she didn't even yell at me.

No way Story wanted me to bang her like an animal. She laid there and took it, and I was so gone she needed to tell me to rub her clit. The ugly rears its head and my stomach knots. I ain't made for this. I need to get out of here.

But she's so perfect lying on her belly, the huge globes of her spectacular ass sloping down into those sweet thighs. She's got her legs parted, and I can see the swollen pink peeking out. My dick is raw, but it's hard in an instant, chafing against the denim.

What do normal men do after they fuck? Spoon, I guess.

I want to; I want to gather all that softness to me, feel her rib cage rise and fall as she breathes. Know she's safe. But I don't feel safe.

I lost it. I was doin' fine, and then I lost it, and I fucked her like a whore. I think it turned out okay, but what if it hadn't? I could have hurt her. For all I know, she's bleeding internally, right now.

Fuck. That's crazy. I'm crazy.

I need a beer.

I duck out, shut the door quietly. Hopefully she'll sleep till morning. I do know I'm not supposed to nail and bail; I'm not a complete asshole. But that uneasy feeling...it's creepin' up my throat. Chokin' me.

When I get downstairs, I realize I ain't gettin' peace and quiet in this clubhouse tonight. We're on lock down, and all the brothers are here, along with the old ladies and club pussy and kids. 'Cause this is an MC, even if we've gone legit, someone's tapped a keg, the jukebox is blarin' Skynyrd, and the prospects are tryin' to slide up on Jo-Beth and Angel like it's slow skate at the roller rink. Dizzy's boys are sneakin' around, polishing off empties.

On a couch in a corner, Charge is cozied up to his new old lady Kayla. Kayla's kid is asleep across them, his head resting on his mama's tits, his feet dangling off Charge's lap. Kayla plays with the kid's hair while Charge whispers shit in her ear. She's smilin', and he's only got eyes for what's beside him. My unease wars with a new urge to go back to Story. I'm stuck in place, playin' Peeping Tom, when I hear my name.

"Nickel!" Heavy waves me over to his seat at the bar.

I slide in and rap the wood for a cold one.

"Church?" There will be a meeting on what went down at Twiggy's today—many—but I'm assuming Heavy's gonna wait until there's word from Forty on the dude who got away and from the dentist on the Raider who got stabbed.

"Check your phone."

I do, and there's a text from Heavy. *Church 2morrow 10 am.* There's another one, too.

Got news on today
meet at midnight Barrow rd
cm alone

It's from Ike.

"What?" Heavy reads me like he always does. I hold my phone up to show him.

"Well, that sounds like a fuckin' trap." Heavy belly laughs, remindin' me of that tattooed dude from that kid's movie about the island girl. Charge and I took his boy fishin' up Lake Patonquin and that movie played up and back. I was like, a few more tattoos, that demi-god could be Heavy.

"Sure does," I agree.

We sit in silence a few moments, nursing our beers. What happened today puts us at a whole new level, and not where we want to be. Heavy took us 100% legit five, six years ago now. We thought warring with one percenters was in our rearview. And then when shit flared up recently, we thought it was gonna be petty posturing. Some vandalism. Big talk.

I saw Fay-Lee. She had a busted lip. This ain't posturing.

"What the fuck were they doing?"

Heavy's face gets tight under his crazy beard. "Fay-Lee told Dizzy they said two thousand for an old lady. A bounty."

"The fuck? Why?" I ask, but I already know. It's 'cause of the past. You think you're out; you're ahead. That things can be different. But the past...it keeps you chained in the dirt.

"'If there is serious injury, you are to take life for life, eye for eye, tooth for tooth, hand for hand, foot for foot, burn for burn, wound for wound, bruise for bruise.'" Heavy's quoting the Bible again.

"Yeah, I'll go eye-for-eye with those meth-head fucks."

Heavy shakes his head. "And as they say, that's how we'll all end up blind."

"Did this all really start over a truckload of cigarettes?"

I never paid much attention before. The beef began before our time, when Slip, Heavy's dad, was president. We inherited it, of course, along with the clubhouse, the nest egg that financed Steel Bones Construction, and Boots and the other old heads sittin' at the other end of the bar.

"In a way. The club was running cigarettes across state lines. A dumb tax scam. Low margins. Dad passed a shipment off to Stones Johnson. Stones was unlucky and got busted on Rural Route 9 past Irving. Turns out there were guns under the tobacco. Stones and his boy Knocker went down for twenty."

"Stones died inside." I remember. I was twenty-one, twenty-two at the time. There was a vigil at the clubhouse. Stones had been Steel Bones before it all went to shit.

"And his boys Inch and Dutchy founded the Rebel Raiders." Heavy spits when he says their names. They're both six feet under now, and it's too good for them. After what they did to Hobs and Crista.

"And now Knocker's out."

"And now Knocker's out." Heavy repeats. "And we know fuck-all about what he's doing, where he's holed up. Nothin'."

"You need to go meet Ike." Heavy sighs, shifts like he's bearing up under a weight. "I know this dredges up shit for you. I wouldn't ask if we didn't need it."

I get it. I been lookin' out for Hobs since I was a prospect. And Crista's been servin' me beers in that long-sleeved sweatshirt, hood up, almost as long. I don't give a shit how we got here. Rebel Raiders fucked with mine; that's all I need to know.

The ugly bursts back to life, and I realize it's been lurkin', all the time with Story when I thought it was quiet, it'd been there. Outside the window lookin' in.

"Brother, you don't need to ask." This is what I'm good for. The hard. The bloody.

I stand, brush my hands down my pants. I need a piece, but there's no way I'm gonna risk wakin' Story up to get mine from under the bed. She's gonna look at me with those big, round eyes, and she's gonna expect shit—whatever men do when they find a woman they can't breathe without, whatever words they say to make her stay—and those blue eyes are gonna go dark with disappointment when I fail to give her what she needs. And I'm a coward 'cause I'd rather walk into an ambush than face failing Story Jenkins.

"I ain't a hundred percent that Ike didn't have his hand in what went down at Twiggy's today."

"From what Fay-Lee and Roosevelt say, it all sounds like a coincidence."

"I don't believe in coincidences," I say.

"Neither do I."

I finish my beer, and I check my phone. It's only ten. I got time.

"You need one of Deb's little white pills?" Heavy's laughin' at me.

"Nah." The ugly is kind of rootin' for this to go south, and I don't need slow reflexes. "I need a piece."

"You've got one." Heavy stands, and the brothers around us glance up. He has that effect. It's like a mountain gettin' up on its feet. "And Nicky? You ain't ridin' alone."

I didn't think I was.

FOURTEEN BARROW ROAD is a rancher on the Patonquin flats that's been slowly sinking into the clay since it was built. I lived there until I turned sixteen and Heavy's ma let me move into their basement. It ain't a place I ever drive by or think about on purpose.

I thought it was abandoned since Markie went upstate, but from the light filtering out around the boards in the front window, I guess it ain't anymore. Ike's bike is in the drive. He opens on the third knock.

"Welcome home, brother." Ike greets me, arms wide, in a stained undershirt, reeking of booze. He squints past me into the dark. My brothers are out there, a hundred yards up the road, hidden by the tree line between this shithole and the nearest neighbor who built on solid, insurable ground.

"You come alone?"

I shrug, noncommittal, as I step in to the living room. My brothers aren't gonna do me much good if there's Rebel Raiders back in the kitchen. The house feels empty, though. Weird how you can sense that about the house you grew up in.

The cigar smoke and reek of mold are so strong, I can't take a full breath. Ike gestures to the couch, the same shit-brown one with pheasants we had growin' up, and I shake my head.

"I'll stand." The ugly's riding me hard.

"Suit yourself." Ike collapses in Dad's old easy chair, fumbles with the remote, and presses mute. Everything in the house is the same as the day I left except the TV. Ike's bought himself a Samsung Q9 big screen. Wonder where he got the money?

"So what you got?" I don't need to spend any more time in this shitty time machine than absolutely necessary. I already feel the memories dive-bombing me like demon ghosts.

"Ain't you gonna sweet talk me some, little brother? Just gonna shove your hands right down my pants?" He cackles and kicks up the footrest.

I let it roll over me. That's weird, too. I don't usually have that capability. I get down to business.

"You have anything to do with what went down today?"

I want him to say yes so I can stop this game and beat the beady-eyed glee off his face.

"Other than happening upon it, no." He's sizing me up, seeing if I believe him. I don't. "Lucky your boys got there in time."

Dizzy's not feeling lucky tonight, I'm sure. Neither am I.

"Where's Knocker Johnson?"

Ike grins and waves his arm at the couch. "Take a load off."

We stare at each other a beat, and I realize that unless I play this like he wants, it's going to be pulling teeth. I sit. I'm gonna have to burn these jeans when I get home. Even the idea of Story gettin' near this place—even as close as brushing against something that's been here—it turns my stomach.

I lean forward, rest my elbows on my knees, and wait. He needs to have his say whether anyone wants to hear it or not. He always has.

He lights a cigarillo, plays with the smoke in his mouth awhile. "You know she wouldn't move back here when Markie got locked up?"

"Who?"

"Jeannie. Who else?"

His ex-wife. I remember her comin' around when they first got together. I was ten or so. She was sweet at first. Then she started to drink, always on edge, and she stopped coming around when Ike dropped by to raise hell with Dad and Markie and Keith. Breaking her jaw and her arm in two places was what got Ike put away.

"I told her it'd be ours, free and clear, no mortgage, but she wouldn't have none of it. Like she was too good for a free house. She said it was a jinx."

I don't disagree with her. Nothing good ever came out of this place.

"You know she has a kid now? With some fucker up in Shady Gap?"

I didn't know. Good for her. This ain't what I came for though. "Why you tellin' me this, Ike?"

"She always liked you best. Did you know that? Said you were a sweetheart. Fuckin' Dudley Do-Right."

I think he's drunker than I reckoned when he opened the door. This is maudlin shit. Maybe he's tryin' to pick a fight, ease the demons that run in both our blood. Get me to say somethin' nice about Jeannie and then try to beat my ass. Sounds like him.

I consider it for a second. Doin' some much needed demolition by throwing his carcass around this place is not the worst idea. Let out the pent up ugly from this afternoon. I guess I think on it too long 'cause he goes on.

"We were gonna have a kid. Jeannie and me. She was five months along. She lost it."

My stomach turns. The reek of mold and smoke seems to grow even thicker. I don't want to know what happened. There's no way this ain't a horror story. "Can we talk about the Rebel Raiders, Ike?"

He ignores me, stares off in space, a watery half-smile on his face. "I didn't even mean to hit her that time. She kind of walked into it on accident."

My knuckles turn white as I clutch my knees. I have to get out of here before the foulness in this house seeps past my clothes and into my skin and no amount of bleeding out will get me clean.

"Why you tellin' me this, Ike?" I ask again, but I know why. He's tryin' to play me.

His boozy eyes, genuinely sad for the briefest moment, turn speculative. Like Dad's. He's playin' an angle.

All of them—Dad and Ike, Markie and Keith—they all thought I was weak. Not physically. I could whup all of them, even when they ganged up on me, by the time I hit sixteen. But the fact I never did Ma the way they all did— they marked me as a pussy and tried to own me every minute I lived in this damn house.

"I ain't never gonna get my shit together—get a woman, a kid—if I don't have work. This pissant money ya'll are fronting me for spyin' on the Raiders ain't gonna cut it. I need a job."

I don't trust him for a moment, and neither would Heavy.

"A job doin' what?"

"I could do construction."

He could do a lot of damage at the sites we work. We specialize in modifications that aren't on the schematics submitted to the county. Safe rooms, underground vaults, tunnels. We got a lot of work now on the up-and-up, and only brothers work the mod jobs, but eventually...he'd catch wind of somethin'. Is Ike tryin' to go double agent?

"I could ask Heavy. If you have something worth opening his mind. Steel Bones don't hire felons."

"Unless it's one of their own."

Yeah. He means Scrap. Brother should have never gone down for what he did; he should have got a medal. Rebel Raiders were behind that shit, too.

The rage rises, pulling me to my feet. I stalk to the china cabinet where Ma kept her keepsakes, these figurines of kids with big eyes and big heads. Kind of like Story must have looked as a little girl. They're all gone, but you can see circles in the dust where they used to be.

"What do you have, Ike?" I need to end this soon before this bizarre chill I'm ridin' burns off.

"Rebel Raiders weren't at Twiggy's on accident. Your boy got lucky they had money ridin' on the Pittsburgh game. Otherwise, your brothers would've never made it in time."

My blood runs cold.

"Why?"

"Knocker's sending men out all over, lookin' for Steel Bones. There's a bounty. Two thousand."

"For old ladies?"

"Old ladies, brothers, prospects, whatever."

"What does he want?"

"That twisted fuck?" Ike acts like he can't fathom the man, but we both know it's a lie. There ain't no depravity a

Kobald ain't intimately familiar with. "Why does anyone do that kind of shit? Leverage, I'd imagine. Collateral. Ransom. Revenge."

"Revenge?"

"The man has a real hard-on for Steel Bones."

"He ain't satisfied with carvin' a woman up and bustin' in a kid's head?"

Ike takes a swig of his beer. "Knocker don't see that as on him."

"It was his brothers."

"You takin' responsibility for what me and Markie and Keith get up to?"

I fuckin' hate it, but I take his point. "Then what's this about?"

Ike snorts. "Thought you were supposed to be the smart one, Dudley Do-Right." He waits a minute, and I wait him out. "Don't matter what has happened since. Knocker Johnson agreed to drive a truck of cigarettes for Steel Bones when he'd barely turned eighteen, and he ended up behind bars for eighteen years."

The Blown Job. That's what the older brothers call it. That shit splintered Steel Bones. Stones Johnson's other boys—Inch and Dutchy—founded the Rebel Raiders after Stones and Knocker got life bids. Took a third of the club with them. It's been hauntin' us now for nearly twenty years.

I glance around the room, the peeling wallpaper and the rusted radiators, the chipped linoleum tiles visible through the kitchen door and the gap where some Kobald or other wrenched out the stove to sell it for scrap. There's mouse shit scattered across the floor. Except for the stove, it don't look much different from when Ma finally hit the skids and gave up.

The past is a mass grave. Can't make no sense of it. Can't be made right.

"What's Knocker's end game?" I don't expect Ike to know, and if he does, I don't expect a straight answer.

"What does Steel Bones have that's worth eighteen years of a man's life?"

Story's perfect face, those big, blinking eyes and that sweet smile, comes unbidden to mind, and I drive it back out. I don't want even the thought of her in this place.

"He has to know this don't end well for him. Rebel Raiders might follow him now cause of his name, but they're a bunch of meth dealers and brawlers. Ain't no army."

"And Steel Bones is? I see a bunch of carpenters and roofers these days, brother. Not that I'm complainin'. I can see myself with a hammer and a tool belt." Ike grins, and the lie jerks the corners of his mouth higher.

I know him. I know his tells. And he knows me. We only had a few years together in this house, him bein' so much older, but a jail is a jail, and time there passes slow.

"I'll talk to Heavy." I wipe my palms on my jeans as if that'll clean off the grime.

"Yeah, you do that little brother." Ike stands too. Walks me to the door, his hand on my shoulder. It's all I can do not to toss it off.

He grabs the knob and opens the door, but when it's less than a foot wide and I can finally smell fresh air again, he stops.

"You would've been an uncle," he says, tightening his grip, a twisted smile on his face. "That would've been somethin', wouldn't it?"

I got no words.

"It looked just like a little person. Jeannie even had it buried."

Acid burns my throat, and every muscle in my body strains to throw off his disgusting hand and drive a fist into his filthy mouth. The only thing that stops me is knowin' my brothers would see and swoop down, and then we'd be driving totally blind with the Rebel Raiders.

But that ain't entirely true. There's also the strange fact that beating Ike into oblivion ain't my driving urge right now.

I want to breathe in the cold night air until my lungs are rid of every trace of this place. I want to ride hard. I want a scalding shower, and then I want to sit across from Story Jenkins and watch her crinkle her nose and lift her sweet lips and bug her eyes so you can't tell if she's surprised or teasing the hell out of you.

I want to listen to her soft, high, bossy voice telling me *be gentle* and *do circles*. So I shake loose, head for my bike, and tear off for the clubhouse. And it occurs to me that this might be the first time I ever left this house that I been ridin' toward something and not away.

I GET lucky for once in my life, and Story's still sleeping when I slip in at three in the morning. After I caught Heavy up on what was said, I rubbed myself raw in the communal bathroom showers. I didn't want to wake her. She had one hell of a day, and even though she can handle her own, she's small and peaceable. She's not a fighter like Jo-Beth or Harper.

I'm careful not to jostle the bed too bad when I climb in, but I guess Story's a light sleeper. She pushes up on her elbows, the sheet falls to her waist, and there is all that skin, milky white and lush in the moonlight comin' in from the window. Her nipples perk up, begging for my mouth.

I should shut the shades so we don't get an eyeful when the sun rises, but there's no way I'm tearing myself away from this girl. She rubs the sleep from her eyes and wriggles up to sitting.

"Where did you go?" Her voice is higher, breathier as she struggles to come full-awake.

"Club business."

She pushes her wild hair back, and she scrubs her face with her hands. And then—like the sun bursting out—she smiles.

"Are you naked?" she asks.

"One way to find out."

And I guess I thought I'd have to start from zero, explain myself, find words to make her come to me again, but I don't. One minute she's eyein' my bare chest, the next she's straddling it, her bare ass cradling my stiff cock. She bounces, making the coils squeak.

She fucking *bounces*. And giggles. The sound goes straight to my dick, and it's throbbing now, and my hips are straining to find a hole to push in because her warm, slick pussy is home, and I'm lost 'cause I ain't there. I have mind enough to reach under the bed, grab a condom, and slide it on.

She's bent forward to kiss me, and when my hands are free, I plunge my fingers in her hair, hold her still while I plunder her mouth, and all the while her unrestrained body is goin' crazy on me, writhing and rocking as she rakes her tits up and down my chest. She's tryin' to seat herself on my cock, but I've got her calves pinned with one of my legs, so she can't get enough height.

Somewhere along the line, her hunger amped up my control. I chuckle. This is gonna be fun.

"Come on, Nickel," she begs.

I ignore her. I free one hand, fisting and wrapping her hair around the other, and I slap her hard on the ass. She shrieks and bucks against me.

I slap the other cheek. "Be good."

Her chest is heaving, and her eyes are shining in the dim light. She calms, and I can feel every inch of her silky skin from her belly to her thighs, her slight weight pressing on me, and I want to roll her and pound into her again until she screams my name, but this is too sweet. I take a sip from her lips, stroke up and down her spine with my fingers and chase the shivers.

"Nickel," she whimpers. "It hurts."

Those are magic words. I don't want my girl to hurt ever.

I cradle her and twist, landing her on her back, eating up her happy shriek of surprise. I slide down, wedge my shoulders between her thighs, and wrap my arms around her hips, lacing my fingers and resting them on her belly so she can't squirm an inch.

"Nickel," she whines, trying to peel my hands away or scoot her ass back and failing. "I haven't had a shower."

I nestle my nose in the curls dusting above her pussy lips and breathe deep. She yelps and slaps my back.

"I can tell," I growl, and she yips and beats at me harder. I can smell myself on her, and my cock punches so hard against the mattress I bet I left a dent. "I love how you smell, baby."

I slip my tongue through her soft folds, exploring, searching out her wet hole and lapping at her hard clit. She's really bucking now, but she can't get anywhere, and she's panting heavy, moaning my name, over and over. She's left off slapping me.

I flatten my tongue and lick her asshole-to-clit and back again, and when a fresh gush of pussy juice leaks from her hole, I lap it up.

"You taste so good." There's a little latex aftertaste, but it's fading with each gush, and I'm drawing the cream out of her. Her thighs are quivering against my shoulders, clenching, and her belly's tightening under my grip. She tries so hard to grind her clit into my mouth, but I hold her steady, make her take what I give.

She jerks her torso, and I have to press down harder to keep her where I want her while she gasps, "Nickel, I want to cum. I want to cum."

And now that she's mine, going wild in my arms, I have to give this woman anything she asks for. "Okay, baby."

I suck hard on her clit, let my teeth graze her, and she flails so much as she cums that I can't keep hold of her anymore without hurting her, so I push up, and I look down and watch her full body seize and jerk through her orgasm. I seen this in porn before but never real life.

She's so beautiful. Her hair's a mess, she's flushed pink head to toe, and her legs are squeezed together and bent at the knees as she cries out her pleasure.

My dick is hard enough to pound nails, but I can't move. I can only watch.

Her blue eyes slowly blink open, and as her legs relax, she points her toes. She has the muscles of a dancer, firm thighs and tight calves, and you can see the defined line of each one as she raises her legs and wraps them around my waist.

"I want you, baby," she sighs. "Quit teasing me."

I don't think I'll ever be able to tell her no again. I grab my cock and guide it into her slick channel, stretching her while she adjusts to let me in deeper.

"Yes," she hisses, her eyelids dropping again as she bites her lip.

I go slow because this is heaven, the highest high. The air up here is crystal clear and my body's at peace with itself for once, every part of me working to make this woman moan and whimper and beg and smile and gasp. The hot grip of her pussy on my cock is amazing, like nothing I've ever felt before, but it's nothing to watching her.

I see her frustration rise, bit by bit, as she urges me faster with her hips and slips her fingers between us to play with her clit, but I'm too selfish. This peace is too perfect. I draw her hand away and pin it on the pillow beside her head.

"Unh!"

I guess she's had enough. She uses her other hand to grab me by the scruff of the neck, and she tugs, trying to roll me with her legs and torso. There's no way she could dislodge me—I've got at least sixty pounds on her—but I'm afraid she'll hurt herself, so I let her put me on my back.

She climbs back on, taking my cock in an almost painfully tight grasp and shoves it between her legs, slipping down, and then she rides me hard, using me, her head tilted back, the tip of her hair tickling my thighs. She has her hand shoved between her legs, working her clit so hard I don't know how she hasn't already cum.

I'm gonna spend any second, my balls drawn tight and tingling, my hips slamming up to go deeper, and she keens my name, and I'm lost. I cum so hard my gut cramps, and then her pussy spasms, the flutters along my spent dick sending jolts of life back into it like I'm sixteen again.

A satisfied smile curls the corners of her lip, and for a

second it seems like she's gonna collapse on my chest, but then it's like she remembers something.

"Gotta get this right away. Don't want a repeat of last time," she mumbles and holds the condom at the base as she hops off.

Then she ducks into the bathroom, and I hear the sink running. I'm punch drunk, a mile high, and it takes her words a long damn time to register.

By the time they do, she's out of the bathroom and across the room, digging in her bag. The sun's come up enough that the room's filled with a grey light.

I swing my legs over the side of the bed so I don't miss a second of her bent over naked.

"What do you mean? Don't want a repeat?"

She finds what she was lookin' for, her makeup bag, and she straightens. "Oh, yeah. You were zonked out the first time. The condom broke."

"The condom broke?" My chest constricts so hard my heart skips a beat. I shoot to my feet.

Story's oblivious, rummaging around in her bag. "Yeah, last night. And it got stuck. We're gonna need to change the sheets."

My gut sours. Why is she so calm? She must be on the pill.

"You're on the pill, right?"

She turns, finally catching on that I am freaking the fuck out. She slowly shakes her head. "No. It makes me nauseous and bloated. I wasn't fucking anyone so I went off."

And it's like a dam breaks. All the shit from last night with Ike that I've shoved as far down as I can comes crashing back, and my skin blanches cold and clammy.

"I didn't even mean to hit her. She walked into it by accident."

Ma huddled on her hands and knees in the middle of the

living room, baby Markie under her trying to crawl out while she desperately tries to shield him from the flying fists and boots, me on my knees hiding behind the arm of an ugly brown couch.

An older me bashing in Markie's face as he punches me in the kidneys, over and over, cracking my ribs. Knocking over the curio cabinet and dozens of figurines of happy boys and girls crashing in a mess on the floor.

This can't be fucking happening.

Furious energy bursts from my skin. I throw on pants and a shirt, jam my feet into my boots, not bothering to lace them.

"Where are you going?" Story's eyes widen.

"The pharmacy. To get a morning after pill." I yank on my cut.

Story pulls a top from her bag, tugs it over her head, and moves in front of the door.

"Calm down, Nickel. It's okay. I just got off my period, like, the day before yesterday. And it broke at the top. It got on the sheets more than anything."

"Get out of the way, Story."

My lungs are seizing and sights and sounds are flipping through my head like a shuffled deck of cards: Jeannie's fat lip and black eye, Ma's head snapping back from a punch she couldn't block cause her arms were wrapped around her rounded stomach, my fists pummeling flesh and breaking bones, the smell of men pissing themselves and the taste of blood in my mouth.

"Let's talk about this," Story begs. "Take a shower. We can go together after."

She's in my way. I have to get out of here.

"Move."

She reaches out to touch me, and I flinch back.

"Baby," she says. "We've got time. It's still the morning after. Let's talk. What's going on?"

She won't move, I'm trapped, and the ugly is free, crackling through my veins, turning everything red.

"Fuck, Story. Move!"

She shakes her head, and that's it, the ugly wins. I swing for the wall.

The air whistles. She cries out.

My knuckles crunch as my hand slams into the dry wall beside the door. The silence is so loud I can hear both our hearts slamming.

A hunk of blonde hair is caught between my fist and the cracked plaster.

Oh, God. She moved. As I swung, she moved away from the door. Right into the arc of my swing. I missed her face by a quarter of an inch. Less. Ice flash-freezes my guts, and my mouth goes dry.

Story backs off now, taking slow steps backwards toward the bed. Her eyes are blown so huge I can see myself in the shine of her pupils. Her hands are trembling. She's terrified.

I'm garbage. And I am *weak*. I know what I am—what made me—and I'm so fucking weak that I couldn't stay away and then I couldn't stop—

If I'd hit her, I could have killed her. Damaged her brain; made her like Hobs.

I search her face, her body. Is she hurt? Oh, God. She's frightened, but there's no bruise. No blood. I missed her, except for that hunk of hair. I missed her. The relief is as powerful as it is sickening.

She holds her palms up like she's trying to appease me. "Nickel. Talk to me." Her voice shakes.

My mind churns up a hundred images of Ma, hands in the air, begging, pleading, apologizing for shit she never did and promising things she could never do. My stomach lurches. I'm gonna puke.

I bolt out the door, the devil on my heels, and I don't stop until I've put a state between me and what I've done. What I've become.

What I've always fucking been.

15

STORY

I*m so sorry. don't be scared, i won't ever come near you again. i'm so fucking sry story.*

I get the text three hours after Nickel loses his mind, punches a wall, and then rides off alone in the middle of a lockdown.

And that's the last I heard from him cause he's a coward, and he's gonna get himself hurt, and how can he give up so easy like that? Like we ain't been inchin' toward each other for years and years?

nick answer the phone. talk to me.

nick im not scared. i don't understand what happened. you have to talk to me.

nick im scared now. what's going on?

nick why you leav me on read???

Now *I* want to punch a wall.

The brothers rushed up as soon as Nickel fled—Charge and Forty and Heavy—three huge men crowding around the door, worry in their eyes. I showed them the hole, but I didn't tell them why Nickel lost his shit. That's our business.

Not that there's an "us." You need two people for an "us," and all I have is myself and a ghost.

The brothers let me be after they made sure I was okay, and I appreciated that. Forty and Charge are definitely pissed enough to beat Nickel's ass, but Heavy looked how I feel. Disappointed. Bone-tired. Powerless.

They say if I want to leave, they'll take me to Sunny's. Apparently, Larry is more badass than I knew 'cause the brothers talk like "the Dentist" can handle any comers. I don't want to leave, but what else can I do? I've been left.

Last night was perfect, sweet in a way I always knew the world could be, but that I'd never seen for myself. Now's it's all a stupid hole in a stupid wall.

And what am I going to do? Sit on this bed and stare at it in between staring at my stupid phone? I need to face facts. He told me, and I should have believed him.

Not about him being some kind of abusive rage-aholic who can't be trusted with anything nice. That's a bunch of crap. He's a bouncer at a strip club, for fuck's sake. He beats down pervs who try to hurt women *for a living*.

But he told me loud and clear that deep down, he believes he's a hopeless case, and he's not gonna try for even one day to be better than the piece of shit he thinks he is. My stomach aches, and my heart's a black hole, but what else can I do but believe him?

Even *if* eventually he comes back, *if* he agrees to sit down and talk about whatever crawled up his ass, and *if* we get back to the perfect place we were last night through some kind of miracle, it would only be a matter of time.

I showed him my tits, and he tossed me out. I kissed him, and he punched a truck. I went after him, and he threw another woman in my face. I gave him everything I have, and he ran off and left me.

I know I'm a bit of a stalker. I know I'm not a winner. I'm in a dead-end job, about to fail out of community college 'cause I can't read a book about teeth, and I can only do what I love one night a week in a dank rec center basement 'cause how I make rent makes me unsuitable for normal, decent folk.

I'm not much, not in the world's opinion, but I have *always* played the hand I've been dealt. No giving up. No giving in.

Electric shut off? Move the food from the fridge to the freezer, and it can last two or three days longer.

Can't read? Sit next to the kid with the adult aide and listen when she reads it aloud to him.

Everyone in school hate you? Join dance and pretend only those hours of your life count.

How do you handle a man who won't even try? You pack up your bags and go home. You can't win a game when the other person won't play. And sometime over the past few weeks since I kissed Nickel in the parking lot, this turned into something way more than the world's most frustrating game of tag. It became real.

I was wrong the night I saw him kiss Danielle. I thought I knew then what heartbreak was. What *over* felt like. I didn't have a clue.

As I sling my duffle bag over my shoulder, my entire body feels creaky and awkward, like I'm beginning a dance without warming up. My body is still sore from taking his cock, and he's in the wind. How sad is that?

I don't bother looking around the room one last time. There's nothing here.

When I get downstairs, it's pretty low key. It's not even noon, yet. Shrieks filter in from the yard out back where the kids are running loose, and all sorts of good smells are wafting from the kitchen. A glance out the huge bay windows shows brothers working on their bikes. It's a real family vibe with the whole club here at once.

The sad drags at me even harder. I been around this club my whole life, but it's never really been mine. And isn't that a sign?

I drop my duffle by the bar and wander back to the offices to find Forty. He's the one who offered me a ride to Ma's. I pass Heavy's office, but I don't peek in. He's a real busy man, especially now, I imagine. Besides, we've only had maybe two conversations in my life, and I can't say I understood most of what he said either time. He favors real big words.

So it comes as a surprise when I hear his deep, bass voice ring out. "Story?"

I'm already down the hall, but you don't ignore Heavy Ruth. I go back and linger in the doorway, unsure. Heavy runs all the businesses from this corner room overlooking the garage and the fire pit. He has a big wooden desk and swivel chair like a boss, but the rest of the room screams biker.

There's a greasy engine sitting on a drop cloth on a side table, and beer bottles littered on a coffee table and the windowsill. There's a poster of a lady from the 70s with feathered hair, propping herself up on a Super Glide, her feet on the handlebars, flashing a very bushy beaver. It's eye-catching, that's for sure.

"Sit." Heavy gestures to a chair. He's on his phone, and he barks orders for a few more minutes while I wait, picking at my nails. This room, this man, makes me feel like I'm in the principal's office, if the principal is a hairy giant who dwarfs the furniture and clacks a message out on his computer with massive meat paws.

I'm surprised when he gets up and comes around the desk, taking an overstuffed chair across from me. He's got to be deep in this Rebel Raiders thing. Don't know why he's made time for me.

"Story," he sighs, and I'm listening, but he doesn't follow it up with anything.

Eventually, I feel like I have to fill the silence. "I was looking for Forty. To take me to Ma— Sunny's place."

He nods, still skewering me with his brown eyes, as dark as Nickel's but so different. Where Nickel's eyes are windows, Heavy's reflect the light, a mirror catching in the sun. Disorienting and freaky as hell.

"You sure you can't hang out?" he asks.

"I'm sure."

"The women are makin' lunch."

"I'm not hungry." Shit. Did that sound disrespectful? "Thanks, though."

Heavy sighs, low and long, and he shifts forward. If I didn't know this man, I'd be shitting myself. He's not the type you say no to without a second thought. Or a third and fourth. But what would I be hanging around for?

"If Forty's busy, I can ask one of the prospects," I suggest. Heavy probably wants all his soldiers at the clubhouse.

"No, no." He shakes his great, shaggy head. "Forty and Wall will take you in the Hummer with the prospects riding front and rear."

"That's—" That's too much. "I can drive myself if you'll give me a loaner."

Heavy snorts. "I like my face as pretty as it is. Ain't sending Nickel's old lady anywhere without a full escort."

Old lady? Once upon a time my heart would have leapt from my chest. Now the words cut. "I'm not his...it's...we're not a thing."

Heavy ignores me. "You know how I met your old man?"

I want to say again that Nickel's not mine, but I'm scared of gainsaying Heavy again. I've never known him as anything but patient and kind to women, but I'd be really stupid not to know there's a reason that men show their necks when he speaks. Even the biggest, baddest guys tread carefully around him.

So instead of saying anything, I shake my head.

"You know Harper?"

Everyone knows Harper. She's Heavy's older sister. The lawyer. The one who ran out Claudette, Dizzy's first old lady, and my Ma's friend Heather Tillage. She's a dragon, and I steer clear.

I nod, but again, I don't say anything. I have nothing nice to say.

"She was a good three years ahead of us in school, and she developed early, so by sixth grade, she was getting attention. She loved it. She had to pick me up and walk me home after school, and she just swished her ass the whole way."

I can totally picture this. Harper has more body confidence than any woman I know, and I work with strippers and dancers.

"There was this dirty scrapper named John Kobald who walked the same direction as us until the intersection at Ford Avenue, but he wasn't in my class, and I didn't know him."

I lean forward. I can't help it. I been collecting pieces of Nickel forever it feels like. It's not a habit I'm gonna break in an hour or a day.

"This one day, three middle schoolers—older kids, maybe eighth grade—decide to start hassling Harper, asking her to show them her tits. I'm in second grade. I was big, I always been big, but I knew I was about to get my ass handed to me. I buck, but before I can deliver, John Kobald is all over those guys, wreaking destruction upon them, rending them piece by piece, a mighty sword of vengeance. All sixty-fucking-pounds of him."

A smile peeks through Heavy's dense beard, and his eyes sparkle with the memory. He tells this story like he's telling me something I don't know, but this is Nickel Kobald. I studied him in school. I float to and from him on an invisible chain screwed into my heart. A flash of temper ruffles my feathers, and even though Nickel isn't mine, I can't help but speak. Heavy's not the only one with stories.

"Remember Anders? Skinny guy, face tattoo?" I settle in. I got stories, too.

Heavy thinks a spell, and then nods, his eyes puzzled. "Ran that chicken shit out years ago."

"He hooked up with Bullet's ex. We were at a party up at Lake Patonquin. One of Bullet's kids mouthed off to him. Something like 'You can't tell me what to do. You're not my dad.' Anders backhanded the kid, and then Nickel broke the dude's jaw."

Heavy's brow furrows. "I remember," he says.

"Remember the time Wall fucked Angel in the kitchen, and she reached back not thinking, and touched the stove? How she screamed like she was dyin' and stumbled out into the main room cradling her hand, Wall on her heels, hollering at her about common sense?"

Heavy shifts in his seat. I think he sees where I'm going now. "Nickel headbutted him," he recalls. "Broke his own nose and Wall's. Almost broke mine before we could get him to understand it was an accident."

"Remember when he threw the Fat Boy at Creech?"

"What had he said again?"

"Creech was mad at Jo-Beth and called her a worthless

whore in front of the whole clubhouse because she wouldn't give him head for free."

Heavy's eyes have changed. They're less kindly now, more assessing.

I raise my chin. "You don't have to tell me stories about Nickel Kobald."

"No. I don't guess I do." He appraises me for another minute before he speaks again. "Any old lady would tell you to get gone. Charge. Forty. Wall. They'd tell you the same."

I know. When Nickel's eyes went full black and his fist flew, my instinct was to run. Anyone faced with such sudden violence would be crazy not to be afraid.

"He scared the shit out of me," I admit.

"He's scared the shit out of me, too, once or twice. That shit he carries—it ain't a joke."

"What happened to him?" I know the basics, and at the end of the day, it won't change anything, but a part of me will always crave any crumb of Nickel Kobald I can get.

"Not my story to tell."

No. I guess not. I sigh, my body registering the fullness of the loss again. My joints hurt, and it's not from the falls yesterday or the sex. It's a deeper ache.

"To tell the truth, I don't even know all of it." Heavy sighs. "I saw the bruises and the broken bones and then the scars, and I guess I thought it'd break him eventually. Turn him mean. But of all the brothers I've rode with all these years, he's the only one who hasn't changed. He's still a violent motherfucker, and he's still got the purest heart I've ever seen."

I know Heavy doesn't mean them to hurt, but the words stab at my heart. Nickel won't change. All the good he has in him doesn't matter. In the end, the world didn't need to break him. It convinced him he was hopelessly broken from the start.

Heavy must see the uselessness of it all, too, 'cause after a long silence he heaves another sigh and calls a prospect to pull a car around.

I excuse myself, get my stuff and drag my duffle out front, sitting on it as I wait for the brothers to muster. I shift so my weight is on my ass cheek, my pussy still throbbing and raw from last night. I cling to each twinge, try to memorize the ache, knowing it's the last hurt Nickel Kobald will ever give me.

Except the flattened heart.

That I think I'll get to keep a long, long time.

16

NICKEL

S *hes gone to her mothers*
get ur ass bk now.
pussy.

Heavy ain't wrong. One thing about when you turn tail and run? You can't pretend you're anything else but a coward.

I get back past midnight. I spent a day tryin' to outride my demons, and I'm back where I started. The irony ain't lost on me.

At the clubhouse, there's a rager goin' down. There's already puke on the floor and tits out. I'm guessin' Heavy's moved the old ladies with kids out to his cabin. With all hands on deck, it's no place for young'uns. You can't coop bikers up in one place for days on end and not expect anarchy, even with a law-abiding club like ours is...more or less.

For sure, the gossips have been at it. All eyes are on me while I try to slip up to my bunk. Fay-Lee takes a few steps after me, pissed as hell, but Dizzy holds her back by that collar she wears. The brothers know me well enough to leave me be.

My ass is saddle sore, my guts are knotted to hell, but when I open the door and see the table and the candle and empty crates...a fresh pain slams me so hard I sag at the knees. No, not pain. Or not only pain. Loneliness, too. Regret. Shame.

What the fuck did I think I was doing? A card table? A folding chair? I'm such a fucking loser I can hardly stand to wear my own skin.

I shrug out of my cut, lay it on the bed. Story made it before she left, even folded the sheets down like a hotel. Just to torture myself, I sit down and lay back. I can smell her, faint but there. Her lotion. The sweet tang of her pussy. The dried-up wet spot.

Halfway to Ohio, the ugly receded enough to let some rational thought back in. This morning, it wasn't no emergency. Story ain't a liar. She said she just got off the rag; that's the truth. Of course, shit can always happen, but that's nothing to the shit I cause all on my own.

I finally roll to face the wall by the door. The hole gapes, crumbling at the edges.If I had been a second slower. If I had swung a fraction to the right. I could have killed her.

I didn't even mean to hit her. She walked into it by accident.

My face burns. There's nothing I can do to make this right. Eventually, I force myself up, walk into the bathroom, and scrounge in the linen closet for a tub of joint compound and a putty knife. I find it behind the Comet and an economy pack of soap. There's dust on the top. It's been awhile.

Too long, it seems. When I get the tub open, it's all dried up.

And suddenly it's too much. I always got nervous energy running in my veins, but in this moment, it all seeps from me, like even the ugly can't stand being part of me no more.

I sink to a folding chair and hang my head, the weight of the world bearing down my shoulders.

I had *everything*. Right in this empty shithole. I had *it all*.

I don't know how long I been sittin' there when the door creaks open. Charge eases his head in, sportin' the same pretty-boy grin I tried to punch off his pretty-boy face for months straight as a kid until Heavy made us be friends, and then later, brothers.

When he sees I ain't gonna come after him, he comes in, carrying his own tub of joint compound, a putty knife, sand paper, and fiber glass tape.

"She safe?" I got no right to ask, considering. I know this, but still...

"Yeah. She's at Sunny's. We left Roosevelt and Wash there. Roosevelt's off his feet, but he can shoot a gun if it comes to it."

My fists clench.

"No reason to think it will," Charge quickly adds. "They didn't take Story at the bar. They don't know she's got value."

Value? She's the only perfect creature this world has ever made. Stubborn and patient and sweet and wide-eyed in every sense of the word. Suddenly my breath is crowded out by the sheer terror of all the things that could close those eyes. The Rebel Raiders. The wrong asshole walking through the door at The White Van.

Me.

"Oh, you got the drive-home look bad." Charge chuckles, slapping the joint compound into my hand. "You're doomed, my brother."

I force myself to my feet and make for the wall. I'm an old pro at patches.

"What does that even mean?" I peel off the tub lid.

Charge sets down on the edge of the bed. I want to yell at

him to get off; I don't want Story's scent replaced by man-sweat and beer, but he'd just double down and make snow angels in the sheets. Asshole.

"This one night, I'm drivin' Kayla and Jimmy home. She's leanin' her head on the window, the boy's asleep in the back, and all of a sudden it hit me like a truck."

"What did?"

"That I'm only a man, and some higher power thought it'd be a good idea to give me two angels. And there was no way in the world I wasn't gonna fuck it up somehow."

"Did you?"

"Not as bad as you have, brother, but yes." I shoot him a dirty look. He's got his phone out, returning a text. "Sorry. Kayla needs me to pick up cupcake liners and Canola oil."

This was the dude I did my first stint in county with? Hard to believe.

"She deserves better," I say when he finally looks up. He knows I'm talkin' about Story.

"Definitely."

"Man, I—" The shame is so bitter it makes my mouth water. "I could have really hurt her."

"Yeah, you could have."

He watches me sand the dry wall.

"You know you're shit at pep talks?" I jerk my head to the door. "Appreciate it and all, but I don't need a heart-to-heart where you tell me what I already know."

"No, you don't." Charge stands and brushes invisible dust off his thighs. "You need help."

The words burn.

"Fuck you." I turn my back.

"I don't mean it that way." Charge stops in the doorway, and he claps a hand on my shoulder, his face dead serious.

"I love you, brother. You need help. You ever ready for it, I'm here. Heavy's here. Forty. We got you."

He leaves, and I didn't think it was possible, but the coil in my guts is tighter; even the air is chafing my skin.

You need help.

What the fuck does that even mean? Some of Deb's little white pills? Anger management? A shrink?

What? Am I going to tell some pencil neck in glasses how my dad and my brothers beat my Ma until she crawled so far up a needle she never came out? And then we turned our full attention on each other?

What's that gonna do? Turn back time? Undo what I am? There ain't no help for the past. Like Heavy would say, it's immutable.

I shove it out of my head and finish up the patch job as careful as I can with the ugly pulsing in my brain.

There's a war on, and Story's out there in a fuckin' subdivision, and I'm doin' home repairs 'cause I can't control my-damn-self long enough to see her safe. And she's with who? A dentist and two prospects, one beat to hell?

Ike saw her at the bar. What if he noticed her at The White Van, too? What if he puts two-and-two together, figures out she's someone to Steel Bones?

She's the club's best dancer. All he'd have to do is describe her big eyes and blonde hair to any man in Petty's Mill, and he'd get a name. Wouldn't be hard after that to get an address. It's a small town.

And I'm doin' what? Sanding a patch? I drop the taping knife and grab my cut.

On my way out the front door, Heavy sees me and rolls his eyes. "Ain't got any guys to bail you out if you find trouble," he calls out.

"Don't need none."

It's calmed down in the main room. Heavy must've sent brothers out to hunt Rebel Raiders. Get them at last call, all drunk and disoriented. It's a smart move. Heavy's a smart motherfucker.

I feel a twinge that I'm not riding with my brothers, but it passes quickly. I need to make sure Story's okay.

My anchor is too far away, and like always, my body leads my mind, dragging me across town to the mansions on the hill. Gracy's Corner. From down on the flats where I grew up, you can see the lights at night, a cluster of harsh white blocking out a patch of stars.

I call Harper from the Humvee when I'm a mile out. She's got herself a big ol' house on the hill. Used to share it with Charge before she put him out. Don't know why she wants to live next door to civilians. She comes from the same place we do, but I guess she's always had champagne tastes.

"The fuck, Nick?" Harper croaks when she finally picks up on the tenth ring.

"I need you to call the gate and tell them to let me in."

"Not up for a nightcap tonight, Nickel."

"What the fuck's a nightcap?"

"It's a—fuck. Doesn't matter. What do you want?"

"I got business with the Dentist."

There's a pause and some rustling. A man grumbles, and Harper hushes him. Probably Des Wade. She's takin' a walk on the white-collar criminal side these days. Don't know how Heavy stands it; the dude's a douche.

Harper sniffs, and I hear a door shut and then the splatter of her peeing. "Bullshit. You got business with Sunny's kid. What's her name? Savvy? Cinnamon?"

"Story."

"Yeah." There's a flush. "The one with the weird googly eyes."

"Ain't as weird as your long-ass monkey toes."

"My toes are below average length, Nick. Just like your dick."

"You gonna call the gate?" I know she will. She's Steel Bones, even if she's a raging bitch.

"Of course, little brother. I got you." I think the call's over, but right before I click off, she says, "Not my business, but—" She makes me wait. I don't have to say nothin'. Harper don't know how to hold her peace. Never has. "That girl's too soft for you. She's a kitten, and I don't think you have any idea how tight your grip gets."

It's mostly the truth. And it riles the ugly. Damn but my friends are shit at pick-me-ups.

"I hear you, Harper. Call the gate."

She does 'cause I get no problems from the rent-a-cop in his shed when I pull up. This is what's standing between Story and the Rebel Raiders? Some retiree with a walkie-talkie? Fuck.

I been to the Dentist's a few times, oddly enough for dental work. Heavy made me get bridges when I started moonlighting as security for Steel Bones construction. Appearances don't mean shit when you bounty hunt or crack skulls, but Heavy wants the legit businesses to look a certain way. Badass, but not broke.

The Dentist lives in the middle of a quiet street with houses down only one side. His place overlooks a field of tall grass with a drainage pond. From a security standpoint, I'm liking the houses all close together, but I don't care for the empty lots across the street. The Dentist's place is your standard McMansion. Big front windows low to the ground.

Lots of shrubs impeding lines of sight. I can see at least three ways to scale to the second floor.

Unbelievable. The business the Dentist does, you'd think he'd have a better eye for home security. I pull to the side of the road across from the house, turn off the engine, and push the seat back. I ain't bein' subtle, but that's the point. Anyone comes, I want them coming at me first.

I crack a window so I can hear if a car approaches, and I stare at the house. It's almost three in the morning, and it's mostly dark except for a room downstairs. I lean back on the headrest, and because it's been a long forty-eight hours and my body's sore and I'm runnin' on fumes at this point, I can't stop my mind from wandering where it shouldn't go.

Usually, I can't control the horror show my mind pukes up every so often, but I can hold back the other memories. The good ones. I ration them out cause I'm afraid I'll use them up, rub the shine off of them with too much wear.

But tonight...I tell myself no, but I can't stop.

Story under a street lamp, up on her toes, her soft lips brushing my chin. The slight pressure of her hands on my chest. The tender hope in her eyes, like she's reaching out for me in the dark, like she needs me. Like I am needed.

Story dancing on stage, tripping and stumbling and then throwing her arms in the air like a gymnast sticking a landing while the whole place erupts in hoots and claps. The shiny smile that bursts on her face as her eyes seek me out. 'Cause she's happy, and I'm the one she takes that to first. Every time.

The day she showed me her tits. Earlier, before that mess in the bathroom, when she's sunbathing on a shed roof, laughing and carrying on with Fay-Lee. All the while, she tracks me, and even though there's fuck-all to do in the yard that day except hang out with whoever's flippin' burgers, I stand there like a

*dumbass because her eyes on me have always made me feel some-
thin' nothing else ever has. Warm. Wanted. Invincible.*

Click-click-click. I stiffen, my hand going to my piece.
Then the floodlights in the Dentist's front lawn are trig-
gered, and I see it's Sunny comin' down the drive, wavin' at
me. She's smokin' a cigarette, wearin' a short leopard print
bathrobe and high heels.

Ain't gonna lie. Story's ma is hot as shit. It's dumb luck I
didn't fuck her back in the day.

I roll the window all the way down, and she leans over,
braced on her elbows, all her bangles clanking.

"Sugar." She smiles. "You thinkin' about movin' into the
neighborhood?"

Actually, I could buy a big ass house on the hill if I
wanted. Our dividends are yielding exponential growth.
That's what Heavy says. Don't know what the fuck it means,
but I do know I don't have to buy Beast no more, though I
still do. Best beer comes from Milwaukee. Fact.

I must be tired as shit if this is what's goin' on in my
brain. I drag in a deep breath of night air and get a lungful
of Sunny's smoke.

"Sorry, Sunny." I hack a little. "Didn't mean to freak you
out." And come to think of it: why wasn't she freaked out?
"The Dentist tell you what's goin' down?"

Sunny flicks her ash. "You can call him Larry. And yeah.
Rebel Raiders. I got some nineteen-year-old called Wash
eatin' me out of house and home and gawkin' at my ass on
the back of it, don't I?"

"And you still waltz out here like the neighborhood
watch?"

"Knew it was you, Nickel. It's a club vehicle." She eyes
the back seat. "I know it well."

I raise an eyebrow.

"Ask Forty." She giggles. "And Wall."

"Bullshit. Ain't no way those two both fit in the back seat."

"It was more like I was in the back seat, and they was standing at each door, but—" Sunny tosses her big, blonde hair and winks. "That's neither here nor there. You come to see my girl?"

A vise tightens on my heart. I want to. So fuckin' much.

I shake my head. "Just keepin' an eye out. I'll be gone by morning."

"You should come in. I'll set you up on the couch."

"Nah. But thank you." The clock reads three forty-five. Morning will be here soon. "What you doin' up so late anyway?"

Sunny glances behind her. "Worrying. About my girl. Can't stand to see her hurtin'."

A lump swells in my throat. "I'm sorry, Sunny."

She sighs. "Can't stand to see her hurtin', but don't want her hurt neither. She said you put your fist through the wall?"

I nod.

"Over a busted condom?"

I stare out the windshield, wrap my hands around the steering wheel. This burn is different than the ugly. Worse. I nod again.

"You got a problem, Nickel."

I fucking *know*. My knuckles blanch white.

"I ain't judging. I did, too. Still do if you go by what they say in basement meetings. I hurt that little girl in there plenty. Left her to fend for herself. Didn't pull myself together soon enough to show her a better path."

I hear what she's sayin'. Story don't need another person in her life controlled by demons. I get that. Not sure how many more people are gonna tell me that today, but...

"I did get help, though. Look at me now. Queen of the Suburbs." She gestures to the houses, bracelets jingling. Then she reaches in and lays a hand over mine. "Would be nice if someone in Story's life was strong enough to get it together for her. Would be nice for her to know she's worth it."

Sunny coaxes my head up with a finger under my chin. "You got to talk to someone. I've got a guy. Well—" She flushes. "Larry and I have a guy, but he does singles, too. He's real good. Has an office in one of those business complexes out on Arrowhead Road." She fishes in her bra for a little white card and then slides it onto the dashboard.

I squint to make out the writing in the faint lamplight. "A shrink?"

"Hey. It's was good enough for that mob guy. Alto? Soprano?"

"Are you serious?"

"Are you?" There's a long pause, and then Sunny pats my arm. "They say you have to do it for yourself, but I don't know about that. I didn't. Besides, if I get a long shot grand-baby out of this whole debacle, don't you want to be the best daddy you can be?"

"Fuck, Sunny," I groan. She's crackin' up. "Funny, is it?"

"Hey, if you don't laugh, you'll cry, right?"

I try to smile, but I get distracted by the dark upstairs windows. "How is she?"

Sunny rolls her eyes. "Oh, she's great. She finally nails the man of her dreams, and he loses his shit over something stupid, disappears, and leaves her on read." Sunny slaps the back of my head. I had it comin'. "That's for makin' my baby do the walk of shame all alone."

Oh, fuck. Yeah. I know how the brothers can be. If any of them said shit, I'll...what? What am I gonna do if not beat the shit out of them?

"You know what she's most upset about?" Sunny says, distracting me from that train of thought.

I shake my head.

"That you didn't even try."

And that—that's a blade in the gut.

"You know, I've watched you all these years." Sunny smiles, so like Story except wonky on the left side, maybe from age, maybe from hard living. "At first 'cause I was worried you were gonna perv on my kid, but then...I liked how you looked at her."

"How was that?"

"Same way I did the first time I held her. Like she's a miracle."

There's a moment when we're frozen, starin' at each other, both knowing the other part but not saying it. Story's a miracle all right, one neither of us deserves.

A bullfrog honks and the moment breaks. Sunny slaps the car door and straightens. "Call the number on the card, Nickel. I think I get a discount for referrals. Mention my name anyhow. Just in case."

I sit in front of the house another hour, flippin' that card in my fingers, watching the sun slowly rise in the distance over the Luckahannock. The air is sharp and cool with dew.

There's maybe fifty feet between Story and me. I could cross it in seconds. All that's holding me back?

It's me.

I am the only thing holding me back.

17

STORY

I hate automaticity, contractility, elasticity, excitability, and extensibility. I hate the endomysium and the perimysium and the epimysium and fascia.

I hate Medical Terminology for Health Occupations, and I hate that Ma and Larry have forked over three hundred bucks for a zero credit class that I have to pass but doesn't teach me anything about teeth. At least it hasn't yet. I'm stuck in the muscular system—on page sixty-four of *Introduction to Medical Terminology*—and I can't get out.

I start reading, and then my mind goes swirling off, and I have to stand and move. A half hour later, I'm doing plies using the dresser in Larry's spare room as a barre.

I'm stuck in this room and this house and this stupid, stupid head that won't give up thinkin' about Nickel Kobald. It's been almost two weeks. I should be bouncing back. Dealing with it.

Wash is takin' me to class and to work, and I've been going through the motions, but everything feels wrong. This bed is lumpy, my steps are off beat at work, and damn and hell but I don't give a flying fuck about dental hygiene.

At least Nickel hasn't been at The White Van. Neither has Forty or Cue. Grinder's been filling in as management, and they've been leaning on Austin and the prospects to do security. They've also been bringing in old timers like Boots and Gus and Eighty to sit in the booths and round out the numbers. I'm really worried someone's gonna have a coronary. I don't think Bev's let Eighty relax and watch some titties in decades.

I'm even more irritable tonight 'cause I don't have to work. I got no reason not to study except I hate it, and I have less than zero interest in it, and it's killing my will to live. I want to quit so bad, but I don't think I can give up on both Nickel and community college at the same time.

If I'm not dealing with shit and sticking it out, what am I doing?

I'm stuck, that's what I am. Alone, going nowhere, with hardly nothin' to my name. Walking around for twenty-one years and still in the same damn spot. When you have your eyes on something out of reach, you don't notice you're happily sinking in place. That's another shitty lesson I've learned recently.

I slam the textbook shut, and I get on my feet. This room is too small to dance, but I shove the bed flush against a wall and make myself a dance floor. I do some rises, using the dresser, and then I do a few more plies before I begin tendus. My blood starts flowing, and I settle some.

I should turn my music on, but there's no song I love that doesn't remind me of Nickel. That's why it's so quiet when I'm mid-ronde jambe that I can hear my phone chirp.

It's probably Fay-Lee. She's been trying to get me to stay with her at Dizzy's for a change of scene. I don't think I can handle hanging with another happy couple, though. Ma and Larry are bad enough.

I finish through the grande battement before I check my messages, and good thing I'm warmed up because when I see the text, my breath leaves me with a whoosh and I wobble on my feet, collapsing cross-legged on the floor. It's Nickel.

He's sent a picture of a hallway. At the end is a wood door with a narrow window running next to it, floor to ceiling. There's a sign on the door I can't quite make out. It looks like an office building, but not a really nice one. The kind with low ceilings and slow elevators. There's a message under the picture.

i am trying.

I can't help it. My skin heats, my pulse races, and I have no idea what this means. After two weeks, this is what I get? A picture of a door? What's he trying to say?

Maybe it's a glitch, a message being delivered after service is finally restored, but no. The time stamp is five minutes ago. Besides, Ma told me she spoke to him the night it all fell apart. He's sent different brothers to watch the house since, but still. His phone has been in range at least once during the past two weeks.

Should I text back?

I shouldn't. I'm done with him. Done with his mind fucks. But what is that a picture of?

Maybe it was an accident. His fingers slipped while he was typing.

Who cares? I'm not curious. I'm pissed. No, not pissed. Over it. I'm totally and completely over it. Well, *getting* over it. Any day now, I'm going to be so over it that it's not even funny.

I zoom in on the sign. It's blurrier now. It could say anything.

What am I doing?

I thump the phone back on the desk as if it bit me. It's too little, too late. Hell, I don't even know what it *is*.

I go back to my dresser and start my plies again. My phone chirps again, and I dig my fingers into the wood. I push myself through my barre exercises, and then I make myself go downstairs and pour myself a bowl of cereal. I force down three bites before I give up and race back upstairs, two steps at a time. My stupid, stupid heart. Leading me at the end of a chain.

i just need you to know im trying
i dont know what to do to fix this but id do anything for you
so ill try this
you dont have to txt bk. i just need you to know

My palms sweat. It's like I'm a yo-yo drooping on a slack string and somebody just snapped me up and spun me around.

An angry voice in my brain screams, *But he gave up!*

The busted, careworn part of me adds, *And didn't you give up, too?*

I had to. I *have* to. I can't be a yo-yo.

I should block him. Why didn't I block him already? Because I'm soft-hearted and weak. That's why it's so easy for this man to squish my heart into pulp over and over again.

I turn my phone off, shove it in a drawer, and then I flop on the bed, staring at the ceiling. It's too early to sleep, and the bed's lumpy. I roll onto my side.

What was that picture? Did he get an office job or something?

A door slams downstairs, and Ma's laugh rings out. She was in the basement, checking on Roosevelt. He's recuperating down there, playing video games with Wash. They're the world's lamest security detail—literally in Roosevelt's case. They were on high alert for like a few hours before they got bored and helped themselves to Larry's scotch.

Ma's rummaging in the kitchen now, and it occurs to me she might know about the picture. All she said was Nickel came by to make sure I was safe, but I know her. He's a man; she's Sunny Jenkins. She definitely chatted him up.

I should leave it. Crack the textbook open again. Get on with the brand new me.

Fuck that.

I snatch the phone on my way out the door and fairly sail downstairs. Ma's chopping veggies for a salad, and she has a roast in the oven.

"Do you know what this is?" I pull up the pic and shove it under her nose.

"Damn, Story. No hello?"

"Hello. Do you know where this is?"

Ma sighs and grabs her cheaters from a basket on the counter. "Let me see."

She makes a big show of putting on the glasses and squinting at the picture. She's loving this.

"Ma!"

And then she makes a soft "huh" noise and passes the phone back to me. "Well, I never thought he'd actually do it."

"Do what?"

Ma takes up her knife again. "That's Dr. Rosenthal's office."

"Who?"

"That's mine and Larry's couple's counselor. That's his office."

"What?"

"What do you mean—*what*? You think making it work

between a Jewish dentist and a Methodist sex addict is easy?"

"Ma, you've never gone to church."

"I'm a *cultural* Methodist."

"What does that even mean?" I shake my head, sigh, and try again. "Why is Nickel sending me a picture of your couple's counselor's office?"

Ma slides chopped carrots into a bowl. "I gave him Dr. Rosenthal's card. The other night when he came over. Dr. Rosenthal doesn't just do couples. He does all sorts."

"So, what? Nickel's going to counseling?" I don't think I've ever been more surprised by anything in my entire life.

"Looks like it. Photo's kind of blurry. Could be the office next door. Maybe he's getting insurance."

Sunny snickers and grabs me under the chin. "It's nice to see you out of that room." She lays a wet kiss on my forehead. "Don't get your hopes up, though. Leopards don't change their spots."

No, I guess they don't. And it's not like Nickel's standing outside my window with a boom box. He sent me a few texts after ghosting on me. I fight the urge to text back, and I leave him on read.

A few nights later, he sends me a pic of a brick wall and concrete steps going down to some basement.

still tryin baby. miss you so fucking much.

After tossing in bed for three hours, I get Larry to lock my phone in his office safe so I can leave it alone and get some sleep.

Next Tuesday, I get another picture of Dr. Rosenthal's office.

still at it, baby
wash says you look good

i want to kick his ass for sayin it but im learning to reframe
my emotions

i want to kick my own ass cause i aint there with you

im happy you are good tho

Friday, I get another picture of a brick wall.

still tryin

aint givin up anytime soon but got to tell you this sucks

A good five minutes later my phone chirps.

aint complainin tho

I don't text back because if I do, I'll say come over. I'll say how could you leave me, and I love you, and I need you like air, and you're suffocating me every second you're not around. I'd beg, and I'm still too bruised to take another hit. That's kind of a lie, though. I'm a bop bag for him; I'd pop right back up.

But I am terrified. This feels so fragile. Like we're playing Jenga, and if I make one false move, whatever he's doing will fall apart, and he'll be lost, not just to me, but all the way and forever.

So I keep him on read, and I go to work and classes. It's quiet. Painfully quiet. The Rebel Raiders have gone to ground again, and things eventually go back to normal. Wash stays with us and keeps driving me places, but Roosevelt goes back to the clubhouse. Cue comes back to The White Van, but still no Forty. And no Nickel.

I make noises about going back to my apartment—it's killing me to pay rent for an empty place—but Larry says that Heavy still has old ladies and kids on lockdown, so I have to stay. I don't really mind. I miss my stuff, but I'm so lonely. It'd be worse at my place.

Dancing at the club feels lonely. Sleeping alone feels lonely. At least at Ma's, I have people to be lonely around.

It's pathetic, but the highlight of my days are pictures of

doors and walls. My phone chirps, and my heart soars higher than a bird for the second or two before I remember that nothing real has changed. Nickel's still not here. This— whatever it is—could be over in an instant. The tower could all fall down, and there's nothing I can do about it.

I should tell him to leave me alone. Tell him I'm done and block him. But here I am, holding on to the thinnest thread, and why?

Because I'm a fool.

No.

Because I'm his anchor. He's floating out there, a hundred miles away, and even if he never finds his way back, I'm not letting him go.

I'm not stupid; I'm hanging tough. It's the only way I know how to be.

18

NICKEL

My first visit to Dr. Rosenthal, we talked bikes for about forty-five minutes. I told him I almost punched my girl in the face, he asked me if I'd done it before, I gave him the short version of my rap sheet and Steel Bones came up, and then he started tellin' me about his bikes—he collects vintage Triumphs—and that was it until the chime on his phone went off.

The next time, we talked roads—he likes heading south along the Luckahannock and the twists and turns up by the bluffs same as I do—and then he made me tell him what it feels like when I *get aggressive.*

I told him about the ugly, and he said there ain't no such thing. It's feelings that got names, and I need to man up and stop actin' like my *aggression* is something I can't possibly control 'cause that's a load of horseshit. He used other words, but that was the gist.

Now this guy is sixty-five if he's a day and no more than a buck twenty soaking wet. He wears thick glasses, crosses his legs like a chick, and his office has got all these pictures of birds on the walls. Dude has brass balls.

The next couple times we talked about my *triggers*, and he taught me *de-escalating strategies*. He talked a shit ton, but it all boiled down to take a deep breath and walk away.

Last time he made me break down all the times I could remember losing my shit, so that was fun. Not sure what it was all about, but I left feelin' like warmed-over shit. I'm a little leery today. It ain't as if I'm proud of what I am. I don't get off on tellin' war stories like Creech or Bucky or some of the prospects who want to look hard.

I sit on the couch across from the doc like usual. Don't care what you're supposed to do, I ain't gonna lay down in front of no dude.

"John!" Dr. Rosenthal crosses his legs and smiles. He always sounds really stoked to see me. "How have the past few days been?"

"Good. Good." Hell, actually. Story's ignorin' my texts, which is fine, but I'm in knots worryin' about her at Sunny's with the Rebel Raiders out there, God knows where, plannin' God knows what.

"Any incidents of aggression since we last met?"

"Nope." I don't think you can count joggin' a Rebel Raider hang-around's memory with a few blows to the head. I wasn't mad or out of control; it was business. Besides, Dizzy went way harder than me on the guy.

"And have you been practicing the lazy-eight breathing I showed you?"

"Sure." No, I have not. I *have* been breathing, though, so I'm countin' it.

"Attend any meetings?"

"Yeah. Sunday night." Now *that* I have been doing. Doc's got me going to the group of random addicts that meet at the Church of Christ. Sex, pills, booze, food...sex with food and booze while on pills. They take all comers. It actually helps. I guess no matter what shit you're tryin' to stop doin', there's common ground amongst fuck-ups.

"So." Dr. Rosenthal clicks his pen. He keeps a legal pad in his lap, but I don't ever see him write on it. "This week I want to talk about something different. I want you to tell me about the first time you remember seeing violence inflicted on another person."

I don't know where to start.

"Like on TV or real life?"

"Real life."

Shit. I don't know. It'd be easier to remember a time growin' up when someone wasn't gettin' beat on. I try to think, but my mind's a blank.

Doc shifts in his seat. "Let's try this. Can you tell me about a time when you saw violence inflicted on another person in high school?"

"Sure." That was any given Friday or Saturday night. "One of my brothers got some of us prospects together to rough up this dude who'd been creepin' on one of his girls." I chuckle, remembering. "We find the guy, and he wouldn't let us get a shot in."

"Okay, okay. How about middle school?"

Heavy, Charge, Forty, and I were always scrappin' back then. It's hard to pick, but I got to grin, sortin' through the memories.

"All right. One time my brother Forty—you got to understand, this guy is a neat freak—anyway, this new kid's messin' with him, tryin' to make a name for himself, and he throws Forty's backpack in a mud puddle. Forty's like, torn, 'cause he can't stand mud on his shit, but he also wants to tear the guy a new asshole. So basically, he's like scrubbin' the backpack with one hand and slammin' the guy's face in the dirt with the other, gettin' madder and madder when the dirt won't come out."

Doc's kind of grinnin', too. This sucks a lot less than last time.

"How about elementary school?"

I tell him about a time when Harper's mouth wrote a check her ass couldn't cash, and Heavy ended up havin' to dive into a six-on-one girl fight. He lost. I stayed out of it.

"And what about before you went to school?"

The temperature in the room dips about ten degrees.

Like the house on Barrow Road, this ain't a place I go voluntarily. My brain spits this shit up, of course, all the time, but I don't ever think about it on purpose. A few memories of neighbors brawling or my brothers workin' something out float through my mind, but it's like when someone says, "Don't think about elephants." And then you can't think about nothin' but elephants.

It's like I've been in denial this whole conversation, and deep down, I knew what Doc was asking for from the beginning. I could tell about something else. I could change the subject. Refuse to talk. Walk out. I got choices, but I told Story I was gonna try.

Besides, no matter how people act like it is, rememberin' something ain't as bad as living it. You ever doubt that, ask someone which they'd rather do.

"My Ma used to make dinner."

Doc nods for me to go on.

"She was raised by her grandmother so she could cook real good. Homemade pies. Meatloaf. Pot roast. She stayed home with Ike and Keith and me, and come about three o'clock, she'd set us in front of the TV and go make dinner."

"That sounds like a good memory."

My gut sours. It's not.

"So one day, she goes into the kitchen to make a pot roast, and we're watchin' Sesame Street or something. And my dad had left his pack of cigarettes on the coffee table. Well, Ike, who's always been a shit, sits there and unwraps them, one by one, makin' a stack out of the tobacco. And Keith, who's also a shit, fake sneezes and blows it all over the carpet."

It's so weird. I must have been four or five, but I can remember exactly where I was sitting—on the floor right up close to the TV.

"Anyway, my dad comes home from work—pissy as usual, probably more so since he forgot his smokes—and he sees what Ike and Keith have done. I can remember—"

His face turning bright red and the veins in his neck popping. Me turning off the TV like that would calm him down. Wondering if I should run.

"He took one look and shouts 'Farrah!' Ma comes out of the kitchen holding the pan with the roast in two pot holders. She was smilin'. She always tried to make dinner so it was ready the minute Dad came home. She was probably thinkin' she nailed it."

I shut up for a minute 'cause my chest is burning. Doc has gotten real still.

"He tried to grab the pan out of her hands, but it was too hot, so he dropped it. That made him even madder. So he picked it up with one of those mitts and slammed it across her face."

I stop. Most people can't handle shit like this. Doc's still with me, though. He's got his pen in his hand, and he seems okay.

"What happened next?"

"Well, pot roast all over the living room carpet for one."

She'd looked so fucking surprised. I don't know why.

Even though I can't remember anything specifically before the pot roast incident, Dad had always been mean and quick with his fists.

"The lip of the pan cut her forehead, and she was bleeding down her face. It left a burn, too. She bent over to, like, scoop the roast up."

Blood in her eye, burned, and she was worried about the fucking roast. It didn't make sense to me until now. This minute. She was probably thinking if dinner was ruined too, she'd get it even worse.

"Fuck."

"What was that?" Doc asks. "What was that thought you just had?"

I lift a shoulder. "I just realized why she did it. Why she went after the roast."

"Why do you think she did that?"

"To stop him from going any further."

"Did he stop?"

"Never." A twisted grin contorts my lips, but I can't force it away. "That night, he made her pick all the tobacco off the carpet by hand while he sat in his recliner and kicked her whenever she got close enough."

"Where were you when this was happening?"

"At the kitchen table with my brothers. Eating the pot roast."

"How did you feel?"

"Like I was gonna puke. Ike and Keith were bitchin' the whole time about how it had been on the floor, but I ate it all. Their leftovers, too."

"Why did you do that?"

It feels like I'm explainin' the obvious. "'Cause if he saw any left, she'd get it even worse."

"That must have been horrible for you."

"Worse for her." After that, she didn't make real dinners no more. She'd microwave ravioli or make a box of macaroni and cheese. She got some pain pills for the burn on her face. That was the beginning of the end.

"You must have felt powerless."

"I was." I couldn't take my dad in a fair fight until I was twelve or thirteen. He was a big guy, but hard living slowed him down.

Doc sighs and leans further back in the chair, re-crossing his legs. "John, I want to point something out to you that you might not be fully aware of."

I shrug. *Lay it on me.* This walk down memory lane cannot possibly suck more.

"There's this thing in psychology. A defense mechanism called compensation. Have you ever heard of it?"

"Like when a dude with a small dick gets himself some boneshakers?"

Doc shakes his head, half-smiling. "You're thinking over-compensation. Compensation is when you try to make up for something by putting your energy in something else."

"Okay."

"You've told me a lot about your episodes of aggression. I've noticed something."

I wait. He blinks like I'm supposed to guess.

"The customer who elbowed the woman you work with." He raises one finger.

"The skip you were telling me about who was running from an assault charge against his grandmother." He raises a second finger.

"How you met Story. The men who were videotaping her without her permission." He raises a third finger and then twists his wrist like I need to count them. "Do you see a trend?"

Well, yeah. When he lists it out like that, of course I do.

"I am going to suggest that your aggression isn't generalized. You're not an angry person like some of the patients I treat. You're compensating for what happened when you were young and powerless."

My chest tightens. What he says...it feels too good to be true. Like a scam to convince me I ain't broken when so clearly I am.

He goes on. "Most of your aggression seems to be in defense of others, particularly women, who you perceive as being abused or in danger."

He's giving me way more credit for control than I deserve. When the ug—when I'm feeling aggressive, I ain't thinking much at all about what I'm doin'. My fist in the wall is a good example.

"What about with Story, then? She wasn't in danger from nothin' but me."

Doc's nodding. "Yes. As you tell it, you believed she was in a sort of danger—caused by you—and you became violent. We can argue about the realities of the situation, but emotionally, what you did was logical considering the coping mechanism you've developed in response to what was, in my professional opinion, a devastatingly traumatic childhood."

"Logical? It was completely fucked up."

Doc keeps nodding. "Yes, it was. But it wasn't out of nowhere. It wasn't from a place of rage or hatefulness."

"I was out of control."

Doc sighs and sets his pen on his blank pad of paper. "John, I want to ask you something. That night when your father assaulted your mother, was he in control?"

It went on for hours. After she picked up the loose tobacco, he made her scrub the gravy stains from the carpet.

The whole time, he was watching *Married with Children*, laughing his ass off.

"Yeah. Yeah, he was."

"You're not your father, Nickel."

I know this, but hearing it? A weight lifts.

The chime goes off, and as I write the man a check, I think maybe I understand all the birds on his walls, their wings spread, gliding through the sky. This must be how they feel.

By WEDNESDAY NIGHT, I'm back down to earth.

My heart's pounding. My mouth's dry. I thought the ride to Shady Gap would settle me, but every mile I got more and more riled up. By the time I turn into the gravel parking lot, I'm so amped my right eye is twitchin'.

Shady Gap Recreational Center

Story's here. It's the night she teaches her adult ed dance class.

I don't feel ready. Dr. Rosenthal says I can make my own decisions, but the people at the support group say I need time, and I guess that's true, but when Gail from group told me about this meditation class, and come to find out it's only offered this night, well...I ain't strong enough to turn down fate.

I could avoid her, duck quick into the class, but my body won't let me. The craving is so deep, at night it takes over my mind, and I wake up in a sweat, my cock hard as rock, groaning Story's name.

If Heavy wasn't keeping me on the road, chasing down leads with Wall, I wouldn't be able to take it. I'd be camped out in front of the Dentist's house like a stalker, and Story'd probably call Heavy to drag me off, and that'd be it. I think she's finally gotten smart. She leaves me on read, and I don't blame her.

She hasn't blocked me, though. Not yet. This shit ain't totally hopeless.

I slide off my cut, stow it in a saddlebag, and jog inside. The building is a converted junior high, and it still smells like a school.

The class I'm going to is in room 102, but I trip down the stairs, slappin' the ceiling on the way like I used to do at Petty's Mill Middle when I started to get some height on me. Reminds me of old times. School was a nice break back in the day. I could nap at a desk knowing no one was gonna wake me up with a fist or a boot, and there was breakfast and lunch.

Story's always bitchin' around the club about having to teach a dance class in a basement, so I know I'll find her down here. I don't know what I'm gonna say or if I'm gonna puss out and bounce without talkin' to her, but I guess I'll figure it out in the moment. What could go wrong?

Everything. That's what.

I follow the sound of Lou Bega. That song with all the girl names.

"Okay, ladies! Kick ball change! And slide. Slide." That's my girl. That's her sweet, bossy voice.

I sidle into the doorway of a dimly lit, open space that smells like sweat and really old, sour milk. There are no windows, but someone has hung a few mirrors up on a far wall. The joint is *packed*. Easily thirty ladies are lined up in Spandex and sweats, not one under fifty.

It takes a second to find her, but there she is, in the front, wearing a headpiece with a mic. Her hair's in a high pony-thingy, and fuck me, but she looks like a 1980s exercise instructor, the kind I jacked off to when I first discovered how my dick worked. She's got on sparkly silver leggings, a hot pink leotard crawlin' up her butt, and a thin, white belt.

It's messed up, but I ain't the only one whose eyes are glued on that ass. You'd have to be dead not to watch that shit jiggle.

"Now grapevine left!" She points left, and everything's bouncing, her hair, her ass.

My cock goes rock hard, tenting my pants. That's one reason why I don't normally wear athletic pants. I duck out real quick to tuck my dick under my waistband. Don't need to give the grandmas a show.

"Sashay! And kick! Two, three. Kick!"

The ladies are huffing and puffing, but they're all grinning or laughing or trying to whip their hair like Story and pop their asses like she does. A few of them in the front row look serious as hell.

I ain't never seen her like this. She's a boss.

"Margie!" she sings out. "Can you take it lower?"

"Not since the Clinton administration!" a short, grey-haired lady hollers back from the last row.

"Well, how about a shimmy, then?" Story shakes her titties, and all the ladies hoot and cackle and follow her lead, big ol' titties flapping everywhere. I didn't think I had it in me, but my face burns. I think I'm blushing.

"Now that I've still got in me!"

"You don't use it, you lose it," Story says, pointing for her class to go the other way.

"I never had it, so I don't miss it," a plump lady in grey sweats calls out, and again, the ladies howl while they dance in unison.

I guess that's when they start noticing me 'cause a ripple of giggles and whispers goes through the room until Story blinks, turns her head, and spots me in the doorway. She don't lose a step, but that loud, fun girl goes on mute, and her walls come up. Now she looks like she does at The White Van. She's still smiling, but she's on guard.

I don't ever want to be the reason she goes on mute. I want to bail, but I done enough time with Doc to know that's an avoidance response. Also, bein' a pussy. I didn't need to sit on no couches to figure that part out.

Story finishes up the song, and then she thanks the class. I duck inside and lean against a wall to let the ladies out. My heart steps up, expecting that any second, she'll be close enough to touch. I ain't caught a whiff of the coconut shit she uses in her hair in too damn long. The need hits me hard.

I didn't count on the ladies.

I guess Story's kind of a celebrity at the Shady Gap Rec Center 'cause she gets mobbed. Five or six ladies, all gabbing up a storm, teasing and joking. And sliding me hard-ass looks out the corner of their eyes. Okay, I see what this is. I guess I don't look totally harmless in my gym gear.

I catch Story's gaze and raise an eyebrow. It's up to her. She gives me the cold shoulder, I'll get lost.

Her chin wobbles, and she crosses her arms. She says something to the ladies, and after they cackle a good while longer, they file out, givin' me the hairy eyeball the whole time.

Story don't come no closer. She stands by an old boombox that she has propped on a chair next to a shoebox full of CDs. She looks so small in the big, empty room, and I can't wait no more. I stalk to her, my hands ready to warm away the goosebumps down her bare arms, every instinct yelling at me to grab her up and kiss away the hurt in her eyes, but a step from her, my body hits a wall.

It's my brain, tellin' me be careful. That what's wrong can't be fixed with hands. Panic rises in my chest, but I breathe through it. I got some words now. I fuckin' pray they'll be enough.

"What are you doin' here, Nickel?" she asks.

"Meditation class." I check my phone. "Starts in twenty minutes."

Her brow furrows. "Doug's class?"

"I guess. If he does meditation."

"He does Tai Chi."

"Yeah, that's what it's called."

"Where'd you hear about—? Why are you—?"

She ain't got a frame of reference for this. To be honest, neither do I. I can't see myself sitting still for an hour straight, but Gail from meeting says it ain't sitting so much as moving slow. These days, if Gail or Dr. Rosenthal says to do it, I do. I'm givin' it over to a higher power, and in my case, that's a really skinny old dude who collects bird paintings and a bossy, middle-aged mail lady.

Eventually, Story gives up on whatever she was tryin' to ask, and says, "I guess you'd better get along then. Don't want to be late."

"I got a few minutes."

She chews on her bottom lip, and I can hardly stand the stress comin' off her in waves. The ugly stirs, and—no. Not the ugly; I can't call it that no more. It ain't outside of me. It's *my* fear or *my* anger or *my* feeling of being out of control. Like Doc says, name it so I can deal with it.

And what I'm feeling now? It's guilt. Plain and simple. I mishandled this beautiful woman, and I'm terrified I can't make it right, and I want to more than anything in the whole damn world. I search for the words, and everything is not enough, so I just say what's in my heart.

"You're so amazing up there. You're an amazing teacher."

And maybe God loves me a little after all 'cause Story's mouth melts into a soft, happy smile. She forces it away right quick, but it was there. My girl's still there.

"Yeah?" She tries so hard not to look like she cares.

"Those ladies were havin' a blast. I thought someone was gonna break a hip."

The smile tries to sneak back, and I'd fuckin' stand on my head if I could get it to stay.

"Don't say that." She bends and raps her knuckles on the wood chair holding the boombox. "I've got a perfect safety record."

"I don't know, babe. You teach them moves like that, somebody's old man is gonna get hurt."

And there's that smile again. Pure sunshine. It fades too damn fast.

"You really here for Tai Chi?"

I nod. "And you. I know I'm supposed to stay away, but..."

Sad crinkles show up at the corner of her eyes. She don't like that.

"Why are you supposed to stay away from me?"

I can't even remember with her so close, smellin' so good —never mind the sweat. Her face is wide open, brimming with that beautiful thing she gives me for free, and that I been runnin' from like a sinner from God. Why am I supposed to stay away? Goddamn, I can't even remember.

"Somethin' about having to keep a plant alive for year," I mumble. "I dunno. I been hanging out with addicts, and they got a lotta rules."

"Like twelve of them, I heard."

My lip kicks up. "Somethin' like that."

"So. What did you want from me?" She squeezes her arms tighter. She must be getting cold now that she ain't moving. This basement is dank, and there's a chill seeping in through the walls. I shrug off my hoodie, and I hold my breath while I drape it over her shoulders. She don't thank me, but she don't shake it off neither.

I push my luck and leave my hands fisting the edges, gently tugging, coaxing her closer still. She don't give an inch, but she stays right where she is, almost in my arms again.

"I guess I wanted to explain. About that night."

I've run these words through my head so many times. I don't want to make excuses, but I got to make sure she don't think it had anything to do with her.

"Well, go on."

"I'd been by my old house on Barrow Road."

"Out on the flats?"

"Yeah. I had to work some things out." With my asshole brother, but I don't want to even say his name here, with her. "Anyway, the house needs to be condemned. It's boarded up. There's a fuckin' RV up on blocks in the front lawn. The place—it just—brought up some shit."

That's an understatement. "The shrink thinks I need to confront the past, but I think that place just needs to be burned down."

I don't know what to say next. I won't let any of the ugly Ike was spewing near her, but I need her to understand. I'm looking for the words, but I guess I take too long.

"It's okay," she sighs. "You don't have to tell me. It's not my business." She steps back, tryin' to shake me loose of the hoodie, but I ain't goin' nowhere.

"It *is* your business. Story, you own me. Every piece. Ever since you booted that asshole in the nuts at that field party."

"You remember that?"

"Yeah. You were badass."

"I was reckless."

I shake my head, smilin' at the memory. "You had my back, all hundred pounds of you."

"It was two against one."

"Yeah, baby girl, but I was the one."

And then she answers, her voice so low, I almost think I'm dreaming it. "You are," she says.

I tighten my grasp, pulling her closer until she's pressed against my chest. "Say it again."

"You are. The one." She lowers her thick black lashes, looking down all shy, and then she raises those big blue eyes to me, and I'm home. "There's not a piece of you that I don't love."

I mean to say it back, but my mouth is on her, desperate for her taste, for her sweet moans. I nip, she parts her lips, and I slide in, searching out that slippery tongue, and it's like she comes unwound, throwing her arms around my neck, pushing her hips forward till my dick is throbbing hard against her belly. I get a good ten seconds of bliss before shouts and banging fill the room.

There's a bunch of kids in white uniforms barreling through the door, followed by a guy dragging a crate of foam helmets.

"Kid's karate." Story's cheeks go pink, and she bends over to unplug her boombox. "They start at seven. That means your Tai Chi is starting now, too."

Fuck Tai Chi.

My cock is hard enough to drive nails, and my girl loves me. I want to throw her over my shoulder, feel her thighs clamp around me on my bike while I—Take her back to an empty room at the clubhouse?

This is not how I told myself I was gonna do this. Story deserves more, and she's gonna get it.

"Gimme this back." I slip my hoodie off her shoulders and hold it in front of my junk, waiting patiently while she grabs her duffle bag and stows the boombox. Then I walk her out to her car.

We stop next to her beat-up Kia—another thing that's gonna change—and then we stare at each other like two idiots.

"You goin' straight home?" I ask.

"Yeah." She reaches up and strokes my jaw with her soft fingers. "You're gonna be late." She's eating me up with her eyes, and it's all I can do not to duck my head and start from where we stopped.

"I heard Tai Chi goes slow. I'm fast. I'll catch up."

I force myself to step back, open her door, and throw her duffle on the passenger seat. "You still staying with Sunny?"

"Nah. Moved back to my place a few nights back." That does not reassure me. Also, where's her fuckin' escort? I scan the parking lot. No bikes.

"If you're looking for the prospect, he'll be here any second." While she's speaking, I hear the roar of Boom's engine. He's cuttin' it rather close. We're gonna have words back at the clubhouse.

Story grabs my chin and forces my eyes back to hers. "What were you sayin'?"

Yeah, right. My plan. "I'll pick you up there tomorrow then. At eight."

She cocks her head like I'm crazy. I stop and try again. Do it right this time.

"I mean if you want to go out. Go to Broyce's. Get some steaks."

"Like a date?" Her lips curve, and her nose scrunches.

"Like a date."

She makes me wait, but her eyes are dancin' in the lamplight. "Okay. I'll go on a date with you, Nickel Kobald. Since you asked."

I can't help but steal another kiss, and then I slap her car door and dash back inside before she can change her mind. A few minutes later, I'm listening to some old dude tell me how the white crane spreads its wings. I know it's backwards, but I don't think I was as happy balls deep in Story's sweet pussy as I am now, Story's sweet words echoing in my ears, no trace of fear or disgust.

Now that I'm getting out of my own way, there ain't nothin' that can come between that girl and me. The road is clear. That nagging feelin' that everything is doomed to go to shit ain't nothin' but bad habit.

Or prior experience, an ugly voice whispers in my head.

And wouldn't you know, it's too damn quiet in room 102 to drown the voice out.

19

STORY

Before I got home last night, Nickel texted me a picture of him lunging with his arm raised.

parts horses mane. srsly thats what its called this shit aint for me

I don't know what I love more: the picture or that he must have asked someone to take it. I saved it as the background on my phone.

An hour later, I got another message.

wear a dress tomorrow. no panties.

And then, while I was changing to go to bed, my phone chirped again.

nvrmd. were takin my bike and itll be too cold.

I sent him a pic of my red thong, asking if he's sure, and then we went back and forth until I fell asleep at three in the morning with my sticky hand still shoved down my pajama bottoms. I wake up with my phone stuck to my cheek and a dick pic in my messages.

I feel bad for nodding off, and I want to call him, hear his grumpy, deep voice and tell him I can't wait until eight o'clock. He needs to come over right now and take care of this ache between my legs that started when he took my mouth after dance class and hasn't dulled since.

But I also want to savor every minute of this day. I have a date tonight with Nickel Kobald. It's like I won the lotto, and I'm walking around with the ticket in my purse.

I go to class, and I don't even care that after the teacher says good afternoon, I'm totally lost. I write down whatever I can catch, and for once, I don't leave feeling like crap. Instead of beating myself up, I call Fay-Lee. She tells me to come over, and she'll do my nails and let me shop in her closet.

When I get to her place, Dizzy's kids are sprawled in the living room, playing video games.

"'Sup?" Parker grunts, giving me a head nod.

"'Sup?" Carson echoes.

These young dudes are way too cool for school.

"We're gonna be upstairs," Fay-Lee says. "Stay out of your dad's beers." She swats the back of Parker's head, and he ducks, keeping his eyes glued on the screen. "And don't bug us or I'll spit in your dinner, and I won't tell you until after you clean your plate."

"So what you're sayin' is that you're makin' dinner tonight?" Parker grins. He's growing his hair long like his daddy. He's got to be breaking hearts at the middle school.

"You should make mac and cheese," Carson pipes up. "With the crumbs on top"

"I ain't your real Mama. I don't have to do what you say," Fay-Lee sasses, tugging me toward the stairs.

"While you're under my roof you will!" both boys shout back in unison, laughing.

"Anyone ever tell you that you have a weird relationship with your stepkids?" I tease. In truth, I have mad respect for her. Before she came around, the boys ran wild.

"I like them; they like me. They stay out of my shit, and I stay out of theirs. It's all good."

She acts like she doesn't care, but she slips those boys cash for pop and chips all the time, and she goes to all their games. I know 'cause she tries to drag me, too, to keep her company.

Fay-Lee pulls me down the hall to the master suite and pushes me down on her big-ass bed. It's made, and the sheets smell fresh, else I'd find somewhere else to sit. Her and Dizzy get down to some freaky shit, I know for a fact.

She rummages on her vanity for a basket full of nail polish, and drops it in front of me while she goes to the en suite.

"Pick," she orders through the open door.

Fay-Lee has about two dozen polishes, like in a salon. She even has some Chanel. Dizzy spoils her rotten. She's got a huge walk-in closet filled with clothes and shoes, and Dizzy just put in a hot tub out back 'cause she asked. I'd be totally jealous if she wasn't my best friend and pretty much the sweetest person on the planet.

I sort through and pull out two glittery pinks while she comes back with cotton balls and her manicure kit.

"Want to watch the soaps?" Fay-Lee kicks off her shoes and sits across from me.

"There are still soaps on TV?"

"Shut your mouth. They're making a comeback."

"They are?"

Fay-Lee ignores me and turns on the television.

I hold up the two pinks, but she snatches them, tosses them back, and pulls out a pale lavender. "This'll match your eyes."

She grabs my hands, placing one on each of her thighs, and dabs some remover on a cotton ball. "You should be happy I like soaps. That's the only way I'm able to keep up with you and Nickel."

I stick out my tongue, and wriggle back so my back is supported by the stack of pillows at the head of the bed.

"So, you gonna tell me how this date happened? You finally text that boy back?"

I blush. "He came to the rec center."

"He bring a dozen roses?"

"He was there to take a Tai Chi class."

"Nickel Kobald?"

I nod.

"The guy who I have literally never seen without busted knuckles or a black eye?"

I nod again.

She's quiet a minute as she scoops up my right hand to examine my cuticles and then starts filing my nails.

"Don't surprise me," she says.

"No?" It surprised the shit out of me.

"You seen my new hot tub?"

"Yeah." I'm not thrown by the change of subject. Fay-Lee has attention deficit like a dog in a yard full of squirrels. "Can we hop in later?"

"You know it. We'll get Parker to bring us drinks. I'm teaching him how to make cosmopolitans."

"Fay-Lee! That's awful."

"I know. He can't get the proportions right 'cause he's got no taste for vodka."

"You're joking."

Fay-Lee shoots me her crooked smile, the faint scar in the corner of her mouth making it adorably wonky. "I am. Kid's more of a whiskey man, but he ain't too bad at mixing." She settles down and starts buffing my cuticles.

"Just sayin'," she goes on. "Steel Bones goes big. After

that shit went down at Twiggy's, I was feelin' it." Fay-Lee's face goes bright red. Bet it wasn't only wrestling that Rebel Raider that put a hitch in her giddy up. "I happened to mention a hot tub would be awesome, and not a week later, prospects were out there digging a foundation."

"Dizzy'd give you the moon. Everyone knows that."

"And remember that Charge bought Kayla a car, and he renovated Boots' place for her and her kid?"

I'm not catching her point.

"Shit. Scrap Allenbach did a dime bid for Crista Holt."

We're both silent, a moment of respect. It don't seem fair. Scrap gave a third of his life for her, and Crista won't give him the time of day. That's messed up business.

"Anyway," Fay-Lee continues. "You want a man who can control himself, I guess Nickel Kobald's gonna become a Zen master. Steel Bones don't do half measures. You watch. That dude's gonna be one of those guys who can catch a fly with his chopsticks."

"Wasn't that from a movie?"

"Yeah. We should watch that after your nails are done."

"I thought we were hot tubbing."

"Get this, we can watch TV from the hot tub." She waggles her eyebrows. "We just open the French doors. It's awesome."

"Won't Parker and Carson be pissed?"

"As their mother, it's my duty to limit their screen time." Fay-Lee presses her lips together all prim. "Besides, Parker's gettin' to be a real perv. If you're in a bikini, he won't wanna be lookin' anywhere else."

"Gross!" I nix the idea of hot-tub-movie-time right quick. "Let's just go through your closet and try on all the stuff that still has tags."

"I am totally spoiled, aren't I?" Fay-Lee sighs.

"You deserve it," I say, and I mean it. Fay-Lee got dealt a shit hand comin' up, and honestly, I don't think there's enough stuff in the world to make her spoiled, but Dizzy's sure tryin'.

"You do, too." Fay-Lee tucks my hair behind my ears and presses her forehead to mine. "You deserve someone who can love you right."

A twinge of pain twists in my chest, popping the happy bubbles that've been flipping around in my stomach all day. "And you don't think Nickel can do that."

It's not a question. It's what my ma and Larry think. And Charge and Forty and Wash and Roosevelt.

"You know what? Here's what I think."

Fay-Lee bends over almost in half and grabs a hand mirror off of the nightstand. She scoots next to me and holds it up, her arm straight so both our faces are framed. Her black hair makes my blonde even whiter, and her tan makes my skin glow like pearl. I think we're pretty, her and I, and I think our eyes are maybe too old for our faces.

She lays her head on my shoulder. "I think that all along the world's been telling both of us it knows better than we do. What's for us. What we can have, and what we can't. And we believe it 'cause we're so used to bad news being true. But I don't think anyone knows us better than we do. We got to play by our own rules 'cause the game we was born into ain't on a level field. You know?"

Fay-Lee presses a kiss to my temple. We stare a little longer into the mirror until Fay-Lee crosses her eyes and sticks out her tongue, and I blurt out, "I hate dentist school. I hate it. I hate it. I hate it."

"Of course you do," Fay-Lee grabs a hand and shakes a bottle of polish. "You're a dancer. You dance. That's what you do."

That's true. All of it.

A few hours later, before I head out, I snag a stretchy pair of black pants from Fay-Lee's closet. Most of her clothes won't fit my boobs and butt, even though we're the same size officially, but I love her style, so if I can squeeze my ass in, I'm gonna borrow it. These pants have tiny diamond studs down the side seam, really teensy and sparkly.

We don't hot tub or watch a movie 'cause it's late afternoon by the time my top coat dries, and I want time to take a long bath before my date.

It only occurs to me on the drive home that this is kinda gonna be the first date I ever had. Dean and I only ever hung out at the clubhouse or at my place, and Evan and I just chilled at home or at parties.

The bubbles in my tummy are fizzing again, and I'm so nervous I have to take a few deep breaths and do barre to get myself loose. I'm out of the bath and about to style my hair when my phone rings. I have two hours to do perfect S-curls. I almost don't answer 'cause who calls anymore but telemarketers?

I glance over though, and it's Forty. I didn't even know I had his number in my contacts. Instantly, a ball knots in my stomach. There's no reason Forty Nowicki should be calling me.

"Forty?" There's noise in the background, the deep murmur of men's voices.

"Hey, Story. You with Nickel?"

"No. We're supposed to go out later. Not till eight."

Forty relays something to whoever's in the background, and then he says, "You don't know where he's at, do you?"

Something's not right. The brothers are like a military outfit. They don't lose each other.

"No. He's not at the clubhouse?"

"No. He ain't at The White Van or the Autowerks or any of the sites. And he ain't pickin' up his phone. He was supposed to be at church an hour ago."

A cold sweat breaks out between my shoulder blades. No one misses a club meeting. Cue always gets someone to cover the guys when there's church.

"Did he work today?" I ask.

"Uh. No. He said he had personal business. But he was supposed to be done by now."

Forty's being cagey as fuck. If it were almost any other brother, I'd call him on it, but Forty's not the one. Dude has a stick so far up his ass he can't hardly nod yes.

"I'll call him, okay?" I say.

"You get ahold on him, tell him to call in."

"I will. If he shows up, have him text me?"

"Will do."

As soon as we disconnect, I'm dialing. Nickel doesn't pick up, and his voicemail is full. What the fuck. I text him, and he doesn't read it. A deep unease begins to weigh down on my chest. I text again.

I try to ignore my nerves and blow dry my hair, but every third second, I'm checking my phone. What if he ran into the Rebel Raiders? What if he was buying me flowers at the grocery store or getting his hair cut—for me, for our date— and the Rebel Raiders found him?

He would do that. He would do some stupid thing like that without backup when there's a war on 'cause for all his bite, he's a puppy inside. The worry is making everything really clear.

I turn off the dryer. I can't take it. I call The White Van, and Austin says he hasn't seen him all day. I call the Autowerks, and a prospect jokes about how everybody's lookin' for Nickel today.

I call Ma and ask for the number of the shrink he's been seeing, but she says Dr. Rosenthal doesn't see patients on Thursdays. I call Nickel, and again, I go to a full voicemail box. I shouldn't panic. He's a grown man, and he's totally badass. Besides, I don't know his schedule. Maybe he was working a bounty gig up in Pyle, and it went long.

But Forty would know if he had a gig. Still, he could be doing anything. Maybe he went for a ride and got stuck in traffic. And didn't call in to say he would be late for church?

Shit. This not panicking isn't working. I'm sweating out my hair so I'm gonna need to blow dry it again before I start with the curling iron, and my hands are shaking.

I give up, and I stalk to my closet and tug on a pair of pink velour sweats. I don't bother with underwear. I keep feeling like my phone's gonna ring any second, and the plan will be back on, and I'll feel stupid for worrying. But the minutes tick by, and my phone's quiet on the coffee table.

Where could he be?

He could be on a ride. He wouldn't take a call on the road. But that's not true. All the guys have Bluetooth and those things that clip in their helmets. He could be in a ditch on the side of the—

No. I start pacing. Fifteen minutes pass. A half hour. An hour.

The phone rings, and I leap half way across the room for it. My heart leaps, and then slams down. It's Forty.

"Forty?"

He cuts right to the point. "Any word?"

"No. Have you heard from him?"

He exhales, his concern poorly hidden. Oh, fuck.

"Not yet, but I'm sure he just let the time get away from him. No worries, sister, okay?"

"Okay."

"Keep me posted."

"I will."

I can hardly swallow past the lump in my throat. I can't just sit here, doing nothing. I pull on some socks and lace up my sneakers.

Where could he be that the guys haven't checked? He could be in one of those basement meetings, but it's been so long now...I can't imagine a meeting would last that long.

I pull up the pictures he sent on my phone, zooming in until I recognize the buildings in the periphery of one of the pics. Christ United, a few blocks over. I'll go, drive past. See if his ride is in the parking lot.

With a plan, the pressure on my chest eases up. I grab my purse and head out. I'm there in less than five minutes. There are no vehicles in the parking lot, and none on the street.

Oh, shit. Where do I look now? I can't go back to my apartment and wait.

I rack my brains, running through every conversation we've had, losing the thread over and over again to mounting panic. And then, almost the instant the street lamps flicker on, it comes to me. His old house. On Barrow Road.

I put the car in drive and head out of town. Petty's Mill is the kind of small town where no one who grew up here needs a GPS to get around. There's so little to do, most kids have explored every dirt road—and partied in every field— by the time they graduate high school.

Barrow Road runs down to the flats, a few miles from the Happy Trails Trailer Park. I'd say it's the wrong side of the tracks, but except for Gracy's Corner, the bluffs, and the new development downtown along the river, there's no right side of this town.

It takes about twenty minutes to get to the turn-off, and I slow down as I drive past tiny ranchers and some pre-fab homes. The sun has set, and there's no lights out here, but the moon's full enough to see by. Nickel had said something about the place being boarded up and a van or something in the front yard. There's plenty of vehicles up on blocks, but most places look lived in.

I'm getting very close to the river before I see a house that fits the bill. There are boards in the front window and a broke-down Winnebago. The place is dark, and there's no bike I can see, but there is a garage with its doors shut.

I pull into the driveway and turn off the engine. I get out, taking only my keys. I'm just gonna peek in the garage, see if I see anyone through the windows, and head out.

It's strangely noisy way out here in the sticks. The crickets chatter in waves, and the rush of the Luckahannock is a muted roar in the distance. Bullfrogs honk from a marshy thicket down behind the house.

Nickel wasn't exaggerating. The place is a shithole. The roof is saggy, and some of the siding is hanging loose. It's bigger than the trailer Ma and I lived in, but it's so much worse—there's no evidence at all that anyone house-proud ever lived here.

We had a flower bed with a short, plastic white fence and ceramic frogs with crystal balls, fairies with rainbow wings that circled in the wind, all sorts of stuff Ma picked up at the flea market when we were flush.

There's nothing but scraggly weeds in this lawn, and the stairs to the porch are wood planks set on cinder blocks. And there's a smell, even so many feet away. Dank mold and cat piss.

I hurry to the garage, peeking in a side door. It's locked, but the window panes have been busted out. There's a lot of junk, but no bike. My skin crawls at the idea of getting close to the house. I consider shouting for Nickel from close to my car, but I can't bring myself to do it. It'd be like hollering in a graveyard. He's most likely not here anyway.

I should check my phone. Maybe he called or texted back while I was poking around the garage. If I get back in my car, though, I'm going to chicken out. I stiffen my shoulders, take a deep breath, and jog up the rickety steps to the porch and peer in the crack between the boards and the front window frame. There's no light. No movement. I knock softly.

An image flashes across my mind. Nickel sitting in the dark, head in his hands, wrestling with whatever happened in this place. All alone. I knock again, louder.

"Nickel?" I call. "It's Story. Are you in there?"

A shadow stirs, rising from an easy chair on the periphery of what I can see, and I jump out of my skin.

"Nickel?"

The door creeps open, and I squint inside, my heart pounding, fear and relief both flooding my mind, keeping me glued in place.

"Baby?"

A thick arm emerges from the door, followed by a thick shoulder, a bald head, and a hideously grinning face. I turn to run, and I make it two steps before my body is jerked back, and there's an arm like a vise around my waist and another at my throat, choking off my air.

"Well, hot damn. Steel Bones delivers," Ike Kobald cackles, his breath reeking of cigars and booze. "Welcome home. *Story.*"

20

NICKEL

I thought cash could buy you anything in this world, including time, but fuck me if I ain't found the one thing where people are slow as shit to take your money.

You want to buy a property, it ain't like you go sign a paper, give them cash, and walk out with the keys. You got to wait for the seller—some old guy who brings his lawyer who's even older and still logy from the liquid lunch they comin' from. Then you wait for the title company guy to get out of his last meeting. You think you're good, but then you gotta wait for the real estate agents. They don't gotta be there, but when they heard the name Steel Bones, they crawled so far up in my business that I felt like they should be buyin' me dinner first.

And then—I guess 'cause I'm payin' cash so they think I'm a whale or somethin'—everybody's gotta try and small talk me instead of giving me the papers.

I know I'm late for church, but I left my phone in my saddlebag, and I wasn't gonna leave that room without the keys 'cause I sure as shit ain't sittin' through that ever again.

Next time, Harper can handle it. That's why she's on retainer with the club. I just didn't want her up in my business.

This purchase ain't exactly smart from a financial perspective. I'm probably over-paying by at least twenty percent. It's my money, though, and honestly, even gettin' ripped off, this ain't making a dent in what I have in savings.

When they hand over the keys in a little yellow envelope, I'm out of there. I ain't surprised I got a shit ton of voicemails and texts. I check voicemail first. I got so many the box is full. It's all Forty and Heavy asking me where my ass is. I delete some to free up space and check the texts.

The itchy frustration from the past few hours disappears when I see my girl's name. I hope it's a pic of her in what she's wearin' tonight. I used to think selfies were stupid, but now all I want is a pic of my girl makin' duck lips in front of a mirror. I miss that pretty face so hard.

I tap and as I read, my shoulders tense right back up. Story's worried. Apparently, Forty saw the need to freak her out. My fault for not telling the brothers exactly what I'm up to, but for Christ's sake, I ain't a sixteen-year-old schoolgirl out past curfew.

I'm gettin' ready to call Story when I see the last message. Ike. Really? He's got something now, an hour before I got a fuckin' date? I almost save it, but for some reason I tap, and my blood freezes in my veins.

There's a picture.

It's Story.

She's huddled on a brown, pheasant-print couch, her arms cradling her middle, huge eyes downcast. She has a busted lip. Adrenaline shoots down my veins, shorts my brain, and it's all I can do to read the message underneath.

get the blueprints for the des wade sites in pyle
you try anything or tell sbmc or anyone, she dies

you got 24 hrs

shes real pretty

you best hustle dudley do-right

A dam breaks and blood roars in my ears, my sight goes red, all the fucking reframing and deep breathing and tai-fuckin'-chi floods away, churned into shattered pieces by the rage animating my body like some fucked up puppet master.

I'm on my bike, racing down Main Street, my only thought to get to Story and end that motherfucker.

Terror looms, huge, crashing waves mixing with fury, seizing my chest in a steel grip and sending sweat pouring down my back.

When I close in on Barrow, I draw my piece from the holster in the small of my back and wedge it between my thighs, ready, my nerves taut, primed to take out, destroy, blow that fucker's skull open and—

My brain screeches, skids, and throws up an image. *A gaping hole. Strands of blonde hair caught in the jagged edges.*

The wind in my face forces cool evening air into my lungs. Trickles of ice cut through the howling in my brain. I ease off the accelerator. What the fuck am I doing?

A shard of sanity glints at the edge of my mind, but it's too new, too fragile. It's instantly swept away by another flood of fear, ten times as powerful as the ugly. I jam my foot on the gas a few hundred yards before I hit the curve at the turn off to Barrow. I'm coming in too hot, and I lean it hard. When I hear the scrape, I force myself to hold the lean, although it's more muscle memory than brain cells at this point. I'm gonna lay it down—hard—and Story's waitin' for me. She needs me, and I've fucked up again.

I can feel the weightlessness when the rear tire loses traction, and I'm flying through the air, luck the only reason my bike don't come down on top of me. Instead it slams into the guardrail. My ears are ringing, and there's a crushing weight on my chest, but it ain't from the crash, it's knowing I let Story down.

I stumble to my feet, limp the few feet to where my piece is laying in the dirt by the side of the road. By some miracle, nothing in my body is broken. Everything fuckin' hurts like hell, but it ain't nothin' if I can get to my girl. I go to pry my bike out of the gnarled guardrail, but the front is mangled and the back tire's blown. It ain't rideable.

I stagger off in the direction I was goin', nothing in my mind but a pounding and the knowledge that a man is about to die. Ike or me if I'm too late. I get maybe a few dozen feet when I hear an engine roar behind me. Forty's Softail Slim. I'd know it anywhere.

I keep plowin' on while he pulls up, walkin' his ride to keep pace with me. My mind ain't clear, but I ain't stoppin' for nothing.

"Where the fuck you been?" he asks.

Shit. What am I doin'? I shake my head as if that'll clear it. "You need to take me to the old place down the way. You got a gun?"

"What's goin' on here, Nickel? Fuck. Stop a minute." Forty pulls off to the shoulder, and I keep on limping forward. He has to jog to catch up, but it don't take long.

"Hey, man." He grabs my arm. I swing with the other, clock him across the face, follow up with a jab to his ribs. He don't even step back. He tackles me, pile drives me into the weeds at the side of the road.

I fight for a while, too crazy to do anything else, but Forty's got sixty or seventy pounds on me, and he's an ornery motherfucker.

"You done?"

"I gotta get Story, man." I kick and flail and Forty takes it all like a Goddamn punching bag. He's got my wrist pinned, the one holding the gun, so I can't get enough momentum to get out from under him.

"Stop, brother. You got to stop."

Slowly, slowly, the madness ebbs. I can't call it ugly. It ain't. It's fear, stark and terrible. It unarms me, and the pain of it is so raw, I'd give anything to lose my mind again. But I can't. I got to get to Story.

"You done now?" Forty exhales. "What the fuck happened?"

"Ike's got Story, man. He hurt her. He says he's gonna kill her."

"Fuck." Forty pushes up and sits next to me. We're both panting, covered in road dust. I still got my gun in my hand. Thank fuck I left the safety on.

"What's he want?"

"I don't know. Fuckin' blueprints."

Forty has his phone out, and he's dialing. I hear Heavy's charred voice bark, "You find him?"

"I got him," he answers, putting Heavy on speaker. "Ike has Story. He says he's gonna kill her. He wants blueprints."

"What blueprints?" Heavy is all business. This request ain't so strange to him.

Forty looks at me. I try to think. What was it? "Des Wade's. The properties in Pyle."

"What would he want with them?" Forty asks. "We did that work years ago."

"Don't worry. I know what this is about." On speaker, I can hear Heavy call the order to mount up. "Where you at?"

"Barrow Road," I say. "Almost to my old place. That's where he's got her. He sent a picture." My guts clench. She was hurt. Her face. Oh, God.

"How long ago did he contact you?" Heavy's breathin' hard like he's jogging while we talk.

I don't even know. I check my cell. Somehow it came out of the crash fine. "A half hour."

"You respond?"

"Fuck. No." I drove off half out of my mind and wrecked my bike a quarter mile away. Shame burns my face. "What should I say?"

"Text him now. Tell him you'll get the blueprints; it'll take a few hours. Tell him you need another pic of Story holding her phone so you can see the date and time."

The fear rears up again, threatens to pull me under. I have to fight to keep my brain straight. "Heavy. We got to get her." My words are as close to begging as I've ever come.

"We will, brother. We'll be there in less than thirty. Forward whatever he texts back, and watch your phone. In the meantime, we need to organize." There's a pause. "Forty? Lou Ellis lives up that way, don't he?"

"Last I heard."

"Let's meet there."

Forty's hard face turns to stone. Lou Ellis is a sore subject. He's an occasional hang around. His sister Nevaeh fucked around on Forty when he was overseas. She's been out of town for years, though.

"Yeah. Okay." Forty gets to his feet and offers me a hand. "We'll meet you at Lou's. Get Wall to bring my rifle."

"Nickel?" Heavy invests a lot in my name, shit we don't need words for.

"Brother—" I don't know what to say, but Heavy hears me anyway.

"Ike ain't gonna hurt her. She's his one way out of this shit. If he's this desperate, he's in deep to the Rebel Raiders, and they got to be pushing him. He wouldn't have done this otherwise. I'm thinking right now these blueprints must be his ticket out of a world of hurt. She's safe. We're gonna get her out of there."

I don't care if Heavy's feeding me lies; I hold those words so tight I can feel them in my hands. "All right, brother."

"You solid?"

I know what he's asking. "I'm solid."

Maybe for the first time in my life. I've lost the ground under my feet, but I will fucking fly if I have to. If my girl needs me to.

"You got me?" I ask Forty. He mounts his bike, shifting as far forward as he can so I can ride bitch.

He knows what I mean. "I got you."

I ain't gonna lose my shit again. I got my brothers, and if that's what I need to keep me even, then so be it. I ain't a proud man. I'm Story's man.

And I'm gonna get my woman back.

21

STORY

Blood is trickling down my chin, and it itches, but I'm so scared, I don't dare move my hand to wipe it away.

I have to pee, too, but I'm frozen in the corner of this couch, and besides, I can't imagine pulling down my pants anywhere near Ike Kobald.

He's merciless, his eyes as dead as a shark's. When he opened the door, he grabbed me, backhanded me so that I tasted metal, and then threw me on this couch. He said if I moved, he'd pop me again so hard my eyes would swell shut, and I wouldn't even see the bullet coming for me.

I would have pissed myself if I'd had to go then.

He's agitated. He'll pace the room for a while, peering out the cracks between the boards in the windows, muttering to himself, checking his phone constantly. Then he sits in that recliner, staring at me and then the phone, sipping a fifth of Wild Turkey and drumming his fingers on the gun resting on the end table next to him.

This was a bad choice.

I didn't tell anyone that I was coming here. I knew Ike

Kobald was bad news, that he's riding with the Rebel Raiders. And I didn't consider that he might be holed up in his old house? It's like I'm fifteen again, following Ryan Alston into the fields, knowing better but doing it all the same.

The knot in my stomach coils tighter and tighter as Ike stands, paces, sits, fiddles with his phone and stares and then checks his phone again. Finally, it chirps. He takes my phone from his back pocket, throws it at me, and makes me pull up the home screen. Then he says, "Hold it up and smile."

He takes a picture of me, and then he snaps. I throw the phone back.

This has to be good. Someone knows where I am, and they care that I'm still alive.

Ike's phone chirps again. He must like what it says because he sinks into the chair, and even though it isn't reclined, it's so old he's leaned back at ease, a guy watching TV after dinner rather than a psychopath holding a woman hostage.

I search the room again for anything I could use as a weapon. Ike took my keys, and he has my phone. My purse —with the expired mace and the nail file—is in the car. There's a coffee table, a brand-new TV, an empty curio cabinet, and not much else. There are two wood-framed pictures hanging on the wall beside me: a young woman in a white dress swayed against a scowling man in a powder blue, bell-bottomed suit and a baby picture.

"That's me. Cute, ain't I?"

I startle. Ike's lit a cigar. He's smirking at me, puffing away like he hasn't a care in the world. "By the time Keith came, Ma kind of fell behind on the home décor."

I swallow, but my throat is so dry, it sticks. I should say

something. They say if you get kidnapped, you're supposed to make yourself human. Talk about yourself, your family.

"My ma covered every inch of our place with stuff." My voice shakes, but I force myself to keep going. "She was big on tie-dye and dream catchers."

Ike raises his eyebrows. He seems surprised I'm calm enough to speak.

"Oh, yeah," he drawls. "Sunny Jenkins is your ma, right?"

I nod.

"Fucked her a few times back in the day. Ditzy bitch. She kept it tight for all that she passed it around."

He sneers, watching to see how I react. I keep my face straight. He isn't the first asshole to talk shit about my ma. Still, my chest hurts. I know what my ma was, but it's not like it doesn't hurt to have it thrown in my face. He does seem to have fond memories. That can't hurt.

"You should let me go."

He snorts and puffs his cigar. "'Cause of some pussy your ma served up fifteen years back?"

"'Cause this is fucked up. No one's goin' to give you money for me."

"Don't need money. Obviously." He waves his hand around the room. "I ain't hurtin' for cash."

He's joking. I'm about to piss myself, and he's being a smartass. "Why, then? Why are you doing this?"

I asked when he first threw me on the sofa, but he just told me to shut up.

"Not your business. Ain't my little brother taught you yet? Old ladies got no place in club business."

"We're not—" I don't know if it'll hurt or help to say that Nickel and I aren't really together. We're not, I guess, but the words feel like a lie.

"Not what?"

I have to try it. "We're not a thing. He's not going to give you anything for me. Ask anyone. We've never even been out together once." My eyes mist up, and I blink really fast.

Ike tuts. "Now, don't lie, little girl. I saw you two. In the parking lot at The White Van." He winks and casually scratches his junk. "Dudley Do-Right. Always tryin' to save the ladies."

It strikes me then, cuts through the terror, leaving a bitter sadness. This piece of shit and me? We both understand something about Nickel Kobald that no one else seems to really get. Nickel *is* the good guy. He's brave and strong and—hell. He's a bouncer and a bounty hunter. He spends all his time protecting women and catching criminals. All he's missing is the badge and a chin dimple.

And—because he is who he is—he's going to bust through that door to rescue me, and Ike is going to take the gun resting on the end table and unload it in Nickel's chest. I can see it clear as day.

How much time do I have?

It's been maybe ten minutes since Ike's stopped obsessively checking his phone. Whatever's happening must be unfolding right now, which means Nickel knows, which means my crazy man is racing to me, guns blazing, straight into disaster. I am not going to let this go down like that.

I draw in a deep breath, and flip the switch in my brain like I do whenever I'm in the spotlight and a hundred people—or a few dozen drunk dudes—are staring at me, and in my head I'm all nerves and stage fright, but I trust my body because it knows and can do things my mind can hardly imagine.

I've made my body strong and graceful, and all I need to do is trust it. Trust myself. There's a way out. Maybe I can't see it, but it's there. My mind is whirring so quick, I hardly realize Ike is rambling on.

"You know that fucking so-called *brother* of mine gave Jeannie the cash for that bitch lawyer she got? She wouldn't have never testified at my parole hearing if she didn't have that cunt's voice in her ear. Jeannie couldn't wait to throw that in my face, either. *Even your own blood knows you're a piece of shit.*"

Ike is amping up, mimicking his ex with a high-pitched voice. I've never seen such hate in a man before.

"Dudley Do-Right cost me a year inside," he spits. "Now his dead body's gonna earn me my patch with the Rebel Raiders, and probably a cool five thousand besides for the shit he's bringing." He laughs, the sound churning my stomach.

"He always did think he was better than the rest of us. His corpse got more cash value, that's for sure. I think I'm gonna make him watch you choke to death on my cock before I kill him. How big are those bug eyes gonna get then?" Ike smirks and winks.

I can't stop the whimper of fear that escapes my lips.

"Now don't get impatient, baby. He'll be here any minute."

22

NICKEL

I'm wearing a path in Lou Ellis' carpet, waiting, straining against my own skin to keep myself from flying off half-cocked again. My brothers are gathered around the dining room table. Heavy, Forty, and Pig Iron are bent over a diagram I sketched of the place, and Big George is getting reports from the perimeter they've set up around the house. Lou and Gus are standing at the exits, eyeing me. Heavy probably put them on guard to hold me back.

When we first showed up, Nevaeh Ellis wandered out of the bathroom wearin' nothing but a towel and Air Pods. Guess she's back in town. Forty went stiff as a board. Lou sent her into town with a twenty and instructions to stay gone 'til he calls. Forty's head seems back in the game now. It better stay there. This all hinges on him. My girl's life is resting on his aim.

Creech, Dizzy, Cue, and Scrap are in position at the house on Barrow. If Ike's at the old place, he's not leaving. If he ain't...I'm not letting myself think that way. There's no car but Story's, no lights except in the living room, so it's most likely Ike's there, and he's alone.

Wall is heading for us with Forty's AR-10 and scope. As soon as he gets here, we move out. The plan is as good as it can be with what we know. Charge had Kayla bring the designs for the improvements he's making to Boots' place. They look like blueprints to me; they'll look like blueprints to Ike.

I'm gonna approach the house alone, get Ike to open the door. Forty will be in the tree line. While I hand the plans over, I duck and wedge myself in the door, open it wide as I can. As soon as Forty fires, Dizzy leads a team in through the back. We got contingencies in case Ike insists on a drop, but if he uses Story as a shield...it's understood. If I need to take a bullet so Forty can get a shot, I take it. Story is the only priority.

Charge is hovering over me like usual, leanin' against a wall, waiting for me to lose my shit which I do every few minutes. When I start lookin' antsy, he claps me on the back, saying "It'll be soon."

Charge glances at his phone, and I spring to my feet from where I'd perched on the edge of the sofa. "You good, brother?"

I scrub my face with my hand. "I look good?"

"To be honest...yeah. Relatively. You ain't never been this, uh, coherent before when there was shit on the line."

"Ain't shit, man. That's my girl."

"Story Jenkins." Charge says it like he can hardly believe it. Can't be pissed at him. I can hardly believe it, too. "She even legal to buy beer?"

"You the one to talk about legal?"

"Kayla's got a kid. Story's...well, I'll put it this way. I always felt guilty staring at her titties at the club. Just sayin'."

"You tryin' to piss me off, brother?"

Charge raises his hands, palms out. "Only tryin' to pass the time."

"Well, you done missed your chance, brother, 'cause after this, my girl ain't dancing no more."

"No?"

"Not strippin' anyway. That's done."

"She gonna be a kept woman?"

"She gonna be whatever she wants to be. She ain't gonna want for nothing, and she ain't never gonna be in a position like this ever-a-fucking-gain."

Charge chuckles, but I can tell that he feels me. "You're far gone, aren't you, my brother?"

"No. Not gone." I shoot him a look he cannot mistake. "Home."

And we don't need to say nothin' else 'cause my brother gets me, bone deep. He still hangs close, there for me, but he loosens his stance. He knows he don't gotta babysit me. I ain't gonna let the ugly take me over.

There's nothin' that owns me but Story Jenkins.

23

STORY

The minutes are ticking down, and Ike's cigar is down to a stub. He's not even looking at me anymore. He's watching a video or something on his phone, giggling every so often. My brain skids between the need to act and all these random memories. I need to focus on escape, but my brain keeps flitting from memory to memory. Maybe what they say is true about how when you're about to die, your life flashes before your eyes.

I remember my first recital when Miss Amy met us as we came off stage and gave each of us a star-shaped lollipop. She said we'd been perfect and beautiful, and my heart was whirling from dancing and the applause. I was hooked. I fell in love, and I never gave up.

I guess I'm supposed to feel regret that all I did in my life was become a stripper like my mom, a stripper on my way to becoming a community college dropout. In this moment, I'm supposed to decide I want more for myself and get off this sofa to fight for a different future. That's what would happen in the movies, but that ain't what's happening in my head.

I'm remembering early on at The White Van, when I was at a loss for what song to request, and all I could think of was Bruce Springsteen's "Born To Run," which I'd heard in the car on the drive in. The guys in the audience came alive at the first chords, went crazy, singing at the top of their lungs, sloshing their beers in the air. I wasn't dancing for them anymore. We were in it together. I don't care that we were in a funky, dark strip club; there was joy in that place.

I remember the day I took over Swinging Seniors, all those old ladies shuffling in and sighing like *let's get it over with*. Fuckin' *exercise*. I thought *hell, no*. We're gonna *dance*, and we did until the laughter and hollerin' could have lifted the stained ceiling tiles of the old junior high cafeteria and floated straight to heaven.

Maybe the world thinks I should want more. Want different. But I don't.

I want joy, and I always have. I ain't never had much, but I've always had that. Dancin' on the pad next to our trailer growing up. Dancin' for Nickel Kobald. I don't ever want to give that up. I want to live with Nickel Kobald in my arms, and I want to dance.

Dance.

Shit. I got an idea.

I flash a glance at Ike. He's still watching his phone. He doesn't notice me start measuring with my eyes.

It's seven steps to the recliner, three steps to the coffee table. The coffee table is six feet long, maybe two feet wide. The pictures are two feet above my head. The picture of Ike's parents is bigger, but the one of Ike as a baby has a thick, beveled wood frame. The end table with the gun is on the left side of Ike's chair. The lever to lower the recliner is on the right.

My heart is pounding. I'm scared, and I'm in way over

my head, but I can't let that stop me. I can trust my body. My brain's a different story, but my body has never let me down. I can do this.

My stomach aches with nerves, and I wait. The timing has to be perfect.

Ike belches, rubs his belly. His phone chirps, and he cracks a smile. "Well, ain't you in luck. Dudley Do-Right came through in record time."

The next moment, I hear the growl of a motorcycle engine and the crunch of tires in the driveway out front. Ike reaches for his gun with one hand while he fumbles for the ashtray with the other.

"It's gonna be like puttin' down a mad dog," he mutters to himself, the faintest note of hesitation in his voice, and I thank God for that cigar nub, cause his grinding it in the ashtray is the only thing that gives me the eight beats I need before his grip is firm on the gun.

One.

I grab Ike's baby picture from the wall.

Two. Three. Four is a *jeté* over the coffee table. Five and six take me to the recliner.

I'm not in my mind. My brain wouldn't know how to do this next thing, but my body knows. I pull the lever on the recliner as I leap onto Ike, throwing my weight forward so that chair falls back, and at the same time, I slam the corner of the picture frame into Ike's right eyeball, over and over.

He screams and bucks, but I clamp my thighs tight and stay on. I hear Nickel in my ear. *Why the fuck you stop then?* And I don't.

Ike's hands rise on instinct to protect his eyes, and as soon as they do, I grab the gun, disengage the safety, press it to the nearest body part, his shoulder, and I shoot.

Bang.

Warm, wet drips splatter on my bare skin above the neckline of my top. I gag.

He howls, flails at me with his uninjured arm, and I fall to the floor. I've got the gun, and I try to keep it raised as I crab walk back, Ike looming above me, stumbling, grappling in the side pocket of his pants for something—a knife?—and I know I need to shoot again, but my hands are sweating so bad, I keep losing my grip.

The door flies open, slams against a wall, and simultaneously, another shot rings out from a distance, a soft pop, and Ike's head snaps backward and he crumples back onto the chair like a puppet with its strings cut.

"Baby, baby." I'm on my ass, staring and shaking, and then there's a hard wall of muscle at my back and strong arms wrap around me, gently lowering my hands and slipping the gun from my fingers. "I'm here. It's okay. You're okay."

Nickel's scent—leather and laundry soap—filters through the reek of this place, and he gathers me up and carries me outside like a bride, and I want to argue that I can walk, but I don't think I can. Every part of me is shaking.

I vaguely register others showing up, a few hushed instructions. An SUV backs up to the front porch, and a large mass is quickly and quietly heaved into the back. Oh, God. That's Ike. That's his body.

My throat seizes so tight air whistles as I try to drag in breaths.

"It's okay. You're okay." Nickel sets me in the passenger seat of my car, shrugs off his jacket and covers me. He grabs my chin and forces me to meet his eyes.

"You took his ass out, baby. Didn't you?" He smooths my hair and strokes his palms down my shoulders. He's shaking, too. His eyes are blown-out, black pools, but there's a quirk at the corner of his mouth. "My badass ballerina. You took him out with a picture frame."

He's freaking out, but he's in control. My body eases. If he's okay, then he's telling the truth; it is going to be okay.

"He was going to kill you," I babble, simultaneously bursting into tears.

Nickel sucks in a breath, surprise and understanding and something else making the hard planes of his face heartbreakingly open. "You were saving me?"

"Of course. You're mine, aren't you?"

He presses his forehead to mine, firm so I can feel him nod. "Always have been. Always will be."

Then he buckles me in, and he drives us to the club-house, obeying the speed limit, both hands on the wheel.

24

NICKEL

"Some people dissolve a dead body in lye. So I've heard." Creech is huffin' and puffin', a black trash bag slung over his shoulder.

We're halfway up the mountain to the burnin' spot. I've got another trash bag, and Wall has a third, twice as big as ours. Creech has the dude with the tear tattoo, I've got Ike, and Wall has the fat guy.

Heavy's got an orange game bag filled with deer over his shoulder. Forty's carrying a sapling.

"Ain't like anyone is going to believe that we bagged two deer and then decided to walk *up* a mountain for the hell of it," Creech grumbles.

"It's tradition." Heavy isn't breathing hard at all, even though he's such a massive motherfucker. I'm drenched in sweat at this point.

"It's bullshit." Creech spits. "It ain't even deer season."

"So we won't run into any hunters," Wall points out.

"We could burn the motherfuckers out back at the club-house." Creech has been bitchin' for the past two hours straight at this point. Ticks that carry Lyme disease. His boots rubbing his heels. The fact that Forty won the coin toss and gets to carry the tree.

"You don't shit where you eat," Forty says.

"I'm just sayin'. There's a middle ground between shittin' where you eat and climbing a fucking mountain to dispose of three bodies."

It ain't just a body, though, is it? It's my brother. It had to happen, and I thank God every day that Forty's aim was true, but still...even with all the blood drained, the bag weighs heavy.

It ain't the first I've humped up this mountain. We've made this trek more than a few times before. As Heavy says, it's tradition. Started back almost the same time Steel Bones did. Slip, Eighty, Grinder, and a hang around named Carl were up on the mountain, hunting elk. It was late at night. They'd been drinking. Carl took offense at something Grinder said, which ain't hard to do. Grinder's an asshole. Carl threw a punch, the two of them threw down, and it wouldn't have been a thing, but Carl grabbed a burning stick from the fire and tried to take Grinder's eye out.

Slip and Eighty jumped in, and Carl didn't make it. They burned him in the campfire and buried him in the morning. A few years later, they passed by on another hunting trip, and lo and behold, a tree had sprung up from old Carl's remains. Seemed like a sign. Steel Bones has buried its bodies in the spot ever since.

We get to the clearing around noon. There's a general groaning as we drop our bags, everyone but Wall. Wall carried the fat man from Twiggy's the whole way, and he didn't bitch once.

Forty and Wall stalk off, probably to see if the shovels we hid up here in a spider hole are still there. Or to get away from the sound of Creech's mouth.

"Carl's doing well." Heavy lowers himself to a fallen log. Carl's birch is at least forty feet tall.

I sit at the other end of the log. "Dutchy's not lookin' too good."

"Yeah. That's that emerald ash borer. Invasive species." Heavy knows all kinds of random shit.

"That what got its leaves?"

"Yup."

"Too bad we couldn't have planted Inch right next to Dutchy."

"Truth."

For what Inch Johnson did to Crista, for all the years Scrap spent locked in a cage because of it...the least we could do is have a place to bring Scrap now that he's out. So he can see it was worth it. Crista sure as shit ain't showin' any gratitude for what he done.

Heavy and I sit in silence a while. Creech wanders off in the same direction Forty and Wall headed. Up this high, there's a stiff wind buffeting the very tops of the trees. It whistles in the branches, shuffling the leaves like paper. It's peaceful.

Maybe it's the calm down by the ground compared to the wildness of the wind whipping high overhead, but there's something in this place that soothes the spirit.

"He deserved to die." I ain't lookin' for reassurance. It's a fact.

Heavy grunts. "He ain't gonna be missed."

He won't. Ike was just another in a long line of Kobalds who made the world worse for bein' born. Uglier. And how much different were we, really? In the end, we were made of the same stuff. Blood and fists and rage.

"He was my brother."

"He was." There's a rustling in the brush, and Forty and

Wall emerge, carrying shovels. Heavy stands, rolls his broad shoulders. "So am I."

I sit there a while longer and watch as Heavy hacks into the short grass, churning up the brown dirt. Forty and Wall join him, and after a time, Creech wanders back, and we spell them, finishing up the pit until it's five feet wide and seven feet deep. Heavy helps me throw the garbage bags in, and Creech douses the lot with lighter fluid.

We back up, and Forty hands me a box of matches. A hawk shrieks overhead.

"Rest in peace, Ike Kobald." I light the match, flick it, and a stream of fire reaches skyward for the shortest moment and then disappears, trapped and dampened by the cold dirt of the hole.

It's not unlike the life we were born into, Ike and I. His fire starved and turned to ash before he ever had a chance to reach for more, but I got lucky. When I had nothing but rage and ugliness, I had a Story to reach for.

And sometimes, that's all you need.

EPILOGUE

STORY

Nickel's been acting very cagey today.

After what went down with Ike, I was worried that it would send us back to square one. No matter how awful the man was, Ike was blood. Nickel keeps insisting all I did was slow Ike down, though. The kill shot was to his head, and if he was gonna hold a grudge—which he isn't—it would be against the brother who took the shot, not me.

No one says who took the shot. No one talks about it at all. It's club business, and that's kind of that.

I have nightmares sometimes, but Nickel's always there to fuck me back to feeling safe. We've been spending most nights at his place 'cause they're doing some kind of renovation in the space below my apartment, and it's loud, and there's fumes.

Nickel asked if we could drop by my place after work today. He wants to do something that requires more privacy than we get at the clubhouse. I'd guess anal if he didn't seem so damn serious about it.

It's been a weird month. Everything's changed, but nothing's changed. Nickel really doesn't want me to dance at The White Van anymore, but Heavy said no one changes their routine until we know what kind of blowback there'll be from the cops.

I'm not sure if I want to quit. Nickel gets that I need a paycheck, and I ain't ever relying on a man to pay my bills. On the other hand, I hate seeing the look on his face when I come out on stage—it's pure misery for him now that he can look his fill at home—but I really, really hate dental hygiene.

Besides, one night a week teaching Swinging Seniors isn't enough. I think I'd waste away if I didn't get that hit of pure joy when my body takes over, and my mind blisses out. I feel really selfish sometimes. I have all I ever wanted—I'm Nickel's girl. Can't I suck it up and give up dancing? I know if I put my mind to it, I can find a way to get through school. And spend the rest of my life cleaning teeth.

Anyway, Nickel disappeared for a few hours this afternoon. Just said he had to take care of something. I'd think it was the doctor or his group, but it's the wrong day. Then he came back to ride me to work, and he was totally silent. He spent my whole shift out front or pacing the club like he used to do when his anger was riding him hard.

I'm definitely gonna make him spill when we get to my place. I've got ways of makin' him talk.

When we pull up in front of my place, it's almost three in the morning. There's no moon out, and the street lamps are mostly busted, but there's light blazing from my building.

It takes a minute to register. There's no brown paper in the windows of the storefront on the first floor below my apartment anymore. The lights are all on, spilling onto the sidewalk out front.

"They must be done with the renovations." I'm excited to

see what it is. A coffee shop would rock. Downtown Petty's Mill is getting just bougie enough that it's a possibility.

Nickel grunts, and I scurry up to snoop.

They must have replaced the glass cause instead of the old, cloudy panes, there's sparkly new ones. They'd better look to putting in a metal gate. My neighborhood is getting fancy and all with Des Wade's new waterfront construction a few blocks over, but my street is still a tad shady.

I'm thinking about that when I catch my reflection on the far wall.

There are mirrors, floor-to-ceiling. And a barre!

"It's a dance studio!" I shriek, clutching Nickel's forearm. He's watching me so closely, a strange expression on his face. His mouth is half-softened in a smile, but there's worry crinkling his eyes.

"Want to take a closer look?"

Do I—

He holds up a key ring, dangling it from his fingers.

Holy.

Shit.

Fay-Lee said Steel Bones goes big. But this?

"Nickel Kobald." I shriek and snatch the keys. "Did you buy me a dance studio?"

"Don't break my fingers, babe," he chuckles, following me while I fling the door open and proceed to poke my nose in every corner. It's amazing.

The studio is wired for sound, the wood floor is sprung and polished to glowing, and there's a locker room with white cabinets and a ballet-pink chaise lounge.

"No pillows?" I'm laughing, giddy.

"You're gonna have to pick those out yourself."

"It's for me?"

"I bought the whole building."

"You did? You bought the whole thing?"

We're standing in the locker room, Nickel in the doorway, blushing. He's actually red in the face.

"Too much?" He offers me a wry smile.

My eyes prickle with unshed tears. "I'll never be able to pay you back."

"Ain't like that." Nickel seems to draw in a deep, steadying breath. "I'm gonna renovate the other floors, too. Combine the second and third, put in a master suite and another bedroom."

"Yeah?" I saunter over to my man, slide my hands up his chest. He grabs them and squeezes.

"I'm gonna marry you, Story Jenkins, and when you're ready, I'm gonna put a baby in your belly. You'll bring our little ones down here, and they'll play in a corner while you teach all the yuppie ladies how to shake their asses. We'll make bank once the waterfront is finished. I talked to Heavy. It's a sound business plan, he says."

"Is that how it's gonna be?" A tear escapes and tickles down my cheek. I'm grinning like a total idiot.

"I'll make you happy, Story. I'll do whatever it takes to be the man you need me to be."

"I know you will." He's made all my dreams come true. I'm gonna work so hard to make his come true, too.

"You trust me?" His breath is hot on my lips as he leans close, his eyes glued to mine.

"Yeah, baby." I wind my arms around his neck, and he sways forward, stepping me back and guiding me down onto the chaise lounge. He's hard and heavy, and his cock jerks against my belly. His black eyes swirl, and I know this man so well, I can pick out the threads of fear...and the overwhelming love.

"I got you, baby," I murmur, holding him closer, cradling him in my arms while he bears down. "I got you."

As I lay there, guiding my man inside me, I can't help but smile. There's joy here in these walls. I can feel it. And I'm never letting go until the joy is spilling out the doors. After all, letting go isn't in me. It's not how I was made.

THE STEEL BONES Motorcycle Club saga continues in *Scrap*!

A NOTE FROM THE AUTHOR

Will Ernestine ever take Grinder back?
Will Creech ever find someone who can love him?
Who was Boots' "California Girl' and why did she leave?

I have no idea! But you will be the first to know if you sign
up for my newsletter at www.catecwells.com.

You'll get a FREE novella, too!

ABOUT THE AUTHOR

Cate C. Wells writes everything from motorcycle club to small town to mafia to paranormal romance. Whatever the subgenera, readers can expect character-driven stories that are raw, real, and emotionally satisfying romance. She's into messy love, flaws, long roads to redemption, grace, and happily ever after, in books and in life.

Along with stories, she's collected a husband and kids along the way. She lives in Baltimore when she's not exploring the world with the family.

I love to connect with readers! Meet me in The Cate C. Wells Reader Group on Facebook.

Printed in Great Britain
by Amazon

21532403R10149